A SILENT JOY

— A —

SILENT JOY

Elizabeth Jenkins

Constable · London

First published in Great Britain 1992
by Constable and Company Limited
3 The Lanchesters, 162 Fulham Palace Road
London W6 9ER
Copyright © Elizabeth Jenkins 1992
The right of Elizabeth Jenkins to be
identified as the author of this work
has been asserted by her in accordance
with the Copyrights, Designs and Patents Act 1988
ISBN 0 09 471610 2
Set in Linotron Plantin 11pt by
Servis Filmsetting Ltd, Manchester
Printed in Great Britain by
St Edmundsbury Press Ltd
Bury St Edmunds, Suffolk

A CIP catalogue record for this book
is available from the British Library

1

The enormous, illuminated indicator spread loftily, widely, above the immense, thronged expanse. On the platforms, travellers were filling up the waiting carriages. The trains throbbed, jerked forward and pulled out, gliding past the big notices that said 'Waterloo', gathering speed as they drew out of the terminus, their routes spread out across a wide landscape under an ocean of purplish cloud, where tiers of windows in factory towers gleamed acidly in the dim evening light.

Grove End, half an hour's run from Waterloo, had been, twenty years ago, a little country town. Now, in 1957, it was more built up, with a high street full of radio and television dealers, garages, estate agencies and dress shops, but there was still a common, with ponds and hawthorn thickets, lying between the high street and the railway station, from which trains to Waterloo ran every twenty minutes.

An irregular row of houses, of Edwardian date, screened by dark, aromatic thuja hedges, was aligned along a quiet road with grass verges. Two were of very comfortable roominess; they belonged to Sir Geoffrey Galbraith, a retired high-court judge, and to the Mercers, of whom Tom Mercer was a retired tea-planter. These two houses had back-gardens running down to the shore of a narrow mere, hedged off by the fences and bushes of the gardens and shaded on its opposite bank by thick-growing trees.

Sir Geoffrey had been one of the travellers on the 6.15. Some of the passengers, coming down the concrete stairs outside the station, had a glimpse of the cameo-like features and rimless spectacles of the judge as he settled himself in the beautiful, sand-coloured leather interior of his car before his man drove it off.

Sir Geoffrey was a childless widower who had never recovered from his wife's death eight years ago. His usual manner was one of courteous severity, and it was a surprise to people who didn't know him to discover how much he was loved by his friends. As it is said of most very successful judges, he was an ordinary man, but with more than ordinary intelligence and a better than ordinary education.

The aching loneliness, though it was muted now, would always strike him as he came back into his house. That he could still find some happiness was in part due to his calm, unselfish temperament, and a good deal to his housekeeper. Mrs Treadgold, widowed herself, had a son and two daughters now living with their families in different quarters of the globe, and she was contented to have a situation where her outstanding gifts as a cook-housekeeper were received with gratitude and admiration. Beatrice Treadgold had an ample, Ceres-like figure, and her gold hair was greying without much alteration of its colour. The first time Hilliard Bartram, the incumbent of St James the Less, had seen her, her name and her colouring and her radiant good humour had brought to his mind the verse in the Revelation of St John: 'The street of the city was pure gold, as it were transparent glass'. He had never spoken of this to Sir Geoffrey, who was one of his dearest friends, because it would have been tantamount to a comment on Mrs Treadgold's appearance, and he knew that though Sir Geoffrey disregarded it, as did Mrs Treadgold herself, it was a standing topic among certain people in the neighbourhood either that old Galbraith might as well marry his housekeeper, why didn't he, or that it would only be the decent thing if he did. But though some Grove End inhabitants were dissatisfied, the position was perfectly acceptable to the two people concerned. When he had engaged her three years ago, Sir Geoffrey had said: 'I shall not marry again,' and Beatrice Treadgold had felt a reliance on his word. She had no intention of re-marrying either. Her present position was very agreeable to her; she always spoke of Sir Geoffrey as 'the master'. At the same time she had an unselfconscious dignity. 'Kindness to everyone, liberties from nobody', was her principle.

6

Sir Geoffrey had arranged for her to have help, though she had at first said she did not need it; but he was inspired by a keen instinct for self-preservation which made him anxious that Mrs Treadgold's post should be made as comfortable as possible. As she had not, at first, wanted another woman about the place (a state of affairs apt to be as much, if not more, bother than it was worth), it was very fortunate that the helper who cast up was Miss Fishwick, known to everybody, high and low, as Gertie. She and Mrs Treadgold had met down at Studland on a coach tour for the Over Sixties, and they were delighted to find, presently, that Mrs Treadgold had come to take up a post in Grove End, where Gertie had been living for years. The congenial acquaintance had now become a firm friendship. Gertie had a spare little frame, a pale and sunken face mounting large spectacles, a cleanness like a sea-washed shell, an irrefragable honesty and a devotion to Methodism. She also had the high standard in domestic work that Mrs Treadgold admired. She came up two mornings a week to turn out rooms, and, as required, to do Sir Geoffrey's mending and, generally speaking, whatever else was wanted. Since some domestic help was, after all, desirable, Mrs Treadgold thanked her stars for Gertie, while Gertie was glad of the money, and very glad of the company of Mrs Treadgold, whom she called Beetriss. She also enjoyed, in complete silence, being a valued member of Sir Geoffrey's household.

The chauffeur Fred replied to Sir Geoffrey's 'good-night' and turned the car into the garage beside the house. Though he was still able to drive a car efficiently, Sir Geoffrey was providing against the time when he would not be able; and when Fred Poulter was already doing part-time work as his gardener, events so fell out that he was able to give him full-time employment as gardener and chauffeur as well.

Fred had married Mavis, a woman of great determination. Her friends had told her at the time that she ought to be able to do better for herself, but he was then earning good money in a local firm of tool-makers, and though he wasn't up to much, she knew that he'd never argue with her. The failure of the firm and the couple's having to live on unemployment assistance had exposed Mavis to sufferings

7

which she felt she ought not to undergo. One evening as Sir Geoffrey was listening to a Chopin Nocturne on the air, Mrs Treadgold appeared at the door of the study. At the sight of her face, he turned off the music.

'It's Fred, sir,' she said. He followed her into the hall. Fred was standing in the kitchen doorway. Sir Geoffrey went in and shut the door after them. The kitchen was a large room and Mrs Treadgold used one end of it as a sitting-room, though her bedroom, also a large room, was furnished as a bed-sitting room. She sat up there now, alternately sewing and listening to the radio, while more than an hour went by. She came downstairs when she heard the front door close. Sir Geoffrey said: 'I'm afraid we kept you out of your kitchen a long time, but he'd sat down and I didn't like to move him.' In the course of the evening, he told her what he had learned. Mavis had left Fred for the well-to-do manager of a local dairy company. She had given him no warning, only telling him that she was going within half an hour of her departure, her suitcases already packed and standing on the front doorstep. She had spoken with such vitriolic contempt of his failure as a husband, both financially and sexually, that he could not bring himself to repeat what she had said. Sir Geoffrey, with a lifetime's practice, had pieced together the halting account. The result was that in six week's time, the council house was given up, and Fred established in a small, out-of-date cottage at the bottom of the garden, within a few paces of the mere, in full-time employment at The Lawn as gardener, chauffeur and handy-man. The cottage was bare. It was connected to main drainage and to gas, but it had no bath. Sir Geoffrey had said, rather dubiously: 'I suppose we shall have to see about putting in a bath. I expect he can manage with a tin tub at present.' Mrs Treadgold knew that he could; she sensed that a Robinson Crusoe-like existence, of simplicity and independence, was just what Fred needed to restore him. Mavis had left behind her the meagre furniture, the pots and pans (after all, she was going to a house furnished in executive style) so Fred had brought basic necessities with him. Sir Geoffrey had said to her: 'Don't let him be in want of anything we can supply from this house.' The only thing she had asked for on Fred's behalf was a small refrigerator. She

8

would have suggested a television set, but he didn't want one. A radio for the sports news, which he had already, evenings spent with the lads, who were glad to see him back, early bed, because gardening took it out of you, come to that, and the great happiness of not having to live with Mavis, was all Fred asked. Kindness and security revived him; from having a hunted look and uttering incomplete sentences in a low voice, he became calm-eyed, his voice was stronger and he spoke coherently, with sense. His weak face, sallow and deeply-lined, was set on a throat with a prominent Adam's apple, and his frame was slight and weedy, but he had large, powerful hands; all his strength, his intelligence, seemed to be in them. He could carpenter, repair, attend to pipes and gutters, re-fix slates. The sense that Fred was there, at the bottom of the garden, and would see to it, whatever it might be, was soon giving Sir Geoffrey great comfort.

One aspect of Fred's affairs caused the judge a little anxiety. People with no experience of the courts might suppose that after the way Mavis had left him, and considering the bettering of her lifestyle which she had achieved with the dairy company's manager, the last thing she would do would be to return to Fred and demand a renewal of marital relations. Sir Geoffrey considered it unlikely, but he did not entirely rule out the possibility. He had therefore made it clear from the beginning of Fred's occupation of the cottage, that he did not rent it or receive it in part-wages. It was an ex-gratia concession which could, legally speaking, be withdrawn at any time. There was no danger that Mavis could claim a share of it as the matrimonial home; but as he knew too well, when people plant themselves in a household, with however little claim, or with none, getting them out of it may be a matter of considerable difficulty.

One bright morning, standing on the gravel outside his front door, he said to Fred: 'Have you or your wife brought up the question of a divorce?' Fred's face returned to its old, bewildered, desperate look. 'No,' he said. 'She's gone, she won't come back; leave her go, I say.'

'Yes, certainly; but if you don't divorce her, she might take it into her head to come back.'

'I wouldn't have her back, not for any money.'

9

'No, but she might be able to annoy you. You'd be safer if you had a divorce.'

At his words, the face looked as it had in that first conversation in the kitchen: clay-pale with unfocused eyes and trembling lips. 'I couldn't stand for all that to come up again,' Fred said. 'I don't want no one to know what she said, not now I've told you, sir.'

'Very well,' said Sir Geoffrey and walked back into the house. Fred went back to giving a sharp edge to the lawn with a pair of long-handled shears. The day was bright and already becoming hot. He saw Mrs Treadgold come out of the back door, making for the bottom of the garden to pick mint. She paused, half-way down the path. A newt, four inches long, greyish green and darkly speckled, with legs and feet that it chose not to use, was wriggling convulsively on its stomach along the hard gravel under a glaring sun. Mrs Treadgold went back into the house and came out again with a glass jar half-full of water. Stooping down, with one touch she startled the newt into slithering to the jar's watery depths. She carried the jar to the bottom of the lawn, made her way through the fence and turned it out on the tree-darkened shore of the mere. Fred had followed her down the lawn at a little distance, for interest's sake. The bees were singing and the warmth was bringing out comforting, delicious scents. As she came back, the empty jar in one hand, a few sprigs of mint in the other, Fred leaned on the shears and said, with a shy, happy smile: 'You do take a lot of trouble!'

Mrs Treadgold said: 'It don't seem fair, not to.' She went into the house, to prepare one of Sir Geoffrey's little Saturday lunch parties.

2

Mrs Treadgold enjoyed these occasions as much as the visitors did. One of the frequent guests was Neil Pepperill, a young man at present lodging with his old second cousin Miss Louisa Bassett in her large, rather shabby Victorian house on the outskirts of Grove End.

He occupied two rooms and a bathroom on the second floor and received a good deal of looking after from her companion, Miss Bumpus, who was quiet and kind. The arrangement was excellent for all parties. Neil would take his jacket off and do things the elderly women didn't know how to do: attend to an over-flowing cistern or an air-lock in the pipes. Once he spent a Sunday morning taking the kitchen boiler to pieces and putting it together again, his face, while he did it, wearing the pre-occupied, intent look of a surgeon's.

From The White House he went up daily to the offices in Thread-needle Street of the engineering firm of Hayes and Hurst. He was doing well in this active company but the double possibilities of sudden expansion and overnight collapse kept the more highly-strung members of Hayes and Hurst in a state of perpetual wariness. Neil was one of these. He was slight and wiry; his expression in repose was both impetuous and severe, but his eyes, dark brown and full of light, were always ready to crease up in laughter.

Living *en garçon* at Cousin Louisa's, he was delighted by invitations to lunch at The Lawn. He and Sir Geoffrey had many sympathies, but their personal experiences were widely different. Sir Geoffrey knew nothing about machinery, except how to drive a car, while Neil regarded machines as sacred and endowed with life. Sir Geoffrey did not think of himself as highly strung but he had a sensitiveness to noise which Neil's generation had grown up without. The former's professional life had encouraged this. In an Assize Court, if he raised his head from his notes, looking even as if he might be going to speak, a dead silence fell; sometimes he had to say pleasantly: 'Go on, Mr So and So.' Neil's favourite pastime was full of loud, discordant noise; he was an enthusiastic partaker in car rallies. Grove End lay on a route often used for these, and Sir Geoffrey found that his complaints of being roused at dead of night by the din of a troop of motor cars forcing their way, banging, throbbing, screeching, through what had once been a village street, though listened to civilly, did not call out the sympathy of his young friend.

'In my youth,' he said, 'there was a reverence for the night. That has gone altogether.'

'Well yes, I suppose you could say so. But apart from traffic difficulties in the day-time, it makes it more exciting to have it at night.'

'And *is* it so exciting?'

'The fun and the scare of it are.'

'Wouldn't track racing do as well?'

'That's different. These rallies are the only things we've got like the mediaeval tournaments. Men were crazy about them, and when you do car rallies, you see why. That jockeying for position by bodies in plate armour, (that's you and your car), inching along among the others, fighting for every bit of space and turn of the road; when I read about tournaments, I recognised it at once: it was neck and neck – good timing was almost the whole of it. And the horses – in plate armour like cars or tanks. It made me realise our mania is just the same as theirs. It's dead exciting.'

'Well, I see you feel it is. I'll try to remember the mediaeval angle next time I'm startled out of my first sleep.' The smile on his lean, usually impassive face was beguiling.

The third member of the Saturday lunch parties was often Hilliard Bartram. Neil was, intermittently, a church-goer, but he would have been pleased to see the Vicar in any case, he was such a sound chap. Hilliard was forty and unmarried but his friends had not yet written him off as a confirmed bachelor; they merely hoped that he would marry one day. His face was thin with an intense expression; it lighted into friendliness when he was spoken to, but the friendliness was turned towards all alike, to people of any age and of either sex.

At quarter to one on this Saturday the three men were in the drawing room and Mrs Treadgold's mind was on the chicken roasting in the oven; the exact moment had almost arrived for turning up the heat for the last ten minutes to produce a crackling, golden-brown skin, when there was a ring at the front door. She hurried to open it, and found on the doorstep little Miss Morwenna Stevens, her purplish-brown face framed in a pixie hood, who presented her with a glossy, expensive-looking manual and said in a hurried, breathless voice that they would be glad to see her at some of the Women's Awareness Sessions, of which the times and places were noted on a slip inside the cover. She then scuttled away down the drive. Mrs Treadgold put down the manual on the hall table and hurried back to the kitchen. She knew Morwenna Stevens by sight as the weak third of a triumvirate who lived together – not merely for comfort and convenience, but as a sort of demonstration of lesbianism. This naturally put them somewhat at odds with the local society. Miss Sobell who was pale and stout and moved slowly, wore a perpetual appearance of calm animosity; Miss Dawson, who was emaciated, one of vigilant antagonism; Miss Stevens' status in the household was like that of a trusted serf, nearly on equal terms with her owners, not quite. She had been told this morning to deliver the progressive literature to Mrs Treadgold, with whom up till now they had not managed to make any contact. They agreed with each other that Morwenna might as well call and see if she could do any good; not that they expected it.

The lunch party had seen Miss Stevens pattering down the drive and Sir Geoffrey asked if she had called for a subscription?

'No, I'll give her that,' Mrs Treadgold said, presenting portions of roast chicken. 'She left a book and said she'd come about Women's Awareness Sessions, which I don't know what they are,' she added candidly.

Neil said sternly: 'They're discussions to make you understand, Mrs Treadgold, that men are selfish and cruel, that they tyrannise over women and rob them.'

'We don't need no sessions to tell us that,' Mrs Treadgold exclaimed gleefully, 'we know that already!' Her face was irradiated as she handed broccoli to the vicar. Removing the first course and bringing in the crêpes Suzette occupied her, but with the coffee she carried in the solid-looking, shiny paper-back and put it at Sir Geoffrey's elbow. He opened it and began to read; in a few moments he exclaimed, 'This is formidable! "We must know about men in order to put them back in their place; they are an aberration and out of control. Men won't exist for much longer."' Neil said, incredulously: 'But won't that be very dull for ordinary women? I can imagine how Phyll would view that!'

'Who is Phyll?' asked Hilliard with interest, stirring crystals of

13

dark sugar into his coffee. Neil seemed to recollect himself. He said: 'Well, it's a bit difficult to explain who she is, actually.'

'Perhaps I can help,' Sir Geoffrey said. 'Bartram, you never met my very old friend Jasper Spedding? He and his family used to live at The Lodge, at the corner of Woodside Road. They moved to London about two years ago. I miss them very much but his wife wanted to live in town. Jasper is Neil's distant cousin. He's got two girls, Phyllida, the elder – about sixteen, is she?'

'Seventeen,' said Neil, firmly.

'And pretty as a picture. Then there's Irina, the little one; eleven, I should think?' (Neil said nothing; Irina's age was of no importance to him.) 'They're both charming, but Phyll is the beauty.' It seemed clear, without the need for further description, that Phyll would not opt for a world in which men had ceased to exist. When Neil had left, somewhat reluctantly, Hilliard said: 'Is Phyll the one, then?'

'My dear fellow, I wish I knew. I hope so. My own marriage was so happy, I want the same for them. They'd be a delightful young pair.' Hilliard's silence was not of the tongue-tied sort; it had the quality of creative listening. As they got up, Sir Geoffrey said: 'Sometimes I can almost see her, standing over there by the French window, just come in from the garden.'

Hilliard Bartram, making his way down Grove End High Street where several passers-by greeted him as he walked along, put a controlling hand on a boy, wobbling on his bicycle and about to tumble off it in the path of a lorry, then turned down the narrow, countrified road that led to his little sixteenth century church. This had subsided so far into the ground that the turf, with waves of long grass and flowering weeds, came up towards the mullioned windows and was so small that on festival days its limited congregation almost filled it. He was on excellent terms with the parish church, a large Edwardian building which provided many attractions: fêtes, club meetings, outings, concerts and a wide, variously-strewn book-stall inside the west door. It was thought in some quarters that Hilliard Bartram was too young a man to have settled himself in the backwater of such a small church as St James the Less. The vicar of St Martin's did not join in this criticism; Bartram was always ready to help him out and Mr Welland had a professional understanding of his work, which was carried on with an almost mystical quietness. Daily matins and evensong were once said with no one present but himself. Now there were about a dozen at these services; at the Sunday ones, fifty or more; at Christmas and Easter the pews were full. There were no remains of the priest's house that had once stood beside the church; Hilliard lived by himself in a small, ugly, yellow-brick villa. He was worked for by a series of women who did the rudimentary cleaning and cooking that his simple existence required; when the supply of domestic help failed, as it sometimes did, he managed for himself. He would think gratefully of the advantages the present age had brought to a man living alone: a launderette, convenience foods, hot water by the instant manipulation of a geyser, a flood of light at the flick of a switch but hadn't there been more hearty satisfaction, on the whole, less distress and despair, in times of dirt and discomfort, pain endured without anaesthetics, light provided by lamps and tallow candles, tainted food and the hardships of cold and hunger for so many? These questions demanded complex answers.

Among his friends Lucinda Fairlight, as an unappropriated and not uninteresting woman, was naturally sometimes present in his mind. All that was generally known of her was that she was of a silent turn, and that anything she undertook to do would be done. He also knew that she earned some of her living by translating French texts and arranging primers of the French language. She had come back to Grove End three years ago; her parents were dead and the lease on which their small house had been let having expired, Lucinda had decided for the time being to live in it herself. It was a little larger than she needed, but space and silence being what she wanted most, she was willing to forego the money she could have made by selling it.

He had first met her in the church porch on Easter Eve two years ago, bringing flowers which Mrs Mercer, who was in charge of the decorations, had asked for. She had light, beautiful but ineffective eyes, a thin, straight figure; she was wearing an old raincoat, for in

15

the spring evening light brilliant drops were still trembling on every stone ledge, and down the stems of the sheaves of grass. She seemed embarrassed, reluctant to speak to the clergyman whose church she did not attend, for she went nowhere. He thanked her warmly for the armful of daffodils and narcissi, and said he hoped she would come to the Easter morning service. Lucinda said she would. There was a second's silence between them and then she surprised herself by saying, as she looked down at the scooped-out flagstones of the porch, over which feet had passed in and out for four hundred years, that it was difficult to know what to think. He said with his impersonal, cheerful air: 'Never mind thinking. Just come if you can.'

Since that evening she had been to the services with increasing frequency, and as he had told her that on one occasion he had called but not found her at home, she had said that she was usually in about six and she hoped he would come in one evening for a drink. He had done this on some evenings at considerable distance from each other; they had had brief but friendly conversations.

Lucinda had held secretarial posts until the work she had done for an educational publisher had made her see that she could do the actual book-writing as well as the book-production, and her inside knowledge made her able to get better terms for herself than the scholarly, impractical creatures who ordinarily did such work were able to secure. She had lived a calmly contented life, self-supporting and self-contained, making, not friends, but agreeable acquaintances who were all she seemed to need.

He was now accustomed to seeing her at the house of their friends the Mercers. Tom Mercer, the retired tea-planter, was perpetually active in his garden; he went to race-meetings, he was interested in local politics, he viewed television and listened to the radio: the day was too short for what he wanted to do in it. His wife Nell also was of late middle age; a thick waistline and a lined face did not prevent her having a most attractive appearance to men of her own years. Her skin was velvety, her complexion the deep coral pink that goes with dark brown eyes. The Mercers were among Geoffrey Galbraith's closest friends. They had recently had a party for their ruby wedding which a dinner at the Mansion House had made it impossible for him

16

to attend. He had sent a basket of crimson roses with a note: 'I am so happy to congratulate you on your ruby wedding. My girl died on the eve of ours.' The next time he went to one of their Saturday mid-morning sherry parties, as Nell came forward with her radiant welcome, he saw that she was wearing a ruby brooch. 'That is very beautiful,' he said. 'To mark the occasion?' She touched it. 'Yes,' she said: 'My dear, generous old man.' Hilliard, who had come into the room behind Sir Geoffrey, said something about the woman whose price was above rubies. Tom called out, from where he was bending over the side-table: 'Come and drink her health.'

Caspar, the Mercers' cat, large, powerful and milk white, was making his way across the room with steady purpose to gain the kitchen. His coat had a luxurious richness as if he were a massive ermine muff. He was a valued member of the household. Nell used sometimes to think sadly of how much her sons as schoolboys would have enjoyed his company. They were now successfully launched: Martin following his father on the tea-plantation in Darjeeling, Colin farming in Kenya. Their photographs, their wives' and children's photographs, gave interest to the mantelpiece, among a procession of little Eastern curios: tiny cloth elephants sparkling with sequins and vigorous little carvings in stained ivory. She was continually happy to think of them as so successful; (impossible not to miss them all the time). They had always wanted a cat, but owing to a chapter of accidents, no cat had ever stayed with them. When she noticed Caspar behaving with quiet majesty as though the house belonged to him, she sometimes felt a pang of regret and pain.

3

It was twenty minutes past eleven on Friday morning and in Elmfield girls' school Irina Spedding should have joined the other eleven and twelve year olds trooping into their classroom after morning break, but when she hurried into the lower school cloakroom to put away in her coat pocket a pink quartz rabbit which she had been told not to bring into class again, she had found Peggy Cromer crouched over the lockers, crying so wildly that Irina was frightened. Peggy was a large, solid-looking child; now her face was crimson, her eyes blood-shot and half-closed, her chest and shoulders heaving with dreadful sobs. Irina saw that something ought to be done: she didn't know what. All the retreating footsteps had died away and the cloakroom was silent except for the sound of loud crying. She knew, because everyone in the form knew, that Peggy's parents were getting divorced and that Peggy would have to leave Elmfield at the end of the term because she and her mother and sisters would have to move away from London, to somewhere much cheaper. A flat had already been found for them, but because it was a flat, they could not take their dog with them. Peggy did not know what was to happen to him. Her mother, plain and forthright, argumentative and unbending, saw the future like a bomb-devastated landscape; her sisters were raging at having to give up the home life which up till now they'd lived unthinkingly like everybody else: its school friendships, dancing classes, birthday parties, seaside holidays; but for Peggy all depriva-tions and miseries were concentrated in the fact that their dog, Turner, who trusted them, must be left behind. This surge of feeling had been swelling for a long time and now something unrecognised had caused the tidal wave to burst, in the lower school cloakroom at twenty minutes past eleven on a Friday morning. She was now crying so hysterically that Miss Wootton, the assistant secretary, trim in a freshly laundered overall, on her way to the stationery cupboard, heard the sounds from some distance off, since all other noises were now behind closed doors. She hurried, alarmed, to the entrance of the cloakroom, saw Peggy Cromer almost prone over the lockers and, without waiting to investigate sped out again, having that instant seen the headmistress coming back to her office. She caught Miss Heck-shire before the door closed behind her. 'Oh, do come!' she exclaimed. 'I'm afraid there's something very bad the matter with that poor child!' and turning on her heel she almost ran back to the cloakroom. The headmistress hurried after her and in half a minute they were standing over Peggy Cromer, whose sobs were now convulsive; her face when Miss Heckshire gently raised it, was a uniform dark red.

'What is it, my dear?' but as she spoke, Miss Heckshire realised that she could not expect an immediate answer and now she remembered that Mrs Cromer had been to see her and given her the picture of what faced the mother of three girls: the cutting off of social life, of dignity, the having to return to the neediness she'd borne cheerfully in the early years of the marriage, when she'd given up her job for the care of the children, while the interloper, the cruel thief, was in well-paid work. 'It's bitter,' Mrs Cromer had said at last, in a voice calmed by exhaustion, 'but it's the wreck of the girls' home I really mind about.' The mother's sufferings and the child's now joined themselves in Miss Heckshire's mind into one terrible whole.

Miss Wootton had an unopened handkerchief in her pocket. She soaked it in cold water at one of the basins and laid it on Peggy's forehead. Irina, not knowing whether to go or stay, was balancing on her toes, with a hand pressed to the rim of a wash-basin. Miss Heckshire was kneeling on the cloakroom floor. She now turned about and said: 'Are you a friend of Peggy's, dear?' 'Not specially,' Irina said shyly. Peggy had stopped the loud crying. She gasped and shivered as the cold water touched her face. She said something under her breath about Turner.

'Who is Turner?' Miss Heckshire asked, kindly but with the obvious determination to find out. 'It's the name of their dog,' Irina said. 'They'll have to get rid of him because of divorce.' Miss Heckshire bent over Peggy. 'Poor little girl,' she said. 'Would you like Irina to stay with you?' Peggy drew a deep sigh. 'No, not much,' she muttered. Miss Heckshire got to her feet, saying: 'We will take her to lie down. Where are you supposed to be now, dear?' 'In French,' Irina said. 'Then you'd better go. Ask Miss Richardson to excuse your being late. Say I kept you.' Irina tip-toed out; the solemnity of the scene imposed soundlessness.

She got herself into the classroom, blushing and downcast before the raking stares of twenty-one of her classmates, many of whom broke into broad grins at the sight of her; they found Irina Spedding's coming in so late insanely funny. Irina said something indis-

19

tinct, in which, however, Miss Heckshire's name was audible and Miss Richardson welcomed and encouraged her. As she opened her French reader, full of up-to-date French conversation, the scene in the cloakroom was half in her mind, half out of it. There had been something, only half-recognised, but frightening.

When Marcia Spedding was persuading and coercing her husband to move the family home from Grove End to London, she had meant to be established in some smart neighbourhood, off Berkeley Square, or one of the better parts of Knightsbridge, but when it came to it Jasper could not afford this sort of situation (or said he couldn't) and they were re-settled in an apartment of two floors over ground-floor offices in Carteret Street, between the Haymarket and St Martin's Lane. The street itself was narrow, loomed over on each side by massive office buildings, with pale stone fronts. Nowhere so near to the Haymarket, Piccadilly and Regent Street could be described as quiet, but Carteret Street was relatively so, and sometimes, on a Saturday or Sunday, the pavements were almost empty.

Marcia was very glad to see the last of Grove End, and Carteret Street was certainly an improvement, though not quite so much of an improvement as she'd hoped for. With her round blue eyes and her curling hair which needed only cutting to take a charming shape round her head, she was so uncommonly pretty it was natural she should be somewhat discontented with her lot. She was, in fact, still almost as pretty as she had been when Jasper had married her eighteen years ago. Then, owing to the fact that none of the several men attracted by her had come up to scratch, she had been in low water. With no training for anything and no wish to train, and with only such relations as were better kept out of the way, she had for a time had nothing to live on except national assistance. She had done her ironing on a suitcase and had borrowed the clothes of good-natured girls: the fur hat, the little black velvet dress, third-hand but a model; the owner had asked for it back four times but, after that, had given up asking.

The engagement to Jasper Spedding was a sunburst. His people had some money, and his salary with an engineering firm, of which he soon became a partner, gave him a comfortable income. In these circumstances it wouldn't, within reason, have mattered what he had been like, but in fact he was generally considered attractive: good-looking if rather too serious, and ready to sacrifice himself, on every possible occasion, to the fascinating creature beside him. He was so happy she had accepted him that, for the first few years, his happiness surrounded them both. His own attitude of devotion did not alter; essentially, Marcia's attitude did not either. Whenever some suggestion had been made which she did not like, her reply had always been: 'Oh, I simply couldn't bear it!' It continued to be, but delivered with rather more petulance and emphasis than before, and for eighteen years this had almost always been enough. The great consolation of his life was now his daughters. He had transferred to them and their society the sense of inexplicable happiness he had once found in his wife's; he would have liked to spend much more time with them than his exacting life allowed.

Phyllida used to be lively but just recently she had withdrawn into herself. Her face with its wild-rose complexion and limpid blue eyes was now always serious and remote-looking. She had a look of her mother but none of Marcia's self-centred energy. Irina was decidedly like her father; she had his agate-grey eyes and smooth dark hair. When Phyllida was six, Marcia had become pregnant once more. She did not want this baby. She was fond enough of Phyllida but she did not want to go through all that sweat again: pregnancy, child-birth and the years of babyhood. She told Jasper she wanted an abortion and for once he absolutely opposed her. On later occasions, she managed better, so that there was no need to talk to him; this time he brought to bear so much persuasion, so much sympathy, so many promises, so much resolution, in fact, that she gave in. Though Jasper loved both of the girls dearly, for Irina he had the special affection that came from having saved her life. Looking back, he dated the realisation of this feeling to a moment when she was three years old and the family were lunching in a hotel in Bournemouth. Marcia had Phyllida with her in the ladies' cloakroom and he had gone into the dining room with Irina to secure a table. The waiter

21

had come up while they were still by themselves, and he had said to Irina rather doubtfully: 'Would you like some fish?' Her face had been suddenly irradiated. 'Oh *yes!*' she exclaimed, 'a *gold* fish!' The waiter laughed and he laughed and then the child laughed too, and the sunlight was pouring in on them through a row of tall windows, on to islands of marblewhite tablecloths, and groves of mitred napkins, standing up like sugar-loaves. Naturally grave as he was, the sight of his laughing child, whom he had rescued from annihilation, pierced him with sensations he could not put a name to. The marriage had gone on, not altogether happy for either but with compensations for both; but attentive, generous, self-denying as he was, always reasonable, almost always polite, Jasper now got on her nerves, simply on her *nerves*, as she said to her friends rather often. There were still times when she was pleased to be seen about with him; he had kept his good looks; his dark hair was greying but his figure was upright; his manner in public had the calmness of a well-to-do man who did not need to assert himself. All this, and the solid comfort of the marriage – for though she was never without some grounds for discontent, on the whole it *was* comfortable – still meant something to her, but she had come to feel the need of someone to whom she could say everything she felt. At this juncture, Mrs Karmiotis appeared, heaven-sent. Elderly, rather large and very handsome, she had light eyes placed curiously near her temples, like a goat's; their usual expression was a wild but watchful gaiety, as she waited to see if something amusing of a scandalous sort might be coming up. She lived a tumultuous social life. She was an energetic and successful hostess. She wore rich clothes, designed, as she said, 'to make a statement'. Her hats were usually of a non-fashionable but striking shape, often with stove-pipe crowns to which gilt chains and large brooches were attached. She had been married to an official in the Greek consular service, but Mr Karmiotis had been phased out long since. One vestige of him remained, beside his surname; she had adopted a Christian name to go with it, and was known to everyone as Theonoë Karmiotis, though she had once been Mabel Gladys Withers.

After lunch on the Saturday afternoon following Irina's experience with Peggy Cromer, Mrs Karmiotis sat smoking in Marcia's bedroom while the latter was making up her face. Jasper was upstairs with the girls in what, for Irina's sake, was still called the playroom. Phyllida was working on a square of gros-point, filling in the background to a wreath, without raising her eyes. Irina looked all round the room, looked at her father with silent joy and then down at the Indian wooden bowl painted in scarlet and gold which held the beads she was threading.

'Who *is* Mrs Karmiotis, actually?' Jasper asked. Irina took up a translucent sea-green bead and threaded it on her string.

'She is a Greek lady,' she said.

Phyllida looked up. '*She* isn't Greek. It's only that she was married to somebody Greek.'

Irina said, perplexed: 'But she wears that hat.'

'Is it a Greek hat?' her father asked.

'I suppose so,' Irina said.

'Well, if it is, that doesn't make her a Greek. I've got an Irish tweed hat, but that doesn't make me Irish, does it?'

Irina gave one of her laughs of which sound was the least part; the rest lay in the gaiety of her face.

'And she and Mummy are going to a film, I hear.'

'Yes, they are,' Irina said, 'with Mr Mosscrop, and he will come back to tea. In fact, he might stop here to dinner.'

'How do you know?' Phyllida asked in some surprise.

'Mummy was talking to Mrs Karmiotis about it.' She narrowed the grey-green eyes between her long black lashes and after a few unsuccessful pokes, threaded a silver bead with a very small orifice.

Jasper was pleased to have a Saturday afternoon that he could spend with his daughters, but he had noticed lately that Marcia's arrangements not only did not include him, he was often not told what they were. This caused him not pain, but a fleeting sense of dissatisfaction. He now asked the girls if he should read to them. Phyllida said regretfully that she must spend the afternoon in revision. She was attending a crammer's with a distant view of trying to enter some college; not that she wanted to, but what *did* she want? Nothing, except the one thing that seemed utterly out of reach: a love affair and then a marriage with her cousin Neil Pepperill. Neil to her, was entirely fascinating. His brown eyes sometimes looked at her as if he loved her, but he had never said he did. She felt altogether changed, a stranger to herself. She did not think anyone could have noticed: not realising that her father had seen it. He had briefly suggested the possibility to Marcia, who had replied with disbelief and indifference, and as he had no insight into Neil's feelings, he did not like to talk to Phyll about the matter in case he might be encouraging her in a false confidence; he felt he must keep his own counsel for the time being. So Phyll, from being light-hearted and ready for enjoyment – and when asked why she was not interested in feminism, saying vaguely, Well, men are more fun, aren't they? – had now become serious and aloof; if anyone except her father noticed the change, they put it down to the fact that seventeen was often a difficult age, retiring and uncommunicative.

Irina now said joyfully that she would like to be read to, and she and her father went downstairs to his study, to leave the playroom quiet for Phyllida. Irina had brought down her bowl of beads and sat on his hearth-rug working at her chain while he read 'Silver Blaze' to her from *The Memoirs of Sherlock Holmes*.

When she had overheard her mother talking to Mrs Karmiotis, she had understood that even if Mr Mosscrop did not come back to dinner, Mrs Karmiotis would. The prospect was not very pleasing. Though they had known her for a short time only, Mrs Karmiotis now appeared to be one of themselves. She had made several visits to the playroom when the girls were sitting there, having been told by their mother where to find them. She had been prepared to like them both, (though she feared that Phyllida might turn out dull, like her father) and she was ready to meet them as a sympathetic adult, prepared to see everything from the young person's point of view. This was partly from the genuine good nature of her exuberant vitality, and partly to enjoy the *cachet* of being in the confidence of such young creatures; but though she felt, justly, that she had a lot to offer that would interest and amuse them, she lost ground by using them as an audience. She greatly relished talking about her current interests; at present she was hooked on the 'Analects' of Confucius.

Their Chinese stylishness appealed to her as the ultimate in intellectual *chic*, and, as most people knew nothing about them, listeners had to give her her head, at least until they tuned out of the conversation.

While she expounded them to the girls in the playroom with dramatic force, smoking and waving a long cigarette holder in the air, Phyllida listened in what seemed an attentive silence, her head bent over her gros-point. Irina was colouring a black and white illustration in one of Andrew Lang's fairy books. She was absorbed and happy. Mrs Karmiotis said suddenly: 'Irina, I don't believe you've listened to a single word I've been saying!' 'No,' Irina said, 'I've been resting my ears.' She went on touching with gold paint the great spherical turban poised on the head of a Persian princess.

Mrs Karmiotis was too sophisticated to show annoyance; she gave a neighing laugh, but she did not forget the failure. Irina, she could see, did not much like her, and she felt that she would find it difficult to like Irina.

This Saturday evening, Marcia and her two guests did not come back in time for drinks before dinner, but when they arrived it was obvious that they had had a good many elsewhere. Phyllida was teaching herself to be a good cook, though in her own despairing mind it hardly seemed to matter whether she were one or not. Her activity was however very useful to her family, as the helper, Mrs Mumford, did not come in on Saturday or Sunday unless by special arrangement. Mrs Mumford didn't know whether she were a widow or not, she had two children: Gloria, now nineteen, in a good job in a chain store, and Darren, who, as far as Mrs Mumford could reckon it out, was about sixteen. He was retarded, what her friends called 'a bit wanting'. It didn't do to leave him alone too long, so sometimes she brought him with her to Carteret Street, where he was as good as gold, never a mite of trouble to anybody. He caught sight of Irina from time to time and wrote letters to her on any piece of paper Mrs Mumford could find for him. She never gave the papers to Irina, but would merely say: 'He's left you another of his letters,' and Irina would take it up, in silence. The letters were difficult to understand, but they seemed to have a meaning apart from their actual words. One of the last ones had borne a recognisable drawing of a daisy;

under it was written, in a hand surprisingly legible: Findsmice is the girl queen'.

Gloria was a different pair of shoes altogether, a proper little madam! Five lurex dance frocks on the go at once. Try to tell her anything, and you'd find she'd written the words and music to it; but she was what Mrs Mumford called 'a good girl, first and last'. Her mother knew that in any crisis, she could be trusted to take care of Darren.

Phyll worked hard and got the meals to table on time. This evening she had made a delicious herb-flavoured soup, and she sent Irina into the dining room with a pile of warmed soup plates. As they sat at table, Jasper was full of satisfaction at his daughter's cooking; he would have liked there to be no guests, so that he could have talked to her and praised her for it, but Mrs Karmiotis was keeping up a high-pressured flow of talk. A printers' strike was imminent, with which she was not in sympathy as it threatened to deprive her of her daily paper. Jasper began to say that the discontent and anger of the workers was understandable; democracy had allowed their unions to achieve almost despotic power and now new technology was taking it away from them. Mrs Karmiotis interrupted him: 'Oh yes, yes, I know,' she said, and taking the conversation back to herself, she launched into the saga of a journalist now standing trial for libelling a member of a fabulously wealthy brewing family. The result, she proclaimed, was a foregone conclusion. No one with that amount of money would lose his case. 'They'll see he goes down, you may be certain.' 'That's for sure,' Mr Mosscrop said.

Jasper retired into silence and was able to study Ivor Mosscrop, whom he was seeing for the first time, with some surprise. Mosscrop looked forty, just about Marcia's age, whereas he himself was nearly fifty. Mosscrop's thick black hair was parted in the middle, right down to the nape; his eyebrows were thick and black; his striking feature was his teeth; they were large and the two front ones were wide apart, giving a fanged look to his mouth. As Irina took away the soup plates, Jasper walked round the table, filling the glasses with claret. When he had poured it out for everyone except Irina, who took orange juice, he left the decanter at Marcia's end of the table.

26

The glasses were cut glass tumblers, holding more than a stemmed wine-glass. Mosscrop emptied his at a couple of draughts and to Jasper's surprise, he then, with an ingratiating grin, pushed it across the cloth to Marcia, who refilled it at once. This was so unexpected, Jasper found himself looking narrowly at this somewhat outlandish guest. Marcia was smiling seductively at him, Mrs Karmiotis was shouting everybody down, Phyllida at the side-board had her back to the room, and Irina was carrying round the plates: Jasper had nothing to distract him from considering Mr Mosscrop. His impressions added up very much to what was thought of him by people who knew him a good deal better.

Mosscrop was a good companion who found it easy to get on with strangers provided they saw with him on basic issues. He believed that everyone who knew what was what, took it for granted that the police were bent; his word for a doctor was 'the quack'; he knew that all judges, and all lawyers, except the useful ones, were inveterate enemies of liberal, sympathetic fellows like himself; parsons, of course, were absurd, except for a few at the very top, who were sinister. In fact the whole set-up was a huge, self-perpetuating conspiracy to defraud him of his rights. He was now forty-three (time to make a killing if he was ever to do it). He had had various forms of employment, which had either let him down or turned out not to be worth his while, but he was now on to a sound thing; this was in the lower reaches of antique-dealing, and he was rapidly gaining a working knowledge of what was worth acquiring. He was fond of women, so long as they didn't get in the way of business, but he'd never been on intimate terms with one who could spend money on him. As he sat at the Spedding's dinner table, laid with Georgian silver and Crown Derby plates, with Marcia Spedding's beautiful eyes shining on him and her lips half open, ready to laugh at what he said, he began to glimpse new horizons.

At the end of the meal, Phyllida, who had prepared the coffee tray, began with efficient promptness to put the dishes and cutlery into the dishwasher. She didn't view the social aspect of the evening as anything to do with her. Irina carried the coffee into the drawing-room in two instalments, the cups on one tray, the pots and sugar bowl on the other, so that a too-heavy load should not invite accident. Unselfconscious, concentrated on the task, she was a delightful object to her father's eyes. His gaze followed her. The cups handed round, she was quietly removing herself when he laid a hand on her as she passed his chair. 'What are you going to do till bed-time?' he asked. 'I want to tidy out the things in the toy-cupboard.' 'Very well,' he said, smiling.

Irina went up to the playroom and opened the double-doored cupboard whose bottom shelf was level with the floor. The contents had never been examined since the Speddings had taken possession of the premises. On their arrival, a good deal of property, Phyllida's and Irina's, had been bundled into it and other things had been put on top, but the shelves had never been thoroughly turned out. At one side of the bottom shelf was a square cardboard carton, which she pulled out, knowing at once what it must contain. This was a family of bears: a honey-coloured one, the largest of the three, with a genial, kindly face, one next in size, with an anxious look, whose plush coat, once white, was now porridge-coloured, and one smaller still, a sharp-faced, white-coated little bear, somewhat *gamin* in appearance. Irina had propped them up in sitting positions when she saw that the youngest bear had a necklace round its neck of very small pearls with a little sapphire and diamond clasp. She recognised this as one she had worn at parties. She must have put it on the bear though she did not remember doing it. When she had thought of it, once or twice during the past couple of years, she always supposed it was lost. She took it off the little bear and laid it on the playroom table, beside a half-smashed cluster of pink glass grapes, and a ball of thick pale blue wool with two knitting needles thrust through it. Her head was inside the cupboard when the playroom door opened, and her mother, with Mrs Karmiotis and Mr Mosscrop, came in. 'We wanted to see how you were getting on,' Mr Mosscrop said in hallooing encouragement. 'I say, you have got a heap of things here, haven't you?' Her mother meanwhile was stooping over the assortment turned out on the floor. 'Whoever gave you those?' she demanded. 'And *that* contraption? I'd no idea there was all this up here. If you don't want them now, you'd better get rid of them. Someone would like to have them, I expect.'

'Yes, hospitals,' said Mrs Karmiotis eagerly, 'or church bazaars.'

'Someone from the Salvation Army came only last week,' Marcia said, 'and I told them we hadn't anything. If I'd known, they could have had all this.'

Irina stood stock still in dismay. She hadn't played with any of these things for a long time, but she hadn't bargained for having them all swept away from her. 'I would like to keep the bears,' she said in a faltering voice.

Mr Mosscrop was standing by the table; he was smiling kindly. 'They're a nice set of chaps, aren't they?' he said in a friendly tone. He touched the grape cluster, now a mixture of shattered globes and glittering fragments. 'And I suppose this came off a Christmas tree?'

'Yes, but I don't remember when, because the things here are quite old.'

'Well,' Marcia was saying, 'you'd better sort out anything you really want to keep, and bring the rest downstairs. It can either be thrown away or put out for the next lot of do-gooders.'

Mrs Karmiotis said: 'I've got to be off, I must say good night.' She came to Irina and kissed her, wafting a smell of rich, expensive scent. Irina accepted the kiss passively. Mr Mosscrop said good night and bowed with humorous politeness. Marcia said: 'Don't be late, darling. Daddy will come and say good night.'

Left alone in the playroom, Irina looked at the litter on the floor. She would leave the sorting-out till tomorrow. She came up to the table. She had a small jewel case and she thought she might as well put the necklace into it. She looked at the table cloth, expecting to see the coil of little pearls. She lifted the ball of wool impaled on two wooden needles, expecting that the very small necklace would have been lying in its lee. There was nothing there. She picked up the ruin of the glass grapes; there was nothing underneath it but an empty expanse of green chenille tablecloth, strewn with sparkling atoms. She knew the necklace could not have been dropped on the floor, but she bent double, scanning the area all round the table's base. When she straightened herself, she was conscious of a pang of fright.

She said nothing about it to her father when he came to say good night. As a rule, she told him of anything unusual that had happened, but when she meant to tell him about this, something kept

29

her lips tight shut. It was her habit to fall asleep quickly, and Jasper, when he came to bed, would open her door and just look at her by the light that came from the landing. When he did so this night, he could see that she was lying spread-eagled, as if she had fallen asleep after tossing about. As he bent over her, she moved her head sideways and cried out, under her breath: 'Turner!' What could that mean? Impossible to guess. She was in some distress, but as she was asleep, he thought it better not to wake her.

Irina let two days go by, and on Saturday she told her mother she'd found the necklace she used to have on one of the bears, when she'd been tidying the toy cupboard that evening; that she'd put it on the playroom table and that when she'd looked for it afterwards it wasn't there. Marcia, who was at her dressing table making up before she went out to lunch with Ivor Mosscrop at a restaurant off Piccadilly, was impatient. 'It must be there if you put it there,' she said hastily, tracing a line under the lower lashes of her right eye with a mauve pencil.

'It isn't. I know it isn't.'

'It's probably somewhere in the toy cupboard.'

'No. It was on the bear when I took him out. I took it off and put it on the playroom table. And then it wasn't there.'

'Well, really, Irina, you've been without it all this time, two years at least. You can't start making a fuss about it now. You must just go on looking for it; and make sure it isn't among any of those things to be thrown away.'

Marcia hurried down the little side street, but, catching sight of Ivor Mosscrop's back and shoulders at the entrance of the restaurant – for he was keeping watch in both directions – she slowed her pace and came down the pavement with casual grace. At sight of her, Mosscrop reacted with appropriate eagerness and decision, and in a few moments they were sitting at a little round table under the wide area window. Across the room the bar was framed in pots of green plants; the air was dim but the stacked bottles ranged on shelves in front of the looking glass all harboured a gleam of brown or golden light in their depths. The place was not quite full, though in a few minutes the habitués would fill it with the swiftness of an incoming tide.

30

The scene was a good one for a rapid increase of intimacy. On Marcia's part it was a swift progress into exhilaration; Mosscrop was delighted, but he was not carried away. Marcia saw the relationship ahead as an emotional one; he saw it as, no less exciting, one for profit-making. As they ate their smoked salmon sandwiches and drank Cinzano, he gave her to understand that he was an antique dealer. From the way he put it, the business sounded a little more dignified than it actually was, but it was true that, along its lowly path, it was humming. The market was expanding steadily, fakes were easily sold and numbers of people didn't know the value of the stuff they had in back rooms and attics. Knock-on-the-door visits to houses in country towns produced a haul of china, brass, pewter objects, put away as lumber, for which the owners were surprised and gratified to get the money Mosscrop so readily handed out. What you needed, besides some knowledge of the racket, was a car, a float of banknotes, a prosperous appearance and a good line of talk. His partner Badger Sneyd could provide the car and the float; he also supplied the know-how, but in a game which depended so much on personal contacts, there were situations in which old Badger's appearance was definitely against him. Badger looked as if he had come out of Wormwood Scrubs, which was not surprising, because he had, though this was some time ago. Mosscrop, on the face of it, seemed to supply what the partnership needed. At this moment he was, for the first time in his life, really successful. The attempts at founding a school of under-water diving, at going into hotel-management, at running a billiard saloon, had failed because the cards had been stacked against him; people had let him down. He didn't mean to think about all that. He was concentrating on this opening of small but increasing gains. Partly owing to Badger's guidance and partly to his own wits, he was becoming able to recognise what you could sell for astronomically more than you gave for it. Wherever he went now, he cast his eye round him. If he saw something worth while he would sometimes ask outright if the owner would consider an offer, or he would say with an impressive shake of the head that it was pricey; or he would seem merely to be struck by its interest and charm.

31

Marcia up till now had been bored stiff by antiques; her dislike of the house at Grove End had sharpened her indifference to Victorian furniture into absolute impatience. The Lodge had been built in 1860; it had gables edged with scalloped white barge boards and pseudogothic windows with arched tops. The large staircase window was a massive sash, of which each half, patterned like frost flowers, had borders five inches wide of crimson glass; each border had a foliated spray of clear glass spread out along it. The contrast with the deep ruby glass gave the clear glass a vividness like quick-silver. When the light poured through it, the window was so arresting in it brilliance and depth of colour, people seeing it for the first time sometimes stopped on the staircase to exclaim at it. 'Yes, it's a funny old thing,' Marcia would say.

She had done her best over the years with refurnishing, but the house had never looked modern, how could it? Jasper did not object to the amount of money she spent, but he did not sympathise with her taste. Though she had now gained more or less what she wanted, Marcia felt injured that he gave her no enthusiastic support, this feeling contributed to the discontent and resentment which now permanently tinged her mind; but under Ivor Mosscrop's influence, though it had been so brief, she was already altering her views. She was beginning to see that antique furniture was not just something to be got rid of, that it had a commercial value which commanded respect. The furniture in Carteret Street, except for the few pieces Jasper had been able to transfer from the Lodge, was all new, but Ivor Mosscrop had detected the few objects that Badger would have picked out. Saying deferentially, 'You've got some nice things in your home,' he mentioned a clock standing between marble columns with a gilded charioteer driving his team above it, and some charming porcelain figures, their clothes painted with flowers. (He had not yet become sufficiently intimate to comment on the Georgian table silver.) Marcia herself didn't care about these things, but she was glad to hear him praise them; it showed that he saw her surroundings in a favourable light.

She had meant to ask him to come in for a drink one evening, but when they were leaving the restaurant she changed her mind and asked him to lunch on the following Tuesday, expecting that on that day she would have the flat to herself. He accepted avidly, but on the Monday morning he was obliged to telephone, saying he must be out of town on Tuesday, he had to attend an important sale at Aylesbury. This was putting the matter rather strongly; he had been given the tip by Badger, who had it from his spy-network, that a widow out that way was moving house almost at once and would probably be glad to dispose of bits and pieces; anything worth having should be picked up at once, before anybody else got wind of it. As Marcia's voice showed how disappointed she was, he said: Could he take the liberty of suggesting himself for another day – today, in fact? Marcia said yes, she couldn't have borne to say no, but, as he rang off, she remembered that not only would Phyll be in to lunch, the crammer's being shut down for a Bank Holiday, but that Neil would be there too; he and Phyll were going to a film matinée and he'd been asked to call for her and lunch first. Marcia realised she must act quickly. She said to Phyll that Ivor Mosscrop was coming to lunch unexpectedly, she had some business to talk over with him; did Phyll think that after they'd all had a drink, Neil could take her out to lunch some-where? Phyll, with the limpid, vague expression she wore nowadays, said she didn't see why not.

4

When Neil came in, Mosscrop was already in the drawing-room, holding a large gin and tonic. Neil's air, though superficially polite, was brisk and formidable. Mosscrop saw at once that there was nothing to be got out of *him*, but they made *de rigueur* conversation: that the number of Bank Holidays now was staggering, the next one following the last before you could turn round and that the problem of where to park your car was making many people give up driving in London.

Marcia gave Neil a drink and replenished Mosscrop's. As she

crossed the room to the drinks tray and looked up at the latter, Neil found himself looking at her with astonishment. He had always carelessly accepted that she was a very pretty woman, but today her vigorous beauty made him feel he'd never really noticed her before. Then Phyll came in, in her coat and scarf, and he put it to her that she didn't really want to stay for a drink, did she? and that they might as well be off. Phyll agreed readily. Going arm in arm with her down Carteret Street he said: 'Where did your mother come across that fellow?'

Phyllida said: 'Mrs Karmiotis introduced them.'

'Fair enough, but how did *she* come to meet him?'

'She found him in a garage.'

'A *garage?*'

'He was running it for a friend, just till things looked up.'

'They've looked up now, I take it?'

'Well, I suppose so. He's an antique dealer now.'

'Does your mother want him to buy or sell something for her?'

'I really don't know.'

'Nothing to do with me, of course, only you said he was there on business. Your father's away this week-end?'

'He's gone down to Sandwich to play golf with Sir Geoffrey. There's a very nice hotel where they always stay. He'll be back tomorrow early.'

'It's wonderful how old Geoffrey keeps going.'

'There's a lot of energy left in him and he's so spare and active.'

'And where's Irina? Doesn't her school pack it in on Bank Holiday?'

'Yes, in a way, but a large party of them have gone to see "Hiawatha".'

'Good.' Neil settled her on a banquette in the bar of the cinema and brought sandwiches and coffee over to her.

The Curzon Cinema was showing one of its excellent films, beautifully mounted and of such emotional fascination that coming out into the street with its blue evening air and moonlight-coloured lamps, and walking down Piccadilly with the railings of the park glinting on the opposite side of the thoroughfare, seemed as a rule still part of the experience; but this evening Neil said he'd have to hurry off. He'd see her back first to Carteret Street. He hailed a taxi and the short ride produced nothing on his part but brief remarks on the night and the technique of the taxi-driver. Phyll bit back disappointment and, in dread of showing it, answered with extra sedateness. At the front door of the building, he got out, helped her out and tumbled back into the cab with a mutter which might have meant that he was wishing her good night. She toiled up the stairs, feeling as if she had done a hard day's work.

It had been said to her before now that Neil, as a young man very keen to make his way and with, no doubt, numerous girl friends, was not likely to be thinking of marriage, but he had, in fact, not so much a conscious wish but an instinctive leaning towards some calm and emotionally settled way of life such as he had never experienced. His mother had died before his father, a quiet, meek lady, worn out, some people said and Cousin Louisa was inclined to believe, by the strain of living with her husband. The latter was a cross-grained dyspeptic of great scholarly distinction. His chief work was a book on the Iron Age so comprehensive and profound that, though invaluable, it was next door to unreadable.

Neil used to say: 'Poor old Pops, he didn't mean any harm, but – God! Difficult was his middle name!' He had always liked talking to Phyll about his past life, because she was so sympathetic and because, one of the family herself though distantly related, she knew what he was talking about. One day he had told her that when he was twelve his father, having no means of disposing of him, had taken him with him to call on a very learned old lady, so old and frail that she was like a skeleton leaf, wrapped in a cloud of shawl. Neil couldn't follow a word of the conversation and sat gazing at the mantelpiece where there was propped up a large photograph of a stone tablet, inscribed 'ATAPAXIA'. Coming away, he asked his father what this word meant and his father said it was the Greek word for peace. Neil said he'd thought perhaps it was the name of something that was the matter with her, and put up there so that people would know what to do if she suddenly came over queer. His father's violent outburst was something he hadn't understood at the time and understood only vaguely now. He said: 'I suppose he thought I didn't appreciate the old bird's importance. I didn't, at that, but I didn't mean to be disrespectful.'

Phyll said serenely: 'Of course you didn't. But I believe people who get duodenal ulcers do often find everything very hard to bear.' It was obvious, even then, that he loved talking to her, but his thoughts of her seemed to go no further. As she went to bed after the evening at the Curzon Cinema, she thought she had made up her mind that she was too dispirited ever to want to see him again, but when, three days later, he telephoned to say that owing to the break-down of a theatre party, he'd been landed with two tickets for the Coliseum for tomorrow night, would she be free, and if so, would she like to come, she said at once that she would like to, very much. She told herself it would be just the same all over again, but she gave way to excitement and was not damped even when the evening turned out very wet. Her parents were out, but her father was coming home to a supper laid out by Mrs Mumford. Irina was sitting in the playroom, poring over Edmund Dulac's illustrations to Hans Anderson's fairy tales, until Mrs Mumford should bring her tray, and Phyll began to dress with steady competence and a resolution not to expect any-thing. The distances to Piccadilly tube station and from the Leicester Square tube station to the Coliseum, though short, were long enough for a heavy rain to make one very wet; finding a taxi on a wet evening was next door to impossible. Her umbrella was a black one whose cover had broken away from one of its spokes, giving it a floundering appearance like the Monstrous Crow, but she remembered to have seen, in the back of her mother's wardrobe, one meant for evening use. Marcia, as she went to all evening engagements by car or taxi, had long ago discarded it, but Phyllida saw that she had been right in thinking that it was there; she pulled it out. It seemed an umbrella that could hardly have been meant for use; but the silver gauze cover, lined with transparent plastic, was waterproof, the silvered handle studded with diamanté and the silvered spokes were workmanlike. She was presently making her way under it from Leicester Square tube station to St Martin's Lane, where the lofty, lighted fronts of the theatres were richly glittering and their reflections shimmered far

36

down into the wet pavements. Neil, standing barely sheltered at the entrance to the Coliseum, eagerly looking out, glimpsed her coming towards him along the curb with flying but cautious tread, her face alight as he'd never seen it before, while raindrops bounced, sparkling, off the taut silver gauze dome and broken lights shivered in the racing gutter at her feet. As he took her elbow, and, the umbrella shut down, steered her across the crowded foyer, Phyll felt she had never known anything like this, and yet that she had always expected it; but it wasn't until the interval, so crushed by people in the densely packed bar that they could talk as if they were alone, that he said, low-voiced: 'I've been trying to tell you for ages how much I love you.' He had his arm round her waist; the crowd was stifling and nearly pushed her off her feet. '*Have* you?' she gasped. A man's elbow covered with black barathea cloth was pressing into her temple, someone's foot trod heavily on her instep. 'Pity we can't run that lot through the machine,' a cheerful voice overcame the others. Neil's arm was round her waist so tightly, it lifted her off her heels. 'I never knew you did,' she murmured; she could have said it aloud without being overheard. 'You didn't?' he exclaimed hoarsely. 'God help us, did you want it put up in lights?' The idea of working themselves near enough to the bar to get any of the drinks on offer seemed an impossibility. Instead they drove their way through the insurgent crowd in the bar, back through the diminishing one in the corridors and found themselves once more in the great, lofty auditorium, now softly lit, miraculously cooler, and though scattered with people who had kept their seats and were studying the programme, talking disjointedly to each other, relatively empty, the orchestra silent. When they had gained their seats and were sitting hand in hand, he said with a heaving sigh: 'It's been so fearfully *long*!' She would have liked to say: 'Whose fault was that? Why didn't you speak ages ago?' but she could not lay her tongue to the words. The audience were coming back, in pairs, in files, struggling along the rows of propped-up red plush seats to slam them down.

'I didn't want it in lights, exactly,' she said, 'but I wanted to feel quite sure.' 'Well, I don't know how you couldn't have felt sure. I should have thought it stuck out a mile.' He was not much taller than she, but turned half-sideways towards her, he was leaning over her. His smile was ecstatic. 'I was afraid of showing anything in case you didn't mean . . .' 'It seems we both meant the same thing.' She laughed, with delight rather than amusement. With her hand in his, she felt as if her veins were running with liquid gold. The renewal of thrilling sounds rose up from the orchestra pit, the lights dimmed, the magic began to diffuse itself once more; the massive folds of curtain parted on a brilliant scene; Neil was to say afterwards: 'I don't remember a thing about the show, but it was smashing; we were charmed out of our minds.'

The telephone rang at eight next morning, just as Jasper was coming out of the bathroom; it was Neil, asking to speak to Phyllida. 'I'll see if she's about,' Jasper said. The door of Phyll's bedroom had opened and her face was looking round it. 'For you,' he said. The conversation lasted till they all came in to breakfast.

'Did you have a nice evening?' Marcia asked casually. Phyll was struck dumb. It didn't occur to her that all she needed to say was 'Yes'. Instead she said: 'I borrowed your tinsel umbrella, my black one's broken.' 'You'd better keep it,' said Marcia good-naturedly. 'I never need it. It's useful for a date on a wet night.'

Phyll said no more about the evening's events. Jasper, as he prepared to go to the office, felt sure that some important stage had been reached so he was extremely pleased when, at ten o'clock, Neil telephoned his office, and asked the secretary when it would be convenient for Mr Spedding to take a personal call? Jasper took the call at once and as Neil began by saying: 'Actually, I've got something rather desperately important to talk about,' and then came to a dead stop, he said: 'Perhaps I can guess what it is. You mean to tell me that you want to marry Phyll: is that it?' 'I mean to tell you that I want to ask you if I may.' Jasper was pleased and touched. He said he thought he and Neil should talk about this, and told Neil to meet him at his club for one o'clock. Neil agreed eagerly, but said in agitation: 'You aren't making up your mind against me, are you?' 'No,' Jasper said. Neil was too anxious to be completely reassured but when they were sitting down to lunch, and he heard Jasper order a bottle of Chateau La Tour, 1945, he realised, as he said afterwards,

38

that broadly speaking they were home and dry.

'How long have you had this in mind?' Jasper was saying.

'Simply ages, in fact I can hardly remember when I hadn't got it in mind.'

'And does Phyll know you're talking to me today?'

'Yes, I told her on the 'phone this morning I was going to try to.'

The recollection of Phyll's face as it looked round her bedroom door came over Jasper. He said, almost absently: 'I want her to be happily married to someone who'll love her and look after her to the end of the chapter.' Neil would have liked to break out into a vehement reply, but he gazed at Jasper speechlessly, his lips ajar, his bright brown eyes filled with moisture. Jasper went on: 'As long as you're sure of yourselves, it's a match I'd be all in favour of, but she's so young, not much more than seventeen, you must allow yourselves time to change your minds if you're going to –'

Neil said in suppressed tones: 'If *she* wanted to call it off, I'd have to take it, that's all, but please God – besides, I think, with her, once is for ever. Of course, I *may* be wrong,' but he spoke as if he didn't think he could be. 'You wouldn't insist on a very long engagement?'

'I think there should be a year before final plans are made.'

After a moment's silence, Neil said: 'I know I'm damned lucky that you don't say anything worse than that.'

'My dear boy, as far as I'm concerned it would be a marriage of just the sort I'd want for her.'

'I suppose I must ask you to see me soon, as soon as possible, about my prospects, income and so on.'

'Certainly, but I don't imagine they'll prove any obstacle. She won't be marrying you for money.'

Neil gave a great sigh, from various emotions, in which relief was paramount. They began to eat, talking about possible places to live, and then Neil began to speak enthusiastically of how the wedding might be arranged. He knew the bride's people were supposed to have the doing of that, but if there were to be *any* difficulty, or inconvenience even, he knew Cousin Louisa would like nothing better than –

'All in good time,' said Jasper with amusement. 'There's plenty of time to work all that out –'

'A sight too much,' said Neil, sighing. 'However,' he added, 'you've been so frightfully decent about it. I mustn't complain,' but he refused pudding or cheese as if he couldn't endure the idea of either.

'As I'm not getting myself engaged,' Jasper said, 'I'll stay and finish my lunch; but if you want to go and – perhaps – telephone, don't let me keep you. You'd better talk to Marcia some time,' he added. 'I don't think she's heard anything about this.' Neil agreed, courteously, but not as if this were a matter of great moment. He did not foresee any strong objection on Marcia's part, or rather, he would not have cared very much if he had; but he knew Phyll wouldn't want to upset her mother, (not actually *want* to, that is); in the middle of so much elation, he didn't stop to ask himself why, or since when, he had begun to count Marcia out. The waiter, an old friend of Jasper's, having seen Neil leave the dining room, came up saying: 'The young gentleman won't take anything more, sir?' Jasper said: 'No, he's just become engaged to my daughter; his mind is rather occupied.' A smile of great benevolence came over the waiter's face and he took Jasper's order for apple pie.

As he walked up Lower Regent Street Jasper was thankful for the prospect of this marriage for her. Thinking over the lunch-time conversation, so abbreviated and so expressive, it occurred to him as odd that the prospective bridegroom seemed to think the bride's mother of so little account that he had suggested having the wedding party at the home of an old female cousin of his own. But Neil was an impulsive lad, he hadn't thought what he was saying; it was important, though, that someone should tell Marcia the news without delay.

Marcia at that moment was sitting beside Ivor Mosscrop on a seat in the Embankment gardens. They had lunched at a kiosk and were now luxuriating in the warmth of the midday pause, which was bringing out a heady scent from the fresh-cut grass. Ivor was saying casually that *if* she ever wanted to dispose of anything in an advantageous way, without fuss, his friend and partner Basil Sneyd was the one. Not that he supposed she *did* want to, but inside gen was always worth filing, wasn't it? Marcia felt that she wouldn't have much chance to make use of this information, but it *was*, certainly, interesting to hear it. The nearness of the man with whom she was becoming infatuated was exhilarating and at the same time soothing; for this blessed moment, air, light, warmth, the whole of creation was on her side. Ivor said: 'Too bad I must think of the time. My watch is in dry-dock,' he added, pushing up her sleeve to see the time on her watch and to note its very expensive Swiss make. It flashed in the sun and Ivor could hardly take his eyes off its gold face and the gold mesh of its bracelet, but Marcia was looking about to see if they might kiss in reasonable privacy. No one was near them; in the middle distance a feeble old man in a threadbare overcoat was eating fish and chipped potatoes out of a newspaper. The paper's astrological advice for his sign that day was: 'Adopt a bold and expansive approach. Mingle with the rich and famous,' but grease from the warm bundle had made the newspaper transparent and the guidance was unreadable. Ivor and Marcia exchanged a lasting, draining kiss, while the sun sent up silvery arrows from the moving river.

Late in the afternoon, Neil put through another telephone call to Phyll, catching her just as she got back to Carteret Street after several hours' struggle to make herself attend to what was being told her at the crammers'.

At the sound of the telephone she lifted her head; life poured through her again. After mutual endearments, he told her again how amazingly decent her father had been, and that he'd forgotten to say that Jasper had said one or other of them must have a word with her mother; so, if Phyll would speak to her and prepare the way, he'd weigh in afterwards. Phyllida had not yet heard her father say anything about the matter, but she had the solid assurance from Neil's words and even more, perhaps, from his voice, that everything was all right, and that being so, if her mother were to be displeased, it would not really matter all that much. In the few short hours since yesterday evening in the crush bar, she had entered the mystical state where nothing mattered except this one only thing. She came into the drawing room where Marcia was lying on the sofa, a drink beside her, cigarette smoke curling about her, her beautiful eyes unseeing, thinking with intense concentration about her own affairs. Phyll said: 'Mummy, Neil and I want to get married. Daddy says we can, presently.' Marcia was for the moment completely taken aback, but she was, on the whole, interested and pleased, and though she had so much of her own to think about, she was willing to give her attention. She raised herself to a sitting position and held an arm out; Phyllida leaned over her, Marcia kissed her and wished her joy but warned her at the same time not to expect too much out of life. The words entered Phyll's ears as if they were spoken in an unknown language. Already she looked different, as Marcia saw at once; the heightened colour in her cheeks made her eyes a darker blue. She felt for the first time a genuine sympathy with the girl. She was not much impressed by Neil's status as a suitor, she would have liked him to be richer and to have some hobby above car rallies: yachting, say, or the turf; still he was eligible, more or less, and the idea of Phyll's marrying him was interesting rather than not, for the moment, at any rate. Phyll would have been glad, now that the ice was broken, to talk to her mother about Neil and discuss their plans, but Marcia was abstracted again. She said no more but lay on the sofa in silence, her spiral of smoke rising towards the ceiling, and Phyll had a sudden access of shyness. Before dinner however she went up to the playroom where Irina was sitting over her supper tray. Phyll sat down at the opposite side of the table and said in gentle tones: 'You like Neil, don't you?' 'I suppose so,' Irina answered. This did not give Phyll the springboard she had hoped to find under her, but she went on: 'We are going to get married.'

'Who are?' Irina asked, wide-eyed.

'Neil and I are.'

'Are you?' said Irina, as if confronted with information she couldn't relate to anything.

Phyll said: 'I thought you'd be pleased – pleased to know, I mean.' Irina stared at her in a state of bewilderment. 'So I thought I'd tell you,' Phyll added lamely. However little the statement conveyed to her, Irina understood that her sister was disappointed. 'Well, I am,'

42

she said. She didn't understand why Phyll should get up and kiss her but she returned the kiss. Going downstairs, Phyll, on a rising surge of excitement, longed to see her father. Marcia's attitude and Irina's had chilled her, but he would make it all seem real to her again. She reached the foot of the stairs as he opened the front door. He saw her, hesitating, brilliant with excitement, on the bottom stair, and saying: 'Well, well, come and talk to me!' he walked into the study and she flew after him. He held his arms out, and, nearly crying, she hugged him round the waist as she had never done before. 'Darling,' he said, 'Neil's been telling me.' 'And you don't mind, do you?' 'I'm very, very glad, *very* glad. But I want you to wait a little. I know you both want to rush into it, but *you* are so very young still. I'd like you to wait a year before your engagement is announced.' With her face against his waistcoat, she made no protest. 'And how long have you felt that you'd like to marry him?' 'A long time, really, but it was only last night he asked me; I never knew before whether he really – that's why I had to keep it all to myself.' She saw that her father was smiling and she said in surprise: 'I never said anything, did I?' 'No, but I must admit I thought you had something on your mind. Have you told Mummy yet?' 'Yes. I don't think she was all that interested, actually, and Irina wasn't either, but *you* are.' 'They will be, pre-sently. I daresay it took them by surprise.'

At Grove End, Cousin Louisa hadn't heard anything to make her so happy for a long time; Miss Bumpus also was illuminated. They asked Neil to join them at dinner. They never drank more than one glass of wine apiece, but the wine was good, and there was a cold pheasant in the larder which would come in very well. As Neil now had that great weight off his mind, and had had nothing to eat since his abbreviated lunch with Jasper, he was extremely hungry and he ate and drank in a way that did Cousin Louisa's heart good and Miss Bumpus's also.

'And your cousin Jasper has actually given his consent to your being engaged?' Cousin Louisa said. The mere idea that this might be in question brought Neil up short. 'Good God!' he exclaimed.

'Yes, of course he has. He said we must wait a year, which seems a fearful imposition, but she's not eighteen yet, let's face it. After that, he won't say anything against it.' The conversation did not actually progress, as it consisted of Neil's saying over and over again everything he'd said before about Phyll and her extraordinary charm (unique, really), and how long he'd been in love, but afterwards, over coffee and Benedictine, Cousin Louisa said: 'I have several old rings by me, dear. I wonder if you'd like to choose one to give her: not an engagement ring, you know, but just to give her, with my love? Ethel dear, would you be so kind as to bring my small jewel case from the bottom of the wardrobe?' Neil was delighted at the idea; anything that Cousin Louisa gave them would be better than anything Phyll would allow him to get for her. The jewel case was shaped like a little trunk. A velvet-covered ridge ran across it with a cleft down its centre, into which a few rings had been pushed: a pearl hoop, a flower-like, dew-laden cluster of diamonds: ('That's stunning!' said Neil involuntarily, but he put it back hurriedly); another with three oval sapphires upright in a row, the mauveish blue of harebells. 'Not very valuable,' Cousin Louisa said, 'such pale stones, just rather pretty.' Finally, there was a large, shallow emerald, a lovely colour but battered and flawed. The culmination of the anxieties and raptures of the day overcame Neil so suddenly that he nearly fell asleep over the jewel case. He tried to say how awfully, awfully good it was of Cousin Louisa, and any of them, he was sure – a yawn cracked his face and he shuddered. 'You get off to sleep,' Cousin Louisa said, and Miss Bumpus withdrew to go to his flat and turn down his bed. How he got up there himself and got his clothes off in a heap on the floor, he didn't afterwards remember.

5

Sir Geoffrey was extremely pleased to hear of the engagement of Neil
and Phyll. Jasper had never said a word to him of any misgiving
about his own marriage, but once or twice lately, and specially on
their last golfing expedition to Sandwich, sitting in the hotel in the
evening, when Jasper mentioned Marcia in passing, Sir Geoffrey had
felt a faint uneasiness on his friend's behalf. If there were an area of
unhappiness there, the prospect of a happy, secure marriage for Phyll
would be particular welcome.

Mrs Treadgold did not know Phyll as she knew Neil, but she had
seen enough of her to know that she was a dear girl, and when Sir
Geoffrey told her that Neil was bringing her to Grove End next
Saturday to call on Miss Louisa Bassett and that he would like them
to lunch with him first, Mrs Treadgold said nothing but her slight
movement of the head and her expression of joyous determination as
she went out of the room made words unnecessary.

The occasion had to be a Saturday for Neil's sake and Sir Geoffrey
was glad as the party could include Hilliard Bartram. He was in the
garden for a minute, speaking to Fred about bringing the car round
after lunch, and as Hilliard came into the hall, Neil and Phyll were
standing in the open doorway of the study, examining the orders and
decorations that had been bestowed on Sir Geoffrey in the course of
his career and were hanging in a case on the wall. Phyll, at least, was
scanning them; Neil's arm was round her waist and he was saying,
quietly but audibly, 'Beautiful as the day.' Hilliard made a heavy step
on the hall floor and they turned round. He said, with his bright,
impersonal smile: 'Neil must tell you who I am, but I needn't be told
who *you* are!' 'Oh, *I* know who you are!' Phyll said. The deep pink in
her cheeks that made her eyes so blue, and the faintly smiling look,
showed such happiness that when Sir Geoffrey joined them, the older
men were touched and their conversation with her had a kind of

gentleness. Sir Geoffrey asked when the wedding was to be and got such a glum reply from Neil, a stranger might have thought he despaired of its ever coming off at all; but Phyll said, they expected it would be in a year from now. 'And all this hanging about and what have you,' Neil said crossly, 'is just to give us the opportunity to change our minds if we want to!' 'The time will go by faster than you think,' said Sir Geoffrey.

Meals at The Lawn were always enjoyable; this one was especially so, with the mutual goodwill and happiness at table and the roast duck, orange salad and straw potatoes, and the beautiful Nesselrode pudding riding at anchor on its lead crystal dish. Before they left, Mrs Treadgold ushered Phyll upstairs and, while she was out of the room, Hilliard said: 'I must congratulate you most warmly.' While Neil was muttering something joyful, he went on: 'With such a very young lady, her father must feel it's only right to give her time to get accustomed to the idea of such a big change in her life.'

'Oh, absolutely,' Neil said, without rancour. He went to the door to watch for Phyll's coming downstairs and met Mrs Treadgold in the hall. She stopped in front of him, assuming suddenly an air of great sternness. 'You be good to her!' she said severely. He ejaculated something the others couldn't hear. Mrs Treadgold relaxed into hearty good-humour and gave him a slap between the shoulder blades. Neil explained that he was taking Phyll to spend the afternoon with Cousin Louisa who'd given them the ring but had not yet seen it on. From Neil's description Phyll had chosen the one with the pale sapphires and Cousin Louisa had sent it with a note full of love, saying: 'Just to wear till you have another one.' 'I shan't want another one,' Phyll had said as Neil pushed it on her finger, and it was difficult to imagine anything more attractive than the row of harebell blue translucent stones on the young hand.

Fred was in the kitchen, waiting to take them in the car, but they decided to walk, in the lovely afternoon. Hearing this he came shyly into the hall while Phyll was saying goodbye to the others. 'Best of luck, sir,' he said, 'you've picked a winner.' Neil thanked him earnestly.

He and Phyll had a charming walk, in which the beautiful weather

46

was thrown away on them, for they would have thought themselves in Paradise whatever it had been, and their afternoon with Cousin Louisa, and with Miss Bumpus when she brought in the tea, was a continuation of their bliss. This naturally reached its height when they were washing up after tea, as they had coerced Miss Bumpus into allowing them to do, and they were in the kitchen for half an hour by themselves, washing up and singing. Phyll had told Neil that she couldn't sing but he had said 'All girls can sing, just as all horses can jump. Some *won't*,' he added. He sang himself, not well, but loudly and in some sort of recognisable tune; under the powerful protection of his voice Phyll lost her shyness and produced her small, sweet notes.

When they had seen the couple off Sir Geoffrey and Hilliard sat down in the drawing room. The vicar said: 'Please God everything goes well with them! It looks as hopeful as can be, it's heartening to see them.'

'Yes, she's the quiet one, but I think she'll manage him for his own good.'

'May it be so. One's had so much experience – heartbreaking – of weddings with any amount of show and glory, bride dressed like a dream, bridesmaids all around, healths drunk, sentimental weeping, every sort of public demonstration, and then, perhaps in two years' time, you hear it's all foundered – the girl finds married life stultifies her or the young man's decided he's found someone else who would suit him better, and the marriage doesn't matter, compared with what they think of as the good life.'

'One feels they'd have done better to get married in a registry office, if the religious aspect means nothing to them, but I suppose they wouldn't forego their saturnalia.'

'Yes, the church is made use of to provide that. But sometimes one is sure the ceremony is undergone in all seriousness and innocence, and then the wreck comes, just the same. One hears about the squabbles and recriminations and divided interests and the wretched split-up and the family misery – and I remember the girl's face in front of me, under the wreath and veil – "bare, ruined choirs where late the sweet birds sang", it's desolating. I think I could say I'm

47

never depressed, but I am sometimes nearly heart-broken. You feel as if you had a million pounds that you're longing to share and give away, and that you can't get it out of the bank.'

Sir Geoffrey said: 'After all, though the divorce rate is increasing, still, the majority of marriages do last, don't they?'

'Yes, though the majority is diminishing while you look, but God forbid I should throw any doubt on this one.'

'No. I can't wish them any happier fate than mine – than mine was. I can't judge other people's temptations to infidelity, I never had the slightest. I think of myself when I remember an old man sitting at his cottage door, being asked by an investigating journalist what he thought of married couples' taking holidays apart from each other. He was bewildered. He said: "But it wouldn't *be* a holiday, if the wife wasn't with me!".'

'Let us hope God allowed them to die at the same time as each other, like Philemon and Baucis.'

Neil had talked freely to Cousin Louisa about himself and Phyll and their marriage. He thought it was not too soon to be looking for somewhere to live, and Cousin Louisa had said, without at all urging the matter, that the upper floor of the White House, in which he had his rooms, could be converted into a self-contained flat: something she had been advised to do before now, as it would add very much to the value of the property. If he and Phyll didn't mind beginning married life out of London, and would like to occupy it for a time, to see how it went, they would be more than welcome. The only draw-back she could imagine, she said, with a look of stern resolution in her faded blue eyes, was that they might feel she and Ethel Bumpus were getting too much to *rely* on them. It would have to be under-stood, she said, and she said it implacably, that the two establish-ments were, and must remain, quite, *quite* separate.

Neil was only afraid that as a consequence of this abnormal good luck, the gods might take it out of him in some way afterwards. It wouldn't do as a permanency – no room for the kids – but as a start-off it was ideal, provided of course that Phyll liked the idea. It was arranged that everyone should come to lunch one week-end, for an intensive viewing of the premises; but when it came to the point, Jasper found, to his disappointment, that he had to be up in Manchester that week-end. Marcia, not altogether surprisingly, had an engagement that would keep her in London; so the party consisted of Neil and Phyll, Irina, who was brought along so as not to leave her behind, and Sir Geoffrey Galbraith, whom Cousin Louisa was always particularly glad to see. She congratulated herself on having made the engagement with the young people, which would be something worth asking him to.

Neil had now bought a car, a Jensen 541 'R' and this was the first time he had driven Phyll in it. She had always known he was besotted with machinery, but until this morning she'd never realised that he regarded cars as if they were people. His *sotto voce* comments on the ones they passed or were overtaken by, spoke of them as if they were sentient beings: 'A very nice little bit of work, that; I don't think he's quite got the measure of her yet,' he murmured, noting with keen eye some manoeuvre on the driver's part which he himself wouldn't have endorsed, and exclaimed with indignation as a shabby Ford shot ahead of them: 'Flogging the guts out of the poor little thing!' As Phyll did not drive herself (as yet), she could not understand what gave rise to his criticisms, but she listened intently. As for Irina, sitting in the back, she did not even try to follow; it was always delightful to her to be in the back seat by herself, lulled into a trance by rapid motion.

Suddenly, the hall of the White House was full of people giving hugs and kisses. They all went into the drawing room where the walls were covered with Morris's Blackthorne Paper: peacock green and indigo, with drifts of starry white flowers across it. Irina had never seen anything so strange. She went up to the wall at once, to examine it, rapt, and was only recalled by Sir Geoffrey's greeting her, over her shoulder. She turned round; people were apt to scold her for being interested in things, but Sir Geoffrey was not cross; his quiet but unexpectedly deep voice was asking if she thought the wallpaper pretty? She said: 'I don't know – not exactly,' and heard Phyll say: 'I would like my cardigan, please. I left it in the car.' Neil at once went out to the car, and Irina thought, if Phyll wanted the cardigan, why didn't she fetch it herself? But this was a passing impression. She never remembered having been in Cousin Louisa's house before, and the room was full of interesting things. There were numbers of pewter objects, boxes and little dishes and jugs, and the fender, of bright brass, held up three heart-shaped shields of turquoise blue enamel. Seeing her fascinated gaze, Cousin Louisa smiled at her. 'All these things belonged to my parents; my mother chose them when she married. Of course, they're very old fashioned now.' Sir Geoffrey said: 'But some of them must be valuable? *Art nouveau* has come back, I never thought it would. I never liked it at the time; it just seemed to me new-fangled and insipid, compared with the eighteenth century pieces, but you have some very charming objects here.'

It had been suggested that Neil and Phyll should thoroughly investigate the possibilities of the upper floor after lunch, but as he already occupied part of it, Neil had no hesitation in slipping upstairs with Phyll for a preliminary look-round. The attention of the other three adults was now concentrated on Irina, and each of them felt that something was wrong with her appearance. Sir Geoffrey thought she looked *distraite*; he could not have said anything further without more time for scrutiny. The two women saw that she looked neglected. Her shoes, though very nearly the same, were odd; the left one was new, the right was one of the old pair which the new ones were meant to replace. Irina had put on the new left shoe and could not find the new right; as the others were calling her to hurry, she snatched up the old right shoe and thrust her foot into it, not liking to spend more time in searching for the new one. They were almost exactly the same, anyhow, but one had a scuffed toe and the other a smooth, shining one. Miss Bumpus said, with gentle forthrightness, 'Shall we brush your hair before lunch?' 'If you like,' Irina said amiably. 'I didn't do it much, because they said to hurry.'

In Miss Bumpus's bedroom she stood with head bent, reading a paperback called *Untrodden Snow*, (126 thousand) which was lying on the dressing-table, while Miss Bumpus brushed out her silky, straight dark hair and combed a few tangles out of it. Irina usually wore a round tortoiseshell comb to keep the hair back when it was

50

not plaited, but this she had not been able to find in her haste, either, so she had pushed the hair behind her ears; as it kept falling forwards, it had needed continual pushes. Miss Bumpus had a bit of scarlet satin ribbon, off a Christmas present, coiled up neatly in a drawer as too good to throw away. This she passed under the hair and tied it on the top of Irina's head in a small neat bow. 'Thank you very much,' Irina said. She put down *Untrodden Snow* rather unwillingly; turning away, she did not look in the glass.

'How nice Miss Bumpus has made your hair look!' said Cousin Louisa when they came back into the drawing room. Neil and Phyll had come downstairs, excited by their reconnoitre, and longing to get upstairs again for a much longer one, but Phyll now felt compunction that she'd never looked to see if Irina were presentable before they set out. 'Good gracious, you've got odd shoes on!' she exclaimed. 'I ought to have seen!' Everyone smiled at her.

As Miss Bumpus had established contact with Irina, the latter followed her into the kitchen where Miss Bumpus was about to dish up. She had the roasting tin in her hands when the front door bell rang. 'Oh dear!' she exclaimed. 'I'll go, shall I?' said Irina and sped out to open the front door.

On the step a somewhat formidable lady was standing, stout, with a white face rather shiny, like candle-wax; she seemed to get wider towards the base; her head was topped by a small black felt beret. Miss Sobell did not as a rule deliver the partisan magazines and notices, but she and Miss Dawson having discovered that they had never put on their list this household of two women, they had decided that Morwenna Stevens had better include it in her next round, with however little prospect of success; whereupon Morwenna had gone down with unmistakeable influenza: temperature, sore throat, aching limbs, all about as tiresome as it could be. While Miss Dawson, somewhat grudgingly, bore the brunt of the nursing, Miss Sobell undertook the colportage, and was finishing a taxing round with a call at the White House. She stood motionless, looking at the little girl with a speculative stare. 'Do you live here?' she asked. 'No,' Irina said, 'we've just come for lunch.' Miss Sobell handed her a copy of the magazine, entitled 'New Orientations'.

'Please give this to the lady of the house,' she said. 'This copy is free, but if they want to see the next one, that'll have to be paid for.' Then she added: 'Perhaps I shall see you again presently.' She gave a strange smile and her spectacles glittered, then she went down the drive with a gliding motion as if she were on wheels. At the gate she paused and turned to look at the house; her massive shoulders and rather hunched back made her head look very small. Neil, who had come downstairs with Phyll and overheard Miss Sobell's last words, seized on the 'New Orientations' and took them with him into the drawing room. Though the magazine had been left, explicitly, for Cousin Louisa, Neil, with characteristic masculine aggression, made no attempt to hand it over but started to read it himself. 'Is it the same publication that was left for Mrs Treadgold?' Sir Geoffrey asked. 'No, this is more of a newspaper,' Neil said. He whisked over the pages rapidly and came upon the Personal Column; he read aloud: 'Divorced, sensitive, caring, non-Tory, mother, teacher, into C.D. and Labour Party, would find life more complete with non-smoking, reliable man, to whom looks are immaterial.'

'She has stated her case with great exactness,' Sir Geoffrey said. 'Let us hope some suitable person presents himself.' 'I suppose there may be some such chap, somewhere,' said Neil doubtfully. 'Oh, I expect so,' said Cousin Louisa with earnest goodwill. 'And after all,' Sir Geoffrey said, 'there's nothing objectionable in saying it; it's merely rather naive. She *wants* to live with a man: she can't be blamed for that. I daresay she will be honest and kind if she can find him.'

'There's a good deal in it that's worse, certainly,' said Neil. Leaving the merely progressive, the paper's leader soared to heights that left him standing. If a woman truly cared about the cause, it said, she *must* be lesbian; it was treachery to give the best of yourself to Man, the enemy. Stupfied, he was at last persuaded to put down the 'Orientations' and go into lunch with the rest. Amid the general enjoyment, he said how glad he was that Miss Sobell, whom he and Phyll had spotted from the bathroom window, wasn't one of the guests. 'I was afraid she might be, as she'd come just at lunch time.'

'Oh dear,' said Phyll remorsefully, 'how sad it must be when you

52

simply delight people by just not being there!' Neil's face lit up with one of his smiles, so brilliant that they made him look almost crazy. 'Much better to delight them by just *being* there!' Everyone laughed.

'Did the lady say anything to you?' Sir Geoffrey asked Irina impassively. 'She asked me if I lived here and I said no; so she said, well, perhaps she'd see me another time.' Sir Geoffrey's silence was not just a refraining from talk; it had a noticeable impact, like speech. Irina went on, 'But I don't want to see her again. She's like Grendel's mother.'

'Who is Grendel's mother?' asked Miss Bumpus in surprise. Irina said: 'Grendel was a fearful monster who lived at the bottom of a mere. In the evenings he used to come up and go across the fields to a hall where people were asleep, and get in and take them away and eat them. His mother lived down in the mere too, and she was worse.'

'How very horrid!' Cousin Louisa cried. 'But I don't think we ought to say Miss Sobell is like *her*.'

'Live and let live,' said Miss Bumpus, but she said it without conviction. Irina gave a slight shrug, relinquishing the discussion, and went on spooning up delicious raspberry pudding.

Neil meanwhile was making remarks between Phyll and Cousin Louisa: he could not keep away from the subject of the conversion of the top floor into a self-contained flat with a master bedroom, a smaller bedroom, a living room and a kitchen. The bathroom was there already, the room that was to be the kitchen would need a sink and a cooker and there would have to be a front door on the landing, none of it very serious builder's work. Cousin Louisa meant to set the conversion in hand as soon as the builders could be induced to begin it. Of course, she said, Phyll must choose the decorations. 'It's so sweet of you,' Phyll said with the deep rose colour rising in her cheeks. When Miss Bumpus carried away the coffee tray, the others went upstairs. Sir Geoffrey inspected everything with keen interest. While he and Neil and Cousin Louisa were in deep conversation, Phyll, already painting the walls with the colours of imagination, took Irina into the little room, empty at present, and told her this would be her bedroom when she came to stay with them. Irina pressed her hands together in speechless delight.

53

When it was time to go, Neil took Sir Geoffrey out to look at his Jensen, and asked if they could give him a lift back to The Lawn. Sir Geoffrey would have enjoyed the mild walk, but he saw Neil wanted to drive him in the new car, so Phyll and Irina scrambled into the back seats and Sir Geoffrey sat beside the driver, listening attentively to Neil's explanations and comments. Set down at his own gate, he looked affectionately at the load of young people and said how nice it was that Neil and Phyll would presently be living in the neighbourhood, for the time at least. Phyll climbed into the front seat again and the smiling faces were turned towards him before they were carried out of sight.

The drive back was spent in eager conversation between Neil and Phyll and plans for consulting decorators and wallpaper firms. Irina listened with interest some of the time; for the rest, she enjoyed the swift passage and the ideas that rushed through her mind, though she could not remember them a moment afterwards. When they drew up in Carteret Street, Phyll said: 'We'll have a quick cup of tea; then Neil and I want to go and look at the wallpaper albums in Bantings'. They're open late on Saturdays. We'll just have time before they shut.' 'You needn't give me any tea,' Irina said. 'I can get it for myself.' 'Well,' Neil began; he obviously thought this was a good idea. 'You'll be all right till your father comes in? Phyll says he'll be back to dinner.' 'Oh yes, quite,' Irina began to say, and Phyll put in: 'Mummy said she wouldn't be late. She's probably in now.' Irina said: 'Thank you for taking me in the car.' They watched her making her way into the entry; she did not look back.

She went upstairs to the playroom and left the door open so as to know when her father came in, and just before six o'clock she heard sounds in the hall. She looked over the banisters but stopped before her foot had descended to the top stair. Below her was a group of three people, all intent and silent. Her mother and Mr Mosscrop stood side by side; in front of them was a little, strange-looking old man. He was holding between his hands, by its head and feet, the porcelain figure of a shepherdess that belonged in a corner cupboard in the hall. The shepherdess's dress was decorated with gilding and sprigs of flowers; her feet rested on a grass-green base that had pink

54

china flowers in high relief scattered on it. The three people stood with bent heads in a moment of utter concentration. Irina drew back and went into the playroom again; she longed to hear her father's key in the lock.

She hovered uneasily, looking out of the window, from which she could see a dusky light with the faint flush over the rooftops which the London sky was never without, then she settled to an exciting read which blocked out uneasiness. Meanwhile Jasper had telephoned from Manchester. He told Marcia that he'd not been able to catch the train on which he'd meant to come back, and would not, now, be at home till nearly eleven. He would have dinner in the restaurant car. Then he said: 'I daresay they've all got back from Grove End by now? Irina's in, is she?' Marcia said: 'I've only just got in myself. I haven't been upstairs to see.' He said, somewhat cautiously: 'I think I'd like to hear that she's safely in. I'll hang on, shall I, while you go and look?' Marcia, smothering impatience, agreed. She was telephoning in her bedroom and as she laid down the receiver, she made an imperative sign to someone not to speak, for fear of the sound's carrying.

Upstairs she opened the playroom door and saw Irina lying on the floor with her heels in the air, reading *The Hound of the Baskervilles*. 'Daddy's just rung up,' she said. 'He won't be back till after you're in bed.' Irina said nothing. Her mother said: 'Shall I tell him you had a nice day at Cousin Louisa's?' Irina said: *'I'll* tell him, when he gets back.' Feeling some resentment, Marcia went downstairs again. Irina was showing a disagreeableness towards her, nowadays, that was becoming marked. She wondered if the child had any idea – but she refused to entertain this possibility. The matter, supremely important, was one for *her* decision, not to be influenced by the claims of anybody else, not *anybody's*, till *she* had decided it: certainly not by Irina's. She picked up the receiver and told Jasper that Irina was upstairs, reading. She'd had a lovely day and presently they'd all be having supper in the kitchen.

Neil and Phyll came back, having made a hurried scamper through wallpaper albums, and agog to engage in further scrutinies and considerations as soon as possible. Neil had the drive back to Grove End

55

ahead of him but Phyll said he must have something quick to eat first. The spasmodic talk was not very different from that of an ordinary family round the supper table. Jasper reached Carteret Street soon after eleven. He was tired and did not want much conversation, but Marcia seemed not to want any at all. Sullen as she appeared, making brief replies, he supposed something had annoyed her, but he hadn't the energy to try to find out what it was. He was anxious to get to bed and sleep. On his way he looked into Irina's bedroom. She seemed to be having a good many restless nights at present. This was one of them. Her eyes were shut but she was moving her head from side to side and murmuring as if at something she saw. As he bent over her, he caught the words: 'The little statue.' The incomprehendible language of dreams! Flotsam on the dark, uncharted tide. He stroked her forehead. Her eyes opened and fixed on him with an uncomprehending stare. Then she said, quietly but distinctly: 'The bear's necklace.' Jasper stroked her forehead again. 'Go to sleep, my darling,' he said softly.

6

The weather forecast prophesied a season of heavy rain but September opened tranquil and warm. Irina went back to school in the second week. She was unusually glad to be immersed in the routine once more; it was a refuge, she did not know from what.

Phyllida was now so often out with Neil in the evenings and weekends that Irina was left a good deal to herself when at home. Though glad of Phyll's company when she had it, her sister's absence did not worry her, and as she did not want her mother's society she passed the time when out of school quite happily, but she looked forward more than ever to hearing her father's key in the door in the evenings, and to the weekends when he would read to her or take her out in the car by themselves to Kew or Richmond. These outings had become more frequent lately; at the same time he had got into the

56

habit of coming home only in time for dinner, spending the time between that and leaving his office at his club. Beside vague, private disquiet, there was a good deal on his mind at present. For some little time, he and his partners had felt uneasy about one of their commitments in Saudi Arabia. An important part of the firm's activities was the designing and installing of heating and ventilation systems in public buildings, in Britain and overseas. In the last two years there had been a falling-off of orders at home, not serious but perceptible, and enough to make it extremely important to secure and carry out efficiently a number of export contracts. The contract in question was for a ventilating system in a new hospital in Saudi Arabia. It had sounded an excellent prospect at first, but now cables were arriving from the site which showed that matters were not going well. Jasper and his partners, Bill Marshall and Ted Wainwright, realised that nothing effective could be done without one of them going to the site. Prompt attention was urgently necessary; the clients were unhappy and dissatisfied and a repeat order, which had been promised, would depend on a satisfactory outcome of the present problems.

All three partners, Spedding, Marshall and Wainwright, were equally competent; from the point of view of the firm's interests, there was nothing to choose between them. All had experience of the Middle East; who should go was a matter to be decided by their private convenience: all were married, all with families. Wainwright rather leaned to the assignment, Marshall was perfectly willing but with no strong bias; Jasper was content to let the others decide it. The journey must be undertaken in a week's time, and word was sent to the superintendent on the site that one of the partners would be coming out; confirmation would follow immediately. Jasper said very little about the matter at home, since he did not expect it to involve his own absence.

Irina had always been known as 'a quiet little thing'; sometimes people had to look about the room to see if she were there. On the afternoon of a half-term holiday, which, as it was a Monday, did not mean that her father was at home, the foretold rains swooped down. Irina had been lying face downwards on the drawing room floor, reading. In front of the bookcase, a large chintz-covered sofa with a

57

valance that nearly touched the floor cut off the rest of the room. She
had *David Copperfield* open in front of her eyes. The position would
have been uncomfortable for adult bones and muscles but she found
no discomfort in it. After a series of restless nights, she suddenly fell
asleep with her cheek on the page. When she woke up, it was much
later in the afternoon; the rain was lashing the windows and sliding
down the glass, and she could see the gleam of the electric fire
reflected in the polished boards at her eye-level. Voices were talking.
Over by the fireplace in two armchairs which she could not see, she
knew from the direction the voice came, her mother and Ivor Mosscrop must be sitting; beside them were the subdued noises of china
on a tea-tray. She was still half-asleep and it was easier to go on lying
with her cheek on the open book than to get up and declare her
presence; but the first instant of complete understanding was one of
breath-taking astonishment.

'My darling,' he was saying, 'you'll have to make up your mind to
it.' The familiarity of his tone took her so much aback, she could not
then have moved to save her life. 'He's got to face it sooner or
later.'

'Yes,' her mother said, 'I know, but –' He went on: 'It'll be hellish
difficult for you at first, but once you've told him, the worst'll be
over.'

(Told him! Told whom? What must they tell him?)

'The way things are, if he's left to find out he could divorce you
without any alimony. Get it out in the open, then you can play it your
way. You've got to be sure he'll do the decent thing and let you
divorce him, that way you could get a hefty settlement.'

The blood pounded in Irina's ears. The words *couldn't* mean what
they seemed to mean! Her mother was saying: 'I'm afraid he mayn't
agree. He may refuse.'

'That's where you come in. You'll have to make him see that
you're so fed up with him that he'll agree to it.

'There's no other way – you can't exactly plead cruelty, can you? If
you run off, it'll take three years and you won't get a penny. Once
he's agreed, and he will if you pitch it strong enough, then it's all in
the bag. I can't say, off the cuff, but if you divorce him you'd be

entitled to a proportion of the value of the house and contents (and don't forget, you've got some pretty pricey things here, it won't do to let him walk off with them) and anything up to a third of his income. It would be much better if you could get him to hand over some capital, plus maintainance for the two girls, of course . . .'

('The *two* girls'. Then it *was* true. The sensation in Irina's chest was as if a sharp knife had entered it at the collar-bone and was sliding down into the lung.)

'Phyll's going to be married quite soon –'

'I'd soft-pedal that, if I were you. Tell her she'd be better off at home for a couple of years, give her a chance to learn housekeeping from her mum. Two years' allowance for her keep would mean a nice little bit over, unless you went and blue'd it all on the wedding.'

'I wouldn't do that. But she's so set on this marriage, and there's going to be so much against us anyway –'

'All right. I daresay you know best. The main point of course is the settlement on *you*. Got a good solicitor?'

'Jasper's got one: Martin Porteous.'

'Seen him, ever?'

'Once. He came to lunch after he'd arranged our move.'

'What's he like? Elderly?'

'Yes. He's the senior partner.'

'Doesn't sound as if he'd be much good to *you*. You'll have to have a separate one. We'll find someone who'll be on your side, a good, active chap who'll be up to all the dodges. I think I know one: Ron Sharpley.'

'I love to hear you talk about it, you make it sound so near.'

'It *is* near, it's being handed to you on a plate. You must be absolutely firm, that's all.'

'All, well, but that's a lot –'

'Hell, you're not going to weaken?'

'No, never. Even if you left me, I'd be determined to get my freedom now. I'd never go on with him any more.'

'Leave you! I shan't leave you.' There was a sound of movement, then a long, deep silence in which Irina lay, almost too frightened to breathe. At last Mosscrop said in smothered tones: 'Of course, don't

59

talk money to him till you've got the divorce firmly into his head. Make him see you're so completely browned-off with him you can't stand this life for another minute, then when he's ready to discuss terms we'll bring in Ronnie Sharpley to turn the heat on.' After a long pause Marcia said:

'Of course he'll feel he's always been generous to me – though I'm not sure that he has, actually –'

'My dear girl, if he's ever been generous to you, as you call it, you've earned it over and over again, you know that. He's had your whole life, so far. There's got to be a change now, a big one, and I'm here to see to it.' There was a sound from her mother, something between a laugh and a sob. 'Only,' he went on, 'you *must* make the first move yourself. Then I'll be here to back you up. When he sees he's got no alternative, old Ronnie will take over. He'll make the pips squeak! Have you any idea what he's got?'

'No. I never heard.'

'Well, we'll see all that later. Old Ron can be trusted to see that he doesn't play any games.' The actual meaning of the words passed out of Irina's ken, but within seconds her mental landscape had changed: from groping bewilderment to a scene completely realised, lit up by a piercing light, forced on her with a speed that made her mind shudder and reel.

Her mother and Ivor Mosscrop had got up and were leaving the room. The rain, which had before been perceptible as myriads of glass rods battering the windows, had now covered each pane with a running sheet of water. 'Where is he?' 'At his club. He'll stop there till he comes back to dinner.' Leaving the door ajar, they moved across the hall to Marcia's bedroom and shut that one. Irina got to her feet, stiff at last with lying in one position so long. Her heart was beating so hard, she couldn't think where to go, what to do. Then, as she rested her arm on the back of the sofa, the idea came that she must find her father. If he was at his club, she must go to him there. She had once seen the beautiful Georgian building from the outside, reminding her vaguely of a temple; she had looked at it through the car window while her father went in to leave a message, and she had been made aware, somehow, that ladies must not go there, but this

60

recollection no sooner recurred to her than it was swept away by uncontrollable force.

The rain was coming down in torrents, bringing a premature darkness, and a drumming sound that carried even into a closed-up house. She gained her bedroom and put on her raincoat and her round felt hat; then she went noiselessly downstairs to the front door. It was a heavy one, and shut behind her with a muffled sound. Marcia who was, as she put it, quite strung up, started from the bed, exclaiming: 'What was that? Irina going out?' 'Probably,' he said. 'She'll get wet but it doesn't matter, does it? She's probably gone out to post a letter to her boyfriend. It's still light; she won't come to any harm.'

By almost unbelievable good luck on so wet a night, a taxi was cruising down the Haymarket, its wheels spraying fans of muddy water. It drew up at the signal of the little girl in the round hat. The driver was somewhat uncertain as to the worthwhile nature of this fare, and even when she gave the reassuring address, he asked: 'Got the money on you, ducks?' 'I have four pounds,' Irina said, in quavering tones. The driver reached out of the cab and wrenched open the door for her, and the drive began, through slashing rain clicking on the taxi's windows, swishing to avoid other traffic, hissing on the flooding road while falling water blurred the street lights. They drew up outside the lofty, solemn portico and Irina pulled all the notes out of her purse and pushed them into the driver's hand. She was halfway across the pavement when he shouted to her, holding out her change.

In the large library on the first floor, exquisite comfort and calmness reigned. Table lamps gave light for reading but overhead the crystal-dropping chandeliers were only partly lit. The softness of this radiance meant that the red-gold firelight from two marble-pillared hearths could be seen reflected, shimmering in the surfaces of wood and brass. All was warmth and silence. Round one of the hearths four men were sitting in easy chairs, reading newspapers. A junior porter, coming over the carpet quietly but rapidly, approached Jasper Spedding and murmured: 'There's a young lady in the hall, sir, who says she must speak to you.' The three companions were too well-bred to raise their eyes from their evening papers, but the announcement was, to say the least, surprising. Two months ago there had been a disconcerting fracas; a lady, discarded by a highly distinguished member of the club, had arrived in the hall one evening, demanding an interview in a loud and drunken voice and had been got outside only with difficulty. Now, the precincts had been invaded again; Spedding, too, that quiet chap. Jasper sat in amazement but when the young porter said in low tones: 'I think it's little Miss Spedding, sir,' he got out of his chair in one movement, striding out of the library and down the wide, shallow stairs ahead of the young man. The hall, floored with black and white marble, was empty, but from his alcove behind the reception desk the head porter came out, saying: 'We've got her in here, sir.' Irina had seen him coming down the staircase and the next instant her damp little form was in his arms, her arms round his neck. She was sobbing wildly. He said with over-mastering seriousness: 'Stop crying, my darling. Try to tell me what's the matter.' After a few seconds' gasping, the tears still racing down her scarlet cheeks, she brought out: 'I heard them. Mummy and he are going to make you be divorced, so that you'll go away and they can have the money.'

Sometimes, when matters appear startling to the conscious mind, it is recognised in the next instant that the subconscious mind has already realised them. Jasper raised his head from over hers, but though he was looking at the black and white marble floor, he did not see it. Then he signed to the junior porter. 'I've left my car too far away,' he said. 'Please get me a taxi.' He led Irina to one of the nooks, of which there was one on each side of the front door. 'Wait for me here,' he said and walking hurriedly to the desk he picked up one of the telephones and dialled his own number. After a longish pause Marcia answered. He said: 'Is Mosscrop there with you?' 'Yes, as it happens, he is. What about it?' 'Just this.' He lowered his voice, though the senior porter had withdrawn to the far side of the spacious hall. 'Irina overheard his conversation with you about divorce. She came to find me at the club –' 'At the *club*?' 'Yes. I'm bringing her back now. She's very much upset and I'd rather he wasn't there when we arrived. Can you arrange that?' After a moment's silence,

Marcia said haughtily: 'Oh, I suppose so.' She put down the receiver. All ideas of choosing the right time, taking a reasonable attitude, playing it by ear, would now have to go by the board. Her face was white and shocked. Ivor put his arm round her and held her closely while she panted out what she'd just heard and that she had guaranteed his absence. 'So the fight's on!' he said. He was circling her waist with a heavy pressure that brought comfort, security, life itself back to her. 'Well, I don't know that that's a bad thing. The sooner the better, after all. The thing is, you mustn't weaken.' 'Weaken!' she said with scorn. 'It had to be done some time,' he said, pressing her head against his shoulder with his palm. After the first shock, he was not sorry the crisis was upon them; he was glad, in fact; but secretly he resented having his hand forced. (Damn the little brute!)

In the taxi Irina sat huddled against her father. The violent rain had stopped but it was still a wet night; though there was much traffic to be negotiated, they seemed to her to be going at great speed, and she was terrified that the journey would end before she had been able to make everything clear to him. If only she could make him understand what was happening the fearful weight would be lifted. She clung to his arm as she told him, almost incoherently, how she'd been asleep behind the sofa, then exclaimed with a rush: 'They're going to take the money away – a great deal of it, and all the things in the house, and get rid of *you*. It'll be a settlement. And you'll have to pay them more money because they'll make Phyll and me live with them. But I don't want to.' Fresh sobs silenced her. Jasper said: 'Don't talk about it any more just now, my darling. We'll hear all about it presently.' The taxi drew up and they got out. Upstairs, Marcia had come out into the hall. Irina's eyes under the tear-swollen lids did not meet her mother's. He put his hands on Irina's shoulders. 'We shall tell Irina all about it presently, but now I think she'd better have a bath and go to bed. She can have her supper in bed, can't she?' 'Of course,' Marcia said coldly, 'if that's what she wants.' He had meant to put off discussion till later, but all of a sudden he found he could not do this. In a few minutes he was leaning against the drawing room mantelpiece, while his wife sat in the chair whose cushions were still crumpled from Mosscrop's visit. He said:

'I've known for some time that we were in a bad way and it *had* crossed my mind to wonder if you might be wanting to suggest a divorce – I'd no idea your plans had got as far as this. Couldn't you have talked to me about it before you and Mosscrop got down to settling the financial details?'

Marcia's face was no longer pale, it was flushed with angry energy. She said: 'I don't expect sympathy and understanding from you. I'll just state the facts.'

'Do that.' She swallowed and said: 'I've been unhappy with you for years. I've – I've decided that I can't take it any longer.'

'Had you decided this before Mosscrop came on the scene?'

'No, but his love, which you wouldn't understand, of course, his – well, his passion for me has made me realise what I've missed in the whole of my life with you. He's made me feel as if I were just getting out of prison – I can't, won't, go back to it.'

He said: 'I've known for years that I didn't make you happy, and it's grieved me bitterly. I did try – when you said you wanted anything, I tried to get it for you. I never stood in your light, except when I persuaded you not to have that abortion –'

'Persuaded! You absolutely forced me.'

'Well, I did. I brought all the pressure I could on you. I can't say I'm sorry about that. But did I ever go against your wishes in any other way?'

She drew a deep breath. 'The way you talk just shows how hopelessly you misunderstand everything.

'Isn't it enough that I'm unhappy and have been for ages? Our marriage has broken down . . .' Jasper looked in bewildered fashion about the room, as if astonished to find that the walls, the furniture, were still solid and intact. Then he said, dazedly: 'Has it?'

'You know it has, only for your own selfish reasons you won't admit it. Of course we've been to bed . . .'

'I supposed so, but though that's painful to me, it isn't a reason for divorcing you. If I decide not to . . .'

'But you can't decide not to! It's not for you to decide, it's *my*

64

decision, and if *I* say we must have a divorce . . .' She sounded nearly hysterical. 'If you're the gentleman you pretend to be, you'll do the decent thing and make out you're the guilty party.'

'Marcia,' he said, 'I haven't shown any passion for you this long time. I thought you didn't want it; it wasn't because I'd stopped feeling any. Can't we begin again? Won't you let me be your lover again? Come away with me, wherever you like, can't we put the life back into it?' His eyes were more eloquent than his words. (Ivor had told her it would be hellish difficult.)

'You simply don't begin to understand,' she said. 'You can't put something back that wasn't ever there.'

'Never there! Are you going to say that you *never* had any happiness, even when we were first married?'

'*Some*, but not what I have now. You simply haven't got it in you to give me what Ivor gives me.' Her face blazed with anger and contempt. In that instant he knew, though he would not acknowledge, that the battle was lost; but he said: 'In the long run, I would be willing, or rather, I would consent, to your divorcing me, if you were absolutely determined that it was the only thing for your happiness; but you can't expect me to agree within five minutes. We've been married nearly nineteen years. We've got two daughters, one grown up; what reason can there be, apart from your fancy for Mosscrop and his for you, to smash up our home? I can understand you feel absolutely engrossed at present, but this sort of thing doesn't last. If we both try, we can get the better of it, between us. I'll do every single thing I can to help you get over it.'

'I don't want to get over it, as you call it. It's the only thing that makes my life worth living –'

'That's why I'm sure it's temporary. You've only known this man – how long? A few months, that's all. And a blinding passion that makes you insist on sacrificing us all, after nineteen years, almost overnight – it *can't* be lasting, at this pitch! It will die down presently, and then we can begin again –'

'Thank you, that's the last thing I want to do!' With a change of tone, she went on: 'You needn't think we meant to spring it on you like this. He and I both meant –'

'You may as well leave him out of it. It's your feelings that matter to me.'

'We were just getting ready –, *I* was, to tell you in a proper, reasonable way. It was Irina's eavesdropping that brought it all out like this, making it look as if we had no consideration for you. It was absolutely shameful –'

'My dear Marcia, hardly worse than what she was listening to –'

'She's always been against me. It's not surprising she should act the spy –'

'She couldn't help overhearing some of it. She was asleep on the floor as I told you, and only woke up to hear you and Mosscrop settling the details. It wasn't surprising, when she heard something so fearfully important to us all, that she came to tell me about it.' He drew a long breath. 'And where have you and he settled to live? or have you arranged to stay on here and turn me out?'

'Really, Jasper, whatever Irina may have told you, we haven't thought about all that. I don't mind where I live. Phyll is determined to be married as soon as she can. Irina of course would be with me. I can't talk any more about it now.'

The last half-hour had been the most exhausting of Marcia's life. She had never before had to explain herself. Now, without warning, she had had to think out, carefully, a statement of overwhelming importance. This mind-bruising crisis had been brought on by Irina. If she and Ivor had been allowed reasonable time to collect themselves, they wouldn't have been caught at this disadvantage, which gave Jasper the chance to be so foul to her.

Jasper had left the room; he was collecting linen to make up the spare-room bed. Phyll would have done this for him, but she was out with Neil and her father was thankful to have one less person to talk to; to talk without speaking of this devastation would have been impossible.

Meanwhile Marcia had arranged a tray with a glass of milk, some bread and butter and a banana and carried it into Irina's bedroom. The child was sitting up in bed, her face still tearstained, clutching the sheet up to her chin. Marcia put the tray on the bed and said: 'I don't want to be cross with you, Irina, but you shouldn't listen when people don't know you're there. And if you do hear something by accident, you shouldn't rush off to tell somebody. I was going to tell Daddy something very important about him and me and all of us, and you've made it much more difficult, rushing about like this. Well, we shall have a lot of talking to do presently and there'll be a lot of changes, but you needn't be upset. Daddy and I shall always take care of you, though we shan't be living in the same house, and we shall make things happy for you.'

Irina's eyes were stretched wide. 'But is he to go away?' What was the use of talking about things being happy for her, with Mr Moss-crop there all the time and her father gone? Marcia, who felt that she'd made a heroic effort, against great odds, to talk to Irina in a calm and friendly manner, nearly lost her temper. When she'd been through so much, it was intolerable. With a struggle, she said: 'I can't talk to you about it all now. There's too much to explain. Children have to let grown-up people decide things.'

'But Daddy doesn't want – I know he doesn't –' Her mother said abruptly: 'I'm not going to talk any more now, Irina, I'm very, very tired.' She was pale, with dark smudges under her eyes.

Next morning the situation, between shock and misery, was unbear-able. Jasper and Marcia could not yet speak of it in front of the girls, and to be all together without speaking of it, that was unbearable too. Jasper had got to look older over-night. He came into the dining room as Phyll was putting down the coffee pot, but then he went out again. Soon after, he left the house without any breakfast. Marcia drank some coffee, then left the table and shut herself in her bed-room, from which she could be heard telephoning.

Phyllida who had come in late the night before and somehow gathered that a heavy calamity was on them, found herself being put in possession of the facts by Irina as they sat over their solitary breakfast. Irina poured out the events of yesterday's afternoon and evening. 'He said old Ron would make the pips squeak. What did that mean?'

'It means, to get a lot of money out of someone, as much as ever they've got, as if you were squeezing a lemon,' Phyll said. She looked sick.

Irina said: 'But it's Daddy's money. How can they –'

'I don't know, actually. It's very difficult to explain.' Phyll broke off, wishing very, very much that Neil was there with them.

Mrs Mumford came in to clear away the breakfast things. With the uncanny capacity of domestic workers to pick up what is going on, the expression on her face implied, not only that she knew everything but that she had foreseen everything. Irina got ready to go to school, her mother still telephoning behind the closed bedroom door. Phyll presently did some telephoning herself from the call box at the corner of Carteret Street. She had already arranged to meet Neil for lunch, but she felt she could hardly get through the morning without breaking the news. Sitting opposite to her over their lunch, Neil gave her such happiness merely by being there that she longed just to enjoy the sensation without disturbing it by these heavy tidings, but when, having ordered for them, he leaned forward and said, 'Now, sweetheart, let's hear about it,' it was a relief to tell him. Neil's immediate response was, that the first time he'd laid eyes on that fellow he'd known he was up to no good. His tenderness for Phyll prevented him from adding that for some time past, he'd had pretty much the same opinion of her mother. 'Well,' he said at last, 'it's a bad show, however you look at it, but of course we don't yet see the outcome, though from what Irina heard, they seem to have got the thing taped. But your father *may* be able to dissuade her (not that *I* would try to, he added to himself). But there's this about it; if everything's haywire, he may be inclined to agree to our getting married sooner than he said –' his eyes lit up – 'almost at once, in fact.' Looking at each other across the small table, they momentarily lost sight of the difficulties and pains outside their enchanted ground.

These, however, rose up in their sombre ranks when Phyll found herself alone with her father that evening. Jasper had dined at his club, Marcia was out, where, they did not speculate, Irina was upstairs in the playroom. Phyll had told her to begin going to bed, and when she came downstairs again, looking for her father, she found him looking for her.

They went into the study. Phyll knew that it was not possible that his hair had become greyer over-night, but it looked to her as if it had; his hair and face, she thought, had an overall greyish tinge.

He said gently: 'Has Irina been telling you?' and stopped.

'Yes.'

'Had you any idea that your mother felt like this – meant to – to separate from me?'

'No. She never said. But I did think she was discontented, or something.'

'How long had you thought that, my dear?'

'Vaguely, for some time, but only, really, since Neil and I got engaged.'

'I'm glad you and Neil are getting married; and if this home is split up, although I said I'd like you to wait a year, now I feel I'd like you to marry as soon as you both feel inclined.' Phyllida smiled, a slowly dawning smile of pure happiness. Then her mind came back to the forbidding present. Her father went on: 'I shall of course keep the door open till the last possible moment, in case – in the hope that your mother might change her mind, but –' he sighed deeply and was silent. Then he went on: 'There must be a divorce, if I am absolutely convinced that her happiness –' he stopped again, then he said: 'It's Irina who worries me, what to do for her.'

'Won't she stay with Mummy?'

'Yes, I think that's almost a certainty, for the time being, at least. I could hardly, at a moment's notice, arrange a household that a divorce-court judge would think as good for her as being with her mother. But presently, I shall do my best – my level best, to arrange something – something that would make it possible for me to have her with me. That's what's so hard to swallow – that our home should be wrecked, and Irina swept away from me in the wreckage, because of that man: someone we never knew till a few months ago. I keep feeling it's some hideous delusion, that it hasn't really happened.' His head moved slightly, as if he were looking about to reassure himself where he was. Phyllida was silent, filled to the brim with sympathy and love. He said: 'I'm afraid she and Mummy have never been very close.'

'No.'

'You have always got on better with your mother.'

'Yes. I like her, really, only –'

'It's natural you should, and I'm glad you do. You and she find it easy to get on?'

'Yes. She's very young, in a way, and she enjoys things. She's fun to go about with, sometimes.' He sighed. 'I daresay she's often found it rather dull, with me.' Phyllida would have liked to say something impetuously, but the words would not come. Her cheeks flushed, her lips quivered, the shining tears came over her eyes. Her father remained silent, looking at her with adoring love. Then he said: 'I was saying a little time ago that we were discussing in the office which of us should go out to Saudi Arabia. You remember?' Phyll nodded. 'It didn't matter which of us it was, and I was leaving it to be decided between Bill and Ted. I didn't much want to go; but now I think I might as well go myself. I think if I got right out of here for three weeks – for one thing, while your mother is in this frame of mind it's rather horrible for us to have to be here in such close quarters – and if she is left quite alone, I think it might help her to come to a decision.'

'But hasn't she, already?'

'Yes, but there's always the chance, the faint hope, that she may change her mind; after all, we're all suffering from shock at the moment, at least she and I are –'

'And we are, too.' Phyll's face was pale again. 'I and Neil and Irina, and so will everybody be who –' she stopped.

'Then I think I shall go ahead with my plans, and take off in about four days' time. Tell me, my dear, if it's not too difficult, what sort of impression does Ivor Mosscrop make on you – you and Neil?'

'Well, *we* can't see anything in him – anything interesting or attractive to make up for his being rather awful. I suppose it's like women being in love with film stars, only then you can usually see why, even though you don't feel it.' Her father said: 'That really is my one hope – that this is a temporary infatuation. It *may* burn itself out.'

It seemed as if the heavy suffering that this sudden confrontation

70

brought on them, *could* not last: it must disperse – so suddenly to face them, so awful in its nature, and for such a trivial cause, for Ivor Mosscrop. Though Jasper told himself this was the reasonable attitude, some deeper instinct conveyed to him a hopeless acceptance of the fact, but he must force himself to struggle against it; divorce would mean the loss of his home, of Irina.

Marcia for her part was suffering too; there was nobody in the family who was on her side. Phyll, when her mother spoke to her about the matter, trying to gain some impression of sympathy, was almost silent, her deep blue eyes wearing their grave, remote look; that she did not say how keenly she felt for her father was the concession she made to her mother. But silence was not a tribute for which Marcia had much use; she would a great deal rather have had vehement speech, assuring her of encouragement and understanding. She had, however, always had some basic sympathy with Phyll; the girl's attitude was natural enough, and at least she wasn't offensive with it. Irina was the thorn in her side. Too young to understand her mother's situation and with no real affection to make her accept, for her mother's sake, what she could not understand, she caused Marcia a burning indignation. It was unbearable! Marcia had of course, in all this martyrdom, the supreme consolation of Ivor's frequent presence and of constant talks with him on the telephone. That Jasper was going abroad in a few days made it seem unnecessary for him to retire to a hotel meanwhile; of course it would have been nice if he had, but Marcia told herself that she'd given up expecting any consideration. As she now took her breakfast in her own room and Jasper was always out to lunch and dinner, the apartment divided itself into two: her bedroom and the drawing room for her, the spare-room and the study for him.

Though there was no one in the family who could see things from her point of view, or cared about what was due to *her*, Marcia had the great advantage of Mrs Karmiotis' friendship and advice. She had told Mrs Karmiotis of Irina's maddening attitude, and of her belief that if only the child could be made to act reasonably, she felt that, allowing for the various inevitable annoyances, the prospect was set fair. Jasper was to take off for Saudi Arabia almost at once; he'd be

71

absent for about three weeks, and on his return, if she hadn't changed her mind – (as if she were likely to!) they'd set about the business of a divorce. She'd been assured by Ivor's solicitor, Mr Ron Sharpley, that as it was to be uncontested, it could be put through at a rate of knots. The only hold-up might be an argument about money, but she did not feel this was at all likely; she'd had nearly twenty years' experience of Jasper's generosity, and Mr Sharpley would be looking after her interests. Though worrying till it was actually through, everything *should* be all right; only, Irina was going to make trouble, she could see that. Mrs Karmiotis said, optimistically, that when the arrangements were actually in force Irina might settle down quite happily. Marcia made no reply to this. She merely said: 'It's all rather hard on me, I must say.' Mrs Karmiotis agreed cordially that it was, and as she always liked to be doing on a friend's behalf, if the matter were in any way dramatic or emotional, she said perhaps *she* would have a word with Jasper, make him *see* how people were expected to behave nowadays? Marcia was perhaps too much involved to be able to put the thing clearly. Marcia agreed that there was no harm in her trying. Jasper was in the flat a good deal. It would be better, probably, not to try to arrange an interview, but to let it come about naturally.

The opportunity occurred late that Saturday afternoon; Jasper came out of the study as Mrs Karmiotis was in the hall, preparing to depart. He was about to greet her with impersonal politeness and pass on, but Mrs Karmiotis said: 'Oh, yes. I've been hoping for a word with you. Can we come in here?' Without waiting for an answer she walked into his room in front of him. Jasper followed, not having said no in time. Mrs Karmiotis sat down and took out her cigarette case. As she also fumbled for a lighter, he did not feel obliged to forestall her with the lighted match which he would have offered to anybody else. He remained standing at one corner of his desk, while Mrs Karmiotis puffed and waved and jangled heavy metal bracelets.

'I wanted to talk to you,' she said, 'because I feel we have to be very careful of Marcia. She's undergoing a great strain at present.' Jasper was silent from astonishment. 'Yes,' she went on, 'I daresay that sounds unexpected, from your angle, but surely it's the understood thing nowadays that if a marriage has broken down, you go ahead with a divorce? Of course it would be up to you to prove you were the adulterer . . .'

He said stiffly: 'I shall have to agree to a divorce if my wife wants it. I don't want it. I want to keep our home so that I can have my daughters with me.'

'That brings me to what I want to say,' said Mrs Karmiotis triumphantly. 'Phyllida, you must admit, is out of the discussion. I hear she's going to be married almost at once, so any plan based on your keeping the home to have her with you is out. But it's Irina. Marcia feels, keenly, that the child will never settle down with her while she senses that *you* are hostile to the arrangement. If you keep up this attitude, you'll make it impossible for Marcia to come to terms with her. Of course Marcia feels it as an injury. It's the mother's right to have the child with her,' said Mrs Karmiotis, with an air of great authority. 'The court would award it to her. It's *your* duty to make the situation workable, to let Irina see that *you* want the divorce, as well as Marcia. You should have a very, very serious talk with her, and explain to her that this is all being arranged for the happiness of everyone concerned.'

'Do you expect me to tell her that I *want* our home to be wrecked, that I *want* her to live apart from me?'

'Yes, yes, I quite see that it's hard on you, but you should remember that *everything's* hard on *somebody*. I think it's your duty to make this sacrifice here, to stop thinking about your own feelings. After all, Marcia has made all the sacrifices up till now –'

'Sacrifices! What sacrifices?'

Mrs Karmiotis said, with an air of audacity and hardihood: 'In being your wife for nineteen years.' She laughed rather awkwardly. 'I'm sure,' she went on hurriedly, 'that the marriage with you was a good one, materially speaking, but there *are* other considerations in life beside money –'

'Did I ever say there weren't?'

She went off at a slightly different angle. 'After all, you know the saying: it takes three to commit adultery.' She smiled slyly, looking mischievously round the room and avoiding his eyes. ('Let him work

73

that one out for himself!') 'And I can tell you this,' she went on, 'that if you don't impress on Irina – we all know that she'd pay more attention to you than to anybody else – if you don't make her understand that the divorce is for everybody's benefit, you'll be making it very, very hard for Marcia. It will need an effort on your part, no doubt – but, it *is* demanded of you. If you don't make the effort, you'll be doing Marcia a serious injury and you'll be depriving Irina of the chance to have a happy home life with her mother, which is every child's right, after all.' Mrs Karmiotis ended with a toss of the head.

She stood up and he seized the opportunity to cross the room and open the door. He said, holding it, 'I am sure you mean your interference very kindly, Mrs Karmiotis, but this is a matter in which I am afraid I must –'

'Oh well,' she said, restored to what she felt was a civilised composure, 'if at any time you should want to talk things over for Marcia's sake, you'll always find me ready.' Jasper bowed and she walked out of the room with stately tread. She did not go out of the front door, however; abandoning her dignified manner, she hurried to Marcia's bedroom, banged on the door and burst in, exclaiming: 'Well, my dear, I did my best. No good, of course; but my God, I don't know how you've stuck it as long as you have!'

That evening Jasper told Marcia that he meant to go on Tuesday. He said candidly that he hoped his absence would be of use to them both. It would not change *his* views, nothing would do that. He wanted to live in the family home for the rest of his life, with her, in close touch with Phyll, with Irina growing up beside them; but complete separation at this point might help them – help her, to see things more clearly. If she was absolutely determined that her happiness required this dreadful – he stopped, unable to continue. His face bore a look of such acute, unmistakeable suffering that she felt, for an instant, almost daunted; but Ivor had warned her that the going would be tough. This was it.

Though he would not have done it on Mrs Karmiotis's advice, he felt that he must have a serious talk with Irina. Among his many last minute concerns, he had managed to buy her an excellent child's

74

book on Arabia, thoroughly illustrated. The pictures named the parts of Arab dress: the keffiyeh, the drapery worn over the head, and the agal, the fillet that wound it round the temples. The illustrations in this book showed Arabs riding on camels, and buildings with domes and slender, soaring minarets, and there were drawings of coffee pots with spouts like the head and neck of a swan and long necklaces of amber and turquoise and large, filigree silver beads. Irina concentrated on the book intently and Jasper told her that though domes and minarets and marble terraces and rose-gardens were still there, the discovery of oil in the Arabian peninsula some years ago had brought in thousands of skilled foreign workers and that Arabia, which was once a very reserved and self-contained country, now had its small population mixed with Americans and Europeans; and its cities were beginning to be built up with hotels and shops and high-rise flats, like cities everywhere else in the world. Where travellers had once ridden camels along the ancient highways, now they went by motor transport, or they travelled through the air, as the prince did on the magic horse, in the Arabian Nights.

Irina was sitting on the arm of his chair, leaning against his shoulder, as she turned the pages with rapt attention, and he said suddenly: 'You know, of course, that Mummy has got to feel that she isn't happy living with me any more and that she wants to be married to Mr Mosscrop instead?' Irina's eyes, widely opened, were dark with dismay. 'But you knew all that before, didn't you?'

'Yes, but I thought you would tell them not to.' He smiled sadly. 'When she says she doesn't want to live with me any more because she has got to be fonder of Mr Mosscrop than she is of me, I can't make her stay with me; she would be unhappy if she couldn't marry him. At least that's what she feels at present. I don't want to make her unhappy.'

'She's making *us* unhappy.'

'Yes, dreadfully unhappy, just now; but –'

'I don't want to stay with her and Mr Mosscrop. I don't!'

'My darling, I don't want you to either. In the end, I want you to come and live with me –'

'Oh, *yes!*'

75

'But it can't be just yet. We must be patient for a little. I must go away for three weeks now, then, when I get back, if Mummy still wants this, I'll think very hard how we can manage. But you see, if she and I are to be divorced, we shall have to come before a judge, and *he* will say where you ought to live –'

'Why *should* he?'

'It's part of his duty to try to arrange what's best for the children of divorced people.'

'He wouldn't know what was best. It's nothing to do with him.' Jasper had not the nervous energy needed to meet the passionate arguments of a child, particularly when he himself largely agreed with them. He said: 'A judge might think that Mummy could take better care of you than I could. I should have to be out all day, shouldn't I, and there would be your meals and clothes to see to. But I think we may be able to manage something presently, only we must be patient –'

'For how long must we?'

'Until I get back, in a week or two. I can't exactly say yet how long I'll be, but less than a month, I expect.' She raised herself and clung round his neck.

'Daddy, Daddy, *please* don't make me live with *them*! I wouldn't be a nuisance to you –' He gathered her in his arms. 'No, I know you wouldn't.'

'I wouldn't need any taking care of, I could do everything for myself, you wouldn't have any trouble, I wouldn't give you any –'

'My darling, I know you wouldn't, but just for a little while we have to wait and see what can be done. But in any case, when I come back, if Mummy goes on living here and I don't, I shall see you all the time, I promise. We shall never lose each other for a moment, never, I promise.' She was crying violently, her head against his neck. He felt the tears on his chin.

The door opened and Marcia came in. She was prepared to join the conversation in a friendly, affectionate manner. Raising his head, Jasper said: 'I think you'd better leave us alone for a few minutes.' The heaving sobs went on. Marcia stopped dead, thinking it hardly possible that he meant to, or could, absolutely shut her out from this

76

scene in which she was every bit as much concerned as he was, but he had bent his head again and seemed unconscious of her being in the room. With a strong feeling of resentment she went out and shut the door.

Theonoë Karmiotis had said, in the most positive manner, that he must, and therefore would, put it to Irina that everybody wanted this divorce, that it was for *everybody's* happiness. He just wasn't doing it, she could see. He was ganging up against her with the child, he wasn't playing fair; not that she'd expected him to, really. She might have known. The sense of being bossed about and put in the wrong was intolerable; the craving for Ivor's presence was like that for a powerful, soothing drug. No further stage in their discussions could be reached until Jasper's return but what chiefly occupied her mind meantime was, that immediately Jasper left for the airport Ivor would be free to come and go: that they could enjoy the comfort of Carteret Street, instead of being restricted to the sparse accommodation of Ivor's lodging (bed-sitting room, scullery on landing, share of bath-room on upper floor), off the Tottenham Court Road. Ivor had said the place wasn't fit to entertain her in, but, until they saw how things were going to go, it seemed the wrong time to launch out into anything better. Marcia entirely agreed, and she was longing to make him free of the comparative luxury of Carteret Street.

When Jasper knew how few days he had at his disposal, he tele-phoned Geoffrey Galbraith, giving him a brief outline of the firm's commitments and saying he would very much like to see him before he took off. Sir Geoffrey would have preferred him to come down to The Lawn for lunch but he saw that it would be less taxing to Jasper for them to meet, as the latter suggested, at his club. He found Jasper looking older, paler and with a new way of speaking, at once faint-voiced and urgent. Over the meal, the latter outlined the position of affairs at the Saudi Arabian hospital and went into considerable detail over the difficulties he would have to deal with. Then he drew breath and said that Marcia was insisting on a divorce so that she could marry Ivor Mosscrop.

Sir Geoffrey's cameo-like features, the sharp nose and light eyes behind the rimless glasses, gave him sometimes an air of impersonal penetration, but when he listened to a friend the effect was one of extreme clear-sightedness combined with gentleness. Jasper gained from his silent attention everything that the most sympathetic ejaculations could have given him. After they had finished their meal they went into the library; it was occupied by only a few people, sitting at a considerable distance from each other. Jasper and his guest retired to a space between a bookcase and a great sash-window, a small round table on a triangular pedestal in front of them, a clock framed in a gilded wreath of bay leaves and berries above their heads. The coffee had scarcely been put down before them when Jasper said: 'It's Irina. When I talked to you down at Sandwich, I'd no idea it had got this far. Phyll, thank God, will be happy with Neil –'

'Yes. A great blessing.'

'But Irina – I suppose she must stay with her mother for the present.'

'Have you any fears of this man, for the child's safety?'

'No, I can't say I have. I imagine he'll think of her as a confounded nuisance rather than anything else.'

'Just as well, so long as there isn't actual harshness.'

'Yes. Well, my aim will be to get some sort of arrangement set up, which will allow me to have her with me. I can't see it clearly just yet, but it'll come. My fear is that a divorce court judge, knowing nothing about the circumstances as *I* know them, will think the child's better off with her mother than with me, and award her to Marcia.'

'We must speak entirely confidentially: you understand that any hint of collusion between you and your wife in this matter could have very grave consequences. But as the object of this pair is to get themselves married and living on your money as soon as they can, I think I would point out to her that if she doesn't fall in with your wishes about the child, unlimited access and so on, you won't agree to her divorcing you. If you divorce her, she won't get the child, and she might not get any money.'

'I suppose so.'

'I never did any divorce work, and it's always chancy, but I think some threat of that sort might have a good effect.'

Jasper drew a long breath and began to regain some of his normal

78

colour. As he stirred his up till now neglected coffee, Sir Geoffrey said: 'May I ask – you have, I take it, made a will? Is it of recent date?'

'No. It was done years ago when Irina was about five. I know I should have up-dated it when the business expanded, but I never got round to it.'

'Well, why not do it before you fly out?'

Jasper said with renewed dejection: 'With a divorce pending, it might have to be altered within weeks of my getting back.'

'Why shouldn't it be? I don't want – heaven forbid – to prophesy disaster, but you're going on a long journey. Wouldn't it be a comfort to leave the girls explicitly provided for, without any risk of confusion? It would be a simple matter to cancel and re-write it afterwards.'

'Yes, you're right. I daresay, in the circumstances, Porteous would see me this afternoon, without an appointment.'

'I don't doubt he would. You may need to appoint trustees, provisionally, for the girls' settlements. If I can be of any use –'

'Thank you! I can't tell you how much I –'

'Then when you come back, if it has to be re-drafted, it'll be just an inconvenience, no harm done.'

'No. It's so obviously the thing. I don't seem to have been all there for the last ten days or so.'

'Naturally. You've had a very severe shock, and with all these business matters on your mind as well –'

They got up. Jasper stayed in the hall to telephone Mr Porteous's office, and, having received a satisfactory reply, they went out together. As they were standing under the portico, about to say goodbye, he said, absently: 'For years and years it worried me; I used to think I wasn't good enough for her. And of course, you might say, if I weren't rather a dull sort, she wouldn't have – this might not have happened.' Sir Geoffrey looked at him, at first with incredulous wonder, then with a dawning compassion that changed into a smile. They descended the flight of steps. Sir Geoffrey hailed a passing cab, and Jasper one that was immediately following, and they were carried away from each other's sight.

7

The brief time was filled with interviews in the office, with visits to the bank, to the Foreign Office, with travel arrangements, Neil, who had already had a meeting with him about taking care of Phyll, (and of the others, of course), rang early on the morning of Jasper's departure, to wish him bon voyage, and to assure him, once again, that he himself was standing by. Bill Marshall and Ted Wainwright also rang, just to wish him all the best and to say they were dealing with something that had come in for him by that morning's post.

Irina had taken herself off to school; she had looked pale and almost sullen; instead of the demonstration she might have been expected to make, when her father embraced her and kissed her, she had stood passively. Phyll, who had come in very late the night before, as she did rather often now, tumbled out of the bedroom not quite dressed and said: 'Shall I come to the airport with you, Daddy?' 'Yes,' Jasper said, and she disappeared to put on the rest of her clothes. The hall-porter came upstairs and carried down two light-weight suitcases and a portfolio. Marcia had done nothing. She had a logical feeling that a show of helpfulness and sympathy at this point would make the final parting, which she had determined was imminent, only the more painful to him. The porter came up again and said the car was already there. 'Phyll will have to have her coffee at the airport,' Jasper said. Then in the brief moment before Phyll came out of her bedroom he said, low voiced: 'I needn't tell you how much I hope you'll change your mind. The door's open. Do come back!' Phyll now came out and picked up her father's light overcoat. She went downstairs. Jasper made a move to kiss his wife, but she stood like a statue. He went hurriedly down.

Convicts when very near release are said to find the last short stretch harder to bear than the long term which has gone before. Marcia, pale and burning-eyed, had found the last few minutes all but unbearable. In the street below, the loaded car started and drove off. Within the doorway of the little pub, The Moon and Stars, open now for its early morning sweeping-out, Ivor Mosscrop stood and watched it; before it was out of sight, he was inside the front door and going up the stairs.

The next few days went by without any trouble above the surface. Jasper sent cables: to Marcia saying he'd arrived safely, to Neil, that the problems were being ironed out and that he didn't foresee having to postpone his return, to Phyll that he was bringing home a wedding-present for her, to Irina that he wished she could see the blue water of the Persian Gulf, and how much he looked forward to coming home again, he hoped on October the third, that was as near as he could fix it. Each morning Irina departed for school after breakfast, a meal which, sitting between her mother and Phyll, she usually ate in silence. When she came back in the afternoon, she had tea in the drawing room if her mother were in; if not, and if Phyll also were out, in the last throes of the crammers', she would find that Mrs Mumford had laid a tea-tray for her in the kitchen, so that she had only to boil the water for her little tea-pot. Phyll and Neil were very good to her, taking her to shows they thought she would enjoy, *A Midsummer Night's Dream*, a Disney film. Marcia was frequently invisible: out, or shut up in her bedroom, from which the sound of conversation, varied sometimes by Mosscrop's deep-toned laugh, could be heard by anyone passing the door.

The light of late September faded out of the skies; a time ensued of gloom, wind and thunder. Irina, going doggedly to school, sitting in class, withdrawn, not questioned as she attracted no attention, thought for long spells how happy she was going to be once her father had come back. Her mind did not travel beyond the prospect of his return; she had ceased to think any further about the imminent threat of separation; his coming home was all she dwelt on. Further cables from Jasper confirmed that he was keeping to the pre-arranged date. On the morning of October the third, Irina for once broke silence at the breakfast table. 'Is it today Daddy's coming back?' 'He said so,' Marcia answered sullenly. She said no more for the moment, then asked Phyll: 'Shall you be in to cook, or shall I speak to Mrs Mumford?' 'Oh, I will,' said Phyll with quiet eagerness. 'Neil's coming,' she added.

But by eight o'clock that night, Jasper had not arrived. They ate their dinner, Neil saying more than once that he might show up at any moment; but when ten o'clock struck without a telephone call from the airport, he and Phyll decided that he must have been delayed, and they wouldn't expect him till tomorrow. If he should come after they'd all gone to bed, he had his keys; even if the hall porter wasn't on duty, there'd be no difficulty in his getting in. Listening to them, Irina determined to stay awake all night in case he did come after all, however late. This resolution made her willing to go to bed without protest when Phyll urged her to; in bed, she managed to keep her eyes open for an hour or more, then she was suddenly asleep before she knew it.

The next day was gloomy too, with leaden clouds and a chill, fitful little wind; the sort of weather to get absolutely on your nerves, Marcia said fretfully; hers, she felt, were in shreds. She and Ivor had agreed, reluctantly, that he'd better not be found in the flat on Jasper's return. As this meant Ivor's absence for what was, at present, an uncertain time, the decision made her nervous and restive and hardly able to speak to anybody.

In the afternoon the air was gloomier and the battering gusts of wind had increased in violence; litter was sent scudding about the streets, and dust and grit into the walker's eyes. Irina, coming back from school, vaguely noticed flapping newspaper placards which said in big letters something about fatality and loss of life. She did not attend to them, they belonged to a world with which she had no concern. When she got in, she knew at once that her father was still not there. Another blank, heavy evening followed. Marcia was taut with irritation and made no effort to appear as if she shared the interest of the other three in her husband's return. Neil and Phyll had the conversation to themselves; though now uneasy, they found

82

their usual pleasure in talking to each other. The four of them were at table, and the dining room was quite brightly lit, but when Irina remembered the scene afterwards, she always saw it in her mind as empty and rather dark.

She was in bed when Neil, having listened to the ten o'clock news, came into the kitchen where Phyll was tidying up, shutting the door behind him. 'My God,' he said, 'there's been a 'plane crash over the Persian Gulf.' She held a damp tea-cloth in both hands, staring in bewilderment and dawning horror. 'They haven't released any names yet, that means they're trying to get into touch with the families.' 'How do they – how would they know whom to –' 'They'd have the names of the people who'd booked in for the flight; I'd better try ringing Marshall, or Wainwright, try to get hold of one of them and see if they've got any news. Of course we don't know what plane he was coming back on. If they know, I'd ring British Airways and see what they'd heard.' She was pale but calm. She put away spoons and forks, gently, with exaggerated care. He took her in his arms. She began to say, crushed against his cheekbone, 'Ought we to say any-thing to –'

'There's nothing to say, yet. Leave me to get what I can. No point in upsetting Irina.'

'No, of course not, but Mummy –'

Neil said harshly: 'I, for one, am not going to talk to your mother just for the sake of talking. When there's any hard news, of course, she's got to have it, supposing it hasn't come to her directly. Where is she now?'

'I think, in her bedroom.'

'Telephoning that swine, I'll bet. Look, I must phone at once if I'm to get through to Bill Marshall. I'll go down to the call box in the hall. Have we got his number, and old Wainwright's? They're in the book, I suppose?'

'Mr Marshall's will be, he lives in London. The Wainwrights are out at Pinner; you'll want a provincial directory.' Neil gave a smoth-ered exclamation. 'But Daddy will have it somewhere, sure to.'

'See if you can find it, angel, in case we need it. Meanwhile I'll look out Marshall's and try him.'

83

Phyll went into the study, wiping her damp hands on the sides of her skirt before she opened the drawer of the desk where the leather-bound address book was lying. She found the Wainwrights' telephone number. Then she went across to Irina's door. She unclosed it with caution, fearful that Irina might be awake, but there was no sound or movement from the bed, which she could just make out across the room in the dim light. She went back to the kitchen to finish clearing up; she was in a state of such anxiety, every breath she drew seemed to cause pain. In ten minutes Neil came upstairs again. He'd spoken to Bill Marshall who had missed the news. He agreed that it was most unsettling, grim in fact. He undertook to get on to Ted Wainwright himself. They'd do what could be done to get the earliest information, and would let Neil hear what success they'd had. Neil gave him the telephone number of his office. The next few hours were going to be ones of excruciating suspense. Saying this, Neil went on: 'Look here, I can't leave you. I'll have to stay the night. Anything will do – an armchair –'

Phyll said: 'There's the spare room Daddy was sleeping in. I'll make the bed up.'

He smiled with a fugitive lightening of care. 'Pity we're not married already.'

Phyll smiled too but she said with decision: 'Well, we aren't.'

He went on: 'I'll have to use your sponge and toothbrush and comb. I'll get shaved in the morning on the way to the office.'

They not only felt that there was no need to seek Marcia's approval of Neil's staying the night, but there was as yet no possibility of doing so. She had made a hurried assignation on the telephone, saying that as Jasper had not shown up she might as well come to Ivor's room for an hour or two. Anyway, she was sick of being indoors, with the others all over the flat.

Next morning Neil did not appear at breakfast. He had a cup of coffee very early and went off to get shaved at an Italian barber's in the Strand, whose shop he remembered from the days when he and others came away from dances in time to see the sunrise from Westminster Bridge. This seemed to him a very long time ago, and he was glad to find the barber still there, dealing with clients at eight o'clock. Marcia did not come to breakfast either. As Phyll had less to say than usual, and was up and down, carrying in cups of tea and plates of toast to her mother, Irina could not bring herself to say: 'Will Daddy come today, do you think?' She went off to school with hardly a word between them.

When she got home at tea-time, instead of taking off her coat in her bedroom as she usually did, she walked straight into the drawing-room; there, she saw at once that a great deal had happened since she left home that morning. Phyll and her mother were there, also Neil and Mrs Karmiotis, all sitting in different parts of the room, looking as if they were waiting for her. Neil came up to her very determinedly and said: 'There's some very bad news, Irina, bad for all of us.'

'When is Daddy coming back?' Irina demanded.

'That's it, chick. He can't come back. He was on the plane and it developed a fault in mid-air: it exploded and –'

'And what?'

'The pieces fell into the sea and everyone was killed or drowned –'

'*Everyone?*'

'Yes, I'm afraid so.' After a second's stunned silence, part of Irina's mind returned, but not the faculty of commonsense.

'But he said he'd come back! He *said* he would! He promised –' Phyll put her arms round her. 'Of course he did, and he would have done, if this dreadful thing hadn't happened to us.'

Marcia stood up. She said 'You and Neil had better take care of Irina. I've had as much as I can stand.' She went, rather unsteadily, out of the room and Mrs Karmiotis got up and followed her. In the dining room Marcia said: 'Of course, poor kid, it's rotten for her.'

Mrs Karmiotis answered,

'Well, yes,' with a certain degree of reserve. 'Where's Ivor? Is he coming round?'

'We're supposed to be going out to dinner. He's to come early, but I wanted to see Irina back first.'

'Let's hope it won't be long before *she* feels able to show some kindness to *you*.'

Marcia made a gesture of hopelessness; then she said: 'Neil's going to Grove End to get his bag and tell it all out to old Cousin Louisa. He'll stay here for a night or two. He and Phyll will manage everything. I'm so – so shot to pieces, I feel I can't do anything without Ivor to take care of me.' She gave a strangled sob.

'Have you got any sleeping pills?'

'No, I've never had any.'

'There are some good ones that you can get off prescription. I'll slip out and get you some before I go.'

'Thanks a million. What should I do without you?'

Meanwhile in the drawing room, Neil was telling Phyll that he'd go off now to Grove End and be back in a couple of hours or so, to stay as long as she'd like him to. Marcia came back, a tumbler of whisky in her hand, and Neil was about to go, when the doorbell rang three times in a pre-arranged signal and Marcia got herself across the hall to answer it.

When Ivor Mosscrop came into the drawing room, Irina was half lying in a corner of the sofa, Phyll was leaning over her and Neil stood with his back to the window, feeling for his cigarette case. Ivor's ally Mrs Karmiotis having crossed him, going out as he came in, he saw that, apart from Marcia (pale and distraught and beautiful), everyone present was rigidly hostile to him. He gave a half-smile; his self-confidence was unmistakeable; his bearing was already more erect that it had been. He would be friendly to anyone who made friendly overtures; if none of them did, that would be all right by him.

'Dreadful business, this,' he said. No one answered. He turned to Marcia. 'I think you'd better come out for a meal,' he said. 'I don't suppose you've had much to eat today.' To Phyll he added: 'I'll take care of your mother for this evening. You'll be all right here, with the young 'un?'

Phyll's lips moved soundlessly. Neil said: 'I shall be staying here for the time being, until we've had time to look round us.' Ivor would have liked to say: 'You mean you've decided to stay in Mrs Spedding's flat?' But as he now felt secure he didn't want to start quarrelling, when the husband had been dead scarcely forty-eight hours. He put his arm round Marcia's shoulders: 'Let's get your coat,' he said.

Marcia spoke in the droning voice of a sleep-walker: 'I shan't be late.' She turned to Irina. 'You'll be good with Phyll, won't you. We must all help each other.' Ivor Mosscrop took her by the elbow and led her out of the room.

Irina still sat, pale and motionless. Neil could see she was in a state of shock; he wished she would start to cry – but then, what a load to heap on Phyll! He said to the latter: 'The sooner I'm off, sweetheart, the sooner I'll be back. I ought to be here again by eight, easy.' Phyll saw him off, and then came back and sat down on the sofa by Irina. She had expected – been afraid of – some devastating outcry, some paroxysm of hopeless weeping, but Irina, after the one outburst, had remained in a trance-like state and Phyll did not dare to speak in case she dislodged the pebble whose shifting would bring down the avalanche. She sat with her arms round Irina, resting her chin on Irina's head, for how long she did not know; but the clock's striking seven roused her. She got to her feet and, pulling Irina up, took her into her bedroom, where she pulled curtains and lit lamps, and getting Irina out of her clothes, for her movements were very vague and slow, she put her into bed and went to fetch a hot-water bottle and heat milk for her. When she had done all this, and had looked into the larder and the refrigerator to see what could be put together for Neil's dinner and hers, alone in the kitchen it came over her that this was the moment she'd been waiting for, when she hadn't to think any more about other people, that she could give herself up to realisation without trying to hold the grief in. When Neil came back she was leaning over the sink on her elbows, crying as if her heart would break. Her weeping was so natural, Neil did not even try to comfort her: he only held her in his arms till the crying fit brought itself to a stop. Then, against half-hearted protests from her which he ignored, he got their meal together and persuaded her to eat a little while he ate a good deal.

Marcia was still out by the time they, exhausted as they were, wanted to go to bed. They found Irina was dozing restlessly, lying with the whites of her eyes showing between lids almost shut. They considered whether to wake her and give her two aspirins to make sure she thoroughly slept, but they decided against this, in favour of leaving her door propped open and Phyll's too. Neil said under his breath: 'I hope that swine won't come in when he brings your mother back.' Phyll was too tired to reply. Once in bed she gave way to a healthy creature's demand for sleep.

Neil, again, was away very early. Before he went, he said: 'We'll simply have to get some sense out of your mother presently. There's any amount to decide on and we must get in touch with your father's solicitors, before we do anything else. Shall I ring them from the office?'

'Oh yes, *please* do. They are Moulton and Wingate, and Daddy's friend is Mr Porteous. He's the senior partner.'

Neil showed great satisfaction at gaining this information. 'And I tell you what,' he added, 'we'll get into touch with old Geoffrey Galbraith right away. I wonder I didn't do it sooner. Ring me if there's anything drastic. Otherwise I'll see you about six this evening, darling heart.'

Irina came in to breakfast, colourless but sensible and calm. Phyll ventured to say: 'Do you want to go to school? You needn't if you don't want to.'

Irina poured milk onto a bowl of cereal and said: 'Oh yes. It's the day of the gym competition and I'm in the team.' Phyll was silently giving thanks when Marcia came in, in her dressing-gown, dishevelled and pale. Phyll had already taken her a cup of tea and Marcia had said she didn't want anything else, but she had now come into the dining room feeling she must make a great and painful but absolutely necessary effort to speak to Irina. She said: 'Irina, it's a very dreadful thing that's happened, for all of us. I'm too ill to talk about it now.' Irina looked at her. Marcia went on: 'We must all be very kind to each other. Daddy would have wanted that.' Irina looked at her plate. 'There are a lot of things to explain to you but I can't do it now.' She put the back of her hand to her forehead. 'So will you try to be patient? Everybody wants to help you but I can't do it now.' She paused. 'Can't you say *anything* to me?' she demanded, her voice rising.

Irina kicked the bars of her chair. 'I suppose so,' she muttered.

'Then say you'll be kind to me and try to help me.'

'Of course she will, Mummy,' said Phyll, removing Irina's bowl and putting butter and marmalade within her reach.

Marcia went back to her room. One would have thought that now, at last, everything would be plain-sailing. Well, it would, soon, but at present the cross-currents were confusing and exhausting beyond words. She had imagined that Ivor would immediately bear her away to realms of happiness. So he would, soon, but he had seemed to think there was a good deal of sorting-out to be done before they took any decisive steps. She was so tired, and with a bad head beginning too, there was nothing she could do for the present except go back to bed.

Neil, whose office was being extraordinarily decent, telling him to take off all the time he needed, found himself next day in the premises of Moulton and Wingate, following a neat typist through the lofty, spacious drawing-room of a beautiful Georgian house, now occupied by desks and filing cabinets. Mr Porteous, in view of his last interview with Jasper Spedding, barely a month ago, was much relieved to be in contact with the young man of whom his client had spoken so warmly as his elder daughter's fiancé, and to hear in Neil's own words that he was standing by. He was also glad to hear that Neil was a friend of Sir Geoffrey Galbraith, and he felt that between them all they should be able to work out something for the girls. He told Neil that at Sir Geoffrey's suggestion, Jasper had made a will immediately before his departure: 'I have it here.' He produced a folded document. Briefly he explained that the capital in the bank was divided into three equal shares between Marcia and her daughters. The flat, whose lease had twenty years to run, was left to Marcia, and all the contents, except for a list of objects, subjoined, which were to be sold for the benefit of Phyllida and Irina, except for any of them that either might wish to keep. ('My wife takes less interest in them,' Jasper had said.) 'The bank are the executors,' Mr Porteous went on, 'and they will want to make sure that none of these objects is removed before they can be sent for auction. There will be a considerable sum from Mr Spedding's share in the firm; that also will be divided into three equal shares, but it is not possible to calculate the amount at present. He hadn't time to make all the bequests he would have liked to make, but he left you, personally, ten thousand pounds, hoping your marriage will take place as soon as possible.' The expression on Neil's anxious young face gave place, momentarily, to a smile of pure happiness; then it reverted to one of harassed concentration. Mr Porteous said: 'Phyllida's share can be made over to her as soon as formalities are completed. Irina's is to be held in trust. I have been appointed as one of the trustees; Sir Geoffrey Galbraith agreed to Mr Spedding's nominating him as the other. Meantime, it's a question of what's to become of the child. Of course in ordinary circumstances, she would stay with her mother.' Neil made an uneasy movement as if he sensed some threat to his own future. Mr Porteous went on: 'I know her father, in the event of a divorce, was determined that ultimately she should live with him, though he realised he'd have to leave her with her mother for the time being; he wanted to have unlimited access to her. But what do you, yourself, think of this man Mosscrop, whom I suppose she'll now marry? I take it he isn't what used to be called a gentleman?'

'No. No, he isn't. I daresay if he had been, she wouldn't have lost her head about him. As it is –' He shrugged.

'As a divorce has been avoided, the question of where the child's to live doesn't arise. It's the mother's right to have her and also the mother's responsibility.'

'Yes. It's a poor look-out for Irina, but as you say there's nothing else to be done. Phyll and I will try to keep an eye on her but we couldn't undertake anything long term –'

'Quite, quite,' Mr Porteous said. 'I will suggest to Mrs Spedding that she should come and see me. She may not know the terms of the second will. All expenses incurred for Irina will come out of the trust: school fees, clothes, holidays and so on but her mother will be able to claim for her support at home.'

'Did you ever see her?'

'Once, as I remember, after we'd conveyed the Carteret Street property. Very pretty, but I shouldn't, I think, have felt inclined to trust her very far.'

'Not farther than you could throw a battleship,' said Neil grimly.

For the next few days the routine of Carteret Street went on as usual, with the single, awful exception. Cooking was done either by Phyll, or Mrs Mumford; Irina went to school, came home, was there at mealtimes, almost completely silent. When she was at home, Phyll spent a lot of time sitting in the playroom with her, but they said nothing about their father. Phyll longed to talk about him but an impassable barrier prevented this with her mother and she was afraid to try to overcome Irina's strange reserve. She could talk to Neil about him, though, and began several times to do this, though she always broke down and cried before she had said very much; even so, the relief was great. She and Neil had been afraid that Ivor Mosscrop would now move into the flat but so far he had not done so. As a rule he spent several hours of the afternoon in Marcia's bedroom and once or twice he was in the drawing room before dinner; neither of them had had any conversation with him. Both sides appeared to be in a state of armed neutrality.

Neil was glad to hear from Phyll's telephone call when he reached his office, that a copy of the will had come by that morning's post; she had taken it in to Marcia with her breakfast tray. Marcia had told her what it was and was now reading it on her pillow.

Marcia was, first of all, astounded by the date on which the will had been drawn: two days before he left! She hadn't had the slightest idea – not that she'd thought, one way or the other. The document was very short; she grasped that a third of the capital in the bank was hers, and the flat and its contents, with certain exceptions. A sensation of delight rose in her breast and spread through her body, warm and thrilling. She reached for the bedside telephone; hearing that she had the will in her hands, Ivor told her to read it to him. When she had done so, he made no comment, merely saying that he'd be round by ten.

Ivor was dressed already, for he was an early riser. The telephone in his lodgings was in the hall and, if he was in when it rang, he was usually the first to answer it. He now went slowly up the linoleum-covered stairs, thinking very hard. The whole thing, while still sound, had gone slightly askew. It had not occurred to him that

Spedding would make a new will, on the eve of his departure for an absence that was to have been so short. He had not of course seen the original will, but Marcia had told him that Jasper had made it about six years ago. The girls would then have been about eleven and five. It was most unlikely that, at that time, the capital would have been divided into three equal shares, with trustees appointed to theirs. Almost certainly, he thought, the whole sum would have been left to their mother, with bequests to them when they came of age. At that stage, the entire fortune wouldn't have amounted to all that much; now it appeared that irrespective of Spedding's property in the firm, it was almost a hundred and fifty thousand. Fifty thousand pounds was a very nice sum, far more than he'd ever expected to get his hands on, but a hundred more would have been nicer still. Or, since Phyll's share would naturally be lost to them on this dam' marriage of hers, another fifty thousand.

When he saw Marcia that morning, his comments on the will rubbed some of the gilt off her prospects. They stood to get – (or she did, it was all the same), just what he'd told her was her lawful expectation in a divorce settlement; but he made it sound as if she'd been shabbily treated, as if Jasper had stolen a march on her. What had exasperated him was the list of objects excepted from Marcia's legacy to be sold for the girls' benefit or kept for them if they liked: the porcelain shepherdess, the clock with the gilt charioteer on top of it, four Regency chairs in the study, a pair of colour prints, one of Nelson, one of Wellington, his early Victorian writing desk, and a Regency silver soup-tureen, long since muffled in its green baize bag, as Marcia had said it was too much trouble to keep cleaning it. These things were just what Ivor would have keenly enjoyed selling; he and Badger would have made a good thing, an interesting thing, out of doing it. Seeing how small the matter was, compared with what he was gaining, it was unreasonable to mind as much as he did, but it rankled. He'd waited a long time for life to come up with something really worth his having; he felt he wouldn't take kindly now to having bits chipped off here and there.

Mr Porteous found, as he had half expected, that the fact of the new will had been a complete surprise to Marcia. He repeated its provisions to her, but though they were of so much importance to her, she seemed for the moment not to be listening to them. Her eyes fixed on the window behind his head, she demanded: 'How had he left things in the first one?'

'I don't think I can tell you, off-hand. In any case, his financial position then was so different, it would hardly –'

'Where is the old one? Can I see it?'

'We destroyed it.'

'Why?'

'It's usual to destroy the old will when a new one is made, and really, Mrs Spedding, it would have no bearing on this present position. Your husband at his – most tragic death – was a much richer man than he was when he made the first one.'

'Well, I don't like these provisions. I think they're very unfair to me. I don't think the girls' shares should be equal to mine –'

'They aren't. You have the possession of the flat for the next twenty years, and all the contents except the objects on this list in front of you.'

'That's another thing. I ought to be allowed to dispose of those things myself. I shall take advice from some other solicitors –'

'By all means; but meanwhile, we ourselves can only execute the will as your husband made it.'

'And as I am providing the home for Irina, her share ought to be in my hands till she's of age to have it.'

'I can promise you, Mrs Spedding, Sir Geoffrey Galbraith and I, as the two trustees, will do everything to meet your claims for her. You need not anticipate any difficulties there.'

'I oughtn't to have to make any claims – the spending shouldn't have anything to do with outside people. The whole thing is an insult to me. I suppose, as you were an old friend of his, you put him up to it?'

'I assure you, Mrs Spedding, he didn't need any advice. He came to this office with his mind made up. His instructions were natural, in view of the fact that you were demanding a divorce.'

'Well, no doubt that's a matter of opinion,' said Marcia angrily. She stood up, collecting her bag and gloves. Mr Porteous also got up.

'Perhaps we shan't get very much farther now,' he said. 'If, presently, you would like the details of your legacy, I shall be pleased to arrange another interview.' He bowed. Marcia paid no attention. She walked into the outer office where, at sight of her, a young man got to his feet and accompanied her on to the landing down the shallow, curving staircase and to the massive, beautiful front door.

As she walked up the pavement, Marcia's mind was in turmoil. Everything about the interview had exasperated her, from the terms of the will itself to the austere reserve of Mr Porteous and the antique beauty of his premises. Just like Jasper, she thought, to go to a place like that! A solicitor's office should be resounding with telephone calls and the whirring, ringing of typewriters, with fitted carpets from wall to wall and very bright strip-lighting; in surroundings like that, one would feel there was some chance of getting up-to-the-minute advice. Walking rapidly, too much preoccupied to look about for a taxi, she was infuriated by a growing sense that old Porteous was probably right, that nothing could be done to alter the will. Not that she could have helped it, she couldn't have foreseen, naturally; but she understood now, that if only she hadn't demanded a divorce so vehemently, if she had led up to the matter quietly and reasonably as she and Ivor had meant to do, Jasper would just have gone off on that trip, to give her a chance to think the thing through; he wouldn't have had that last-minute idea of making a new will; the old one, she was sure, now that Ivor had put it into her head, would have left her in a much more favourable position. It was her absolute insistence on a divorce, (she admitted that she'd been driven nearly hysterical), which had made him take this maddening step; and her insistence had been the result of Irina's idiotic, unpardonable bursting out with what she'd overheard.

Though Ivor now spent several hours a day in Carteret Street, he had not given up his business activities. He and Badger rented a small warehouse in a street off New Oxford Street, where the narrowness of the roadway and the height of the houses on each side made it look like a canyon. At ground level most of the premises were anonymous-looking, concealed behind blank walls with small doorways, kept locked and bolted. Here Ivor would bring what he'd gathered in, and Badger passed the goods on to various dealers, all in a humble way but steadily profitable. He'd been looking forward pleasurably to bringing in the china shepherdess and the clock with his own hands; among the very things this dam' will had deprived him of: Badger would have priced them right away and given him something on account, but he hadn't got where he was without the exercise of strong common sense. He knew he must put on one side all minor dissatisfactions, however irritating, and play the last few rounds carefully. Marcia, on her return, sat on the sofa in the drawing room at Carteret Street, leaning against him and almost crying with vexation. She had wanted so much for him to be really thrilled with satisfaction and delight. Ivor, having mastered his disappointment, set to work to dispel hers. He reminded her that, all told, their circumstances were satisfactory; (besides, hadn't they got each other?) She was so much soothed by his cheerfulness and encouragement that as they sat, with her head on his shoulder, she suddenly felt an impulse of magnanimity. She sat upright and exclaimed: 'I wouldn't have had any harm happen to him for the world! It was the most frightful shock to me when I heard.'

'Of course it was,' he said tenderly.

They now felt that the date of their wedding must be settled. Marcia said that once that was fixed, unalterably, then everything else would fall into place. Could they aim to be married at the beginning of the New Year? Ivor said that would suit him fine, except that he wished it could be tomorrow. Marcia wished it too, with a yearning intensity she'd never known before. She felt that after everything she'd been through, if she couldn't get away with Ivor for a long honeymoon, she simply couldn't go on. But were Phyll and Neil to be married first? If so, they would move out to the flat being made ready for them in old Louisa's house. Would they be willing to take Irina with them? Or would Phyll stay here in Carteret Street till she, Marcia, came back? Marcia was perfectly willing to have the child, in fact, she wanted to; (and in any case, she'd got to), but she could not allow Irina, or any earthly thing, to get in the way of her honeymoon. Something *must* be settled about that, the taking of Irina off their hands for – say – a month. Marcia would have liked to be away, away from everything except happiness, for much longer; for several months, to recover; but now that he had almost secured control of her money, Ivor had become very prudent with it. He agreed to a month abroad, but longer – why stay away at great expense when this flat would be eating its head off? Ivor had, in Carteret Street, domestic surroundings far more comfortable, luxurious even, by his standards, then he had ever been made free of before: constant hot water, a glossy bath with solid-looking taps, large, thick bath towels, the Crown Derby china, the silver (which he must get Badger round to look at right away), the comfortable study, which he meant to take over as a kind of office, though that pricey desk had been filched away from him, the telephone laid on, for nothing, every dam' thing you could want, and Marcia into the bargain. Till he had thoroughly got used to all these benefits, he found the idea of staying at home in Carteret Street, for free, more alluring than their paying heavily for several weeks in some continental hotel. He said that after a month's honeymoon they could be just as happy here, with each other, as anywhere else; in fact, *he'd* prefer it. His low tone, warm and sensuous, made her translate this economic proposal into a lover's prospect of domestic happiness. And, he went on, it would be much easier, in fact there couldn't be any difficulty, in getting somebody to take on Irina for just one month. Several months might present a problem, but nobody could refuse to take her for just *one*. How about that old girl down at Grove End, Cousin What-have-you? Didn't she live with a companion? Then she was a natural for the job. Between her and Neil and Phyll, the kid would be absolutely water-tight. Marcia agreed, then she said: 'I'll have to tell her we're getting married.'

'Doesn't she know?'

'I daresay Phyll has told her, but now we can give them the date.'

Ivor said with narrowed eyes: 'Phyll won't make a row. I hope Irina won't. If she does, you must jump on her. Tell her she must take it as read.'

'I don't know that she will make a row, exactly. She's been wonderfully quiet ever since the news. Phyll says she never speaks about him.'

'Well, so much the better. I don't suppose she's short on sense. Phyll is the smasher, but I always thought Irina had the brains.'

Marcia looked at him admiringly. 'You see into things, don't you. Will you stay to dinner?'

'I think I won't. I might look in afterwards, for a coffee. But, tell the truth, that Neil gets on my wick. I don't see why he's to quarter himself here indefinitely.'

'No; but he was useful at the time.'

'All right, but that time's over now, in my opinion.'

'We want to keep him in tow, if they're to take Irina.'

'Right again. Well, we must just tread water.'

Phyll now came in; she greeted Ivor calmly but she had so much quiet charm about her that even her impersonal manner conveyed a sense of welcome. Marcia said: 'Ivor won't stay to dinner.'

'But you've asked Mrs Karmiotis.'

'Good Lord, so I did. Then that'll be you, Neil, Theonoë and me.'

'And Irina.'

'Yes, of course,' said Marcia hurriedly. 'You're seeing to it?'

'Yes. I'd better get started.' She left the room.

'Nice girl that,' Ivor said. As Marcia said nothing, he added softly: 'Not a patch on her mother, though.' At his words the expression of her eyes was like sunrise on dew. She got up. 'Theonoë will be here any minute now. *Do* come in after dinner. She'd like to see you.'

'She wouldn't be the only one, I hope?'

Mrs Karmiotis had been the first of Marcia's friends to hear the fatal news. It had both shocked and elated her. As she had always been on Marcia's side as against Jasper, the death, though mind-blowing, was in her view a piece of actual good fortune, opening the way to vividness, drama and the birth of spring. She had strenuously encouraged the idea of a divorce and she now felt how fortunate Marcia was in having gained everything the divorce might have given her without trouble or delay. Marcia had told her briefly the surprising date on which the will had been made, and its rather tiresome provision of trustees for Irina's inheritance, and Mrs Karmiotis wanted the opportunity to mull it all over.

At ten minutes to eight, she swept in like a shore-pounding wave tossing a crest. With her prune-coloured satin dress trimmed with long-haired black fur and her necklace of gleaming jet, she was the magnetic centre of the room. Compared with her's, everyone's voice sounded rather weak; they all appeared undecided. Phyll said good evening with her usual quiet sweetness, then excused herself to go to the kitchen. Neil's greeting was rather abrupt. Marcia asked Mrs Karmiotis what she'd like to drink; the latter said whisky, and when Marcia said she'd have the same, Neil wheeled the trolley up to them and left them to it, while he went out to the kitchen to help Phyll dish up, or at least to talk to her while she did.

'And have you made all the wedding plans?' Mrs Karmiotis asked eagerly.

'Not all, but we've been fixing the date: the first week in January. We only did it this evening.'

'And those two?'

'I don't think they've quite decided yet.'

'I suppose they're sleeping together?'

'Well, they have separate rooms here.'

'Still, that doesn't –'

'No, I know.'

'Not that it matters, of course. In fact one would rather despise them if they weren't.' Marcia's lack of interest was so blatant, Mrs Karmiotis did not pursue the topic. She realised that she would have to rely on her own perceptions, as to whether to despise Neil and Phyll or not. She was inclined, after an evening's observation, to feel that she must.

Phyll was now carrying pâté and triangles of hot toast wrapped up in a napkin into the dining room. Neil looked into the drawing room and said: 'I think we're about ready.' His tone was quiet but Mrs Karmiotis hadn't waited for this evening to find out that he had been entirely and whole-heartedly on Jasper Spedding's side, and she wondered how long Ivor Mosscrop was going to put up with his being there at all. She was glad Ivor was coming in after dinner; she liked him very much, particularly for his quality of what she called 'animal warmth'. She hoped that when he was there, there might

98

presently be some sort of *éclaircissement* which would fill her in with all the details.

When they went into the dining room, Irina was there, climbing on to her chair; she was very pale and answered Mrs Karmiotis' cordial, exuberant greeting with an almost inaudible mutter. All of them at the table were to some extent out of kilter, but Mrs Karmiotis rounded them up and held them together. A good deal of the conversation was recitative on her part, but it brought them all in except Irina who, clearly, was counting herself out.

Mrs Karmiotis related the tale of a woman who had attempted to get a divorce on the grounds of cruelty; the judge had refused to understand that her husband's hopelessly insensitive behaviour *did* amount to cruelty. Any intelligent person could see that it did, 'but,' she added, 'you know what judges are.' Neil said submissively: 'Judges don't make the law, they only administer it, as they understand it.'

'Oh yes, yes,' Mrs Karmiotis interrupted in friendly agreement, 'I daresay they do the best they can, though one feels they're a rather dreary lot, doesn't one?'

Neil said: 'I only know one, and he's a good deal sharper than I am.'

'That's Sir Geoffrey Galbraith, isn't it? So you say he isn't dreary?'

'Not at all.'

'He was Daddy's friend,' said Phyll in a muffled voice. Mrs Karmiotis made a courteous gesture; privately, she thought that this confirmed any estimate of Sir Geoffrey's lack of dashing qualities. Marcia had often said that Jasper objected to anyone with any *go* in them.

As they were leaving the table, Ivor appeared; he did not now make the statutory three rings, he had his key: Phyll disappeared to deal with the coffee and the dishwasher while Marcia and Mrs Karmiotis took him into the drawing room and sat down with him by the fire; they began an intimate, affectionate conversation with him. On the other side of the room, Neil sat beside Irina on the sofa. She had a book on her lap and he said: 'Would you like to be read to?' 'Oh *yes*,' she said, 'but will they? –' 'We shan't disturb *them*,' Neil said, nor did it seem likely, the conversation by the fire was going on in

99

crescendos of disbelieving protest and shouts of laughter. Neil waited till he had his coffee beside him, then he opened the book Irina put on his knee. It was a collection of ballads and she seemed to know them already; leaning over him and turning the pages, she kept saying: 'Let's have this one,' or, 'Now this.' Neil read simply, in a low-voiced, decisive manner. Though she knew the ballads so well, some almost by heart, it gave her intense, soothing pleasure to hear him read them, the voice vibrating in his chest close beside her ear. They turned the pages to 'The Three Ravens'.

The dead knight was lying in a field; his hounds guarded him on the ground, his hawks hovered above him and kept off other birds of prey; then his sweetheart came and dragged his body away to bury it.

> *God send every gentleman*
> *Such hounds, such hawks and such a leman.*

Neil had unconsciously raised his voice. In a brief pause of the conversation beside the fire, it sounded across the room almost like a reproach. Mrs Karmiotis, fitting another cigarette into her long holder, called out in displeased tones: 'Rather demeaning, to put the girl into the same catalogue with the hounds and hawks!' They were just taking up again the matter of the peer whom an enterprising journalist had managed to photograph in bed with three whores at once, one black and two white, when Irina stumbled onto the hearth-rug, scarlet in the face, the tears racing down her cheeks. 'It wasn't,' she screamed. 'It wasn't what you said –' She sobbed and gasped: 'The dogs and the hawks and her, they all loved him and nobody else did. They took care of him when he was dead. It was lovely! It was!' Her heaving chest made it impossible for her to get out more words. They all stared at her, aghast. Her crying was getting louder and more frantic. Ivor got to his feet and muttering: 'Leave you to it,' he made for the door. The sight of his back, moving relentlessly away, left Marcia appalled and terrified. 'Ivor!' she shouted in despair. Over his shoulder he said: 'Be back later,' and disappeared. Phyll had now hurried in from the kitchen. She tried to put her arms round Irina; Irina fought her off; she was beside herself. She yelled, between sobs: 'They made him go away! They did! They did! They killed him. I wish someone would kill *them*!' Neil had come across the room. He said harshly: 'That's enough, Irina. Stop that row!' Seeing that his words had no effect on her, he seized her shoulder with his left hand and gave her cheek a heavy stinging slap with his right. Irina subsided into long, painful gasps. Phyll took this opportunity of pulling her out of the room, to get her to bed. Once she was undressed and lying down, she began crying again, unrestrainedly but in a natural manner. Neil said, from the doorway, 'Better not try to stop her, let her cry it out; best thing for her. Has that swine mucked off?'

'I think he has,' said Phyll cautiously, looking out. Saying: 'We'll damn well have to come to some sort of arrangement,' Neil retired with her into the kitchen.

Marcia and Mrs Karmiotis were pouring out stiff whiskies. Marcia had made no move to comfort her child or to go anywhere near her. The most powerful element of the scene, the one stamped on her mind unforgettably, was the sight of Ivor's back as he walked away. Even to think of it filled her with panic. At the same time she was resentful. Pale and distraught, she exclaimed: 'It's too bad of Ivor, clearing off like that. Men all over!' Then she said, 'Not that Jasper –' and stopped, as if surprised at the direction of her thoughts.

Mrs Karmiotis took an invigorating swallow. 'Irina was his kid,' she said firmly. 'Of course he wouldn't have walked out on her. That's entirely different. In fact, if he'd paid less attention to her, things wouldn't be so difficult now.' Marcia was relieved to hear this. She dropped ice into her tumbler. Mrs Karmiotis went on: 'What plans are you and Ivor making? Would those two take her over altogether, do you think?'

'No. I know they wouldn't; Neil wouldn't; and of course I'm prepared – I *want* to have her with me, but she makes it *impossible*.'

Marcia knew already that the people in her immediate circle were against her. Their attitude was *wickedly* unfair; they behaved as if she and Ivor had been responsible for Jasper's death, as if they'd murdered him. Their opinion was completely cock-eyed. They confused the fact that she'd demanded a divorce with the fact of a fatal air-accident, the sort of thing that was happening all over the world, all the time; and she traced the cause of all this back to Irina. If only she had been given the chance to take her own time in bringing up the matter of the divorce: however it had been done, Jasper would have made it difficult for her, of course, but at least in other people's eyes it would have been the sort of affair that nobody was blamed for, the sort of thing that was almost a recognised part of family life, not something that gave other people the right to regard you as a criminal!

Marcia, leaning back weakly on the sofa, had never felt so nervously ill in her life. The picture of Ivor, walking out of the door, made her almost hysterical. Something must, absolutely *must*, be done to make sure that never happened again. Once she and Ivor were married, he'd help her not to mind anything, and he'd take a firm line with Irina. She decided that all their arrangements must be set up without delay. She said so aloud and Mrs Karmiotis agreed fervently. It was now nearly an hour since he had left them, so that he would have had ample time to get back to his lodging, Marcia went into her bedroom to telephone him. She was nervous in case he should still be antagonised by Irina's scene, but from a different angle he was as eager for a rapprochement as she was, and delighted to find her welcoming him back with what amounted to an apology. She was so much relieved, so happy, that fatigue overcame her suddenly. She suggested they shouldn't meet again that evening but very, very early tomorrow morning, to which he enthusiastically agreed, with a mental reservation that he'd calculate the time of Pepperill's departure first.

Coming back into the drawing room, still pale and tear-stained but now smiling, she settled herself for a final conversation with Mrs Karmiotis; the latter had refilled their tumblers. In her relief, Marcia said generously: 'Of course, poor kid, it's rotten for her.'

'Well, yes,' said Mrs Karmiotis, 'but that's no reason why you should be sacrificed to her.' She also had received the impact of Ivor's departing back. 'And of course she'll build her father up *now* into a sort of mythical relationship.'

Marcia said with a beautiful candour: 'They *did* see a lot of each other, actually. He always got on better with her than I did.'

'Oh well, she'll just have to take it. After all, what about *you*? She hasn't a thought to spare for you. I should say she's got very little natural affection.' Marcia sighed sadly. 'However, you should find out when those two mean to get married and see if they can take her for a month over your honeymoon, or plant her on that old party, Louisa Somebody, isn't it, down at Grove End? I'd offer to have her myself, but she's never liked me, and she wouldn't fit in with my sort of life, but I'll do it if you can't arrange anything else.'

'You *are* an angel,' said Marcia faintly.

8

After a long spell of crying, Irina had fallen asleep and did not know that Neil and Phyll had come in to look at her before they went to their own beds. She woke next morning with her eyes still red and heavy and a stiff, sore feeling in her throat which made her unwilling to talk. Phyll, who was always up early to get Neil's breakfast and see him off, now came in with Irina's. She wanted to say something to her about last night's scene, something consoling and loving but she did not know how. Now that Irina's frozen state of grief had melted, she seemed ready to cry all the time. Her tears had overflowed while she was washing and dressing and were brimming her eyes as she put cornflakes and milk into her mouth. The sight made Phyll want desperately to cry herself; she had to struggle hard not to.

Irina having taken herself to school, Phyll acted on Neil's urgent advice; when she came in to take away her mother's breakfast tray she brought up the topic of the immediate future. Marcia was sitting up in bed wrapped in a fleecy, rose-pink bed-jacket lined with pink chiffon. She looked fair, young, sulky, and the sort of person with whom it would be impossible to argue. Phyll, who felt the morning chilly, wore a cardigan of Neil's over her dress and looked anxious. Marcia said: 'Ivor and I want to get married as soon as possible.

103

We've fixed the first week in January. But of course that leaves Irina in mid-air. Can you and Neil stay on here – we meant to be away a month – to caretake the flat and look after her?'

'Well, I'll see if we can,' said Phyll doubtfully. 'Will Mrs Mumford stay on?'

'I should think so,' said Marcia vaguely.

'How would we pay her?' Marcia had not thought of this; the financial aspect of her affairs now struck her with unpleasant force. Jasper's weekly cheques had always covered the house-keeping expenses and left something over; her own bank account which he kept in funds supplied everything else. He had left cheques with her to cover his absence and she had banked them without thinking where the next instalment would come from. All this information was waiting for her in the offices of Moulton and Wingate and she had so far refused to ask for it. She said, with an air of being driven to desperation: 'I simply don't know how everything's left.'

'But didn't Daddy leave you a third of all the money?'

'Yes he did, but where is it? I shall have to go to old Porteous again, though I must say I'd rather die – almost.' She groped for her handkerchief. Phyll saw it half under the pillow and handed it to her. She said: 'I should think Neil could find out all that, if you'd like him to.'

'I would,' Marcia declared at once. 'Get him to find out where the money that belongs to me is put, in my bank account or wherever; and we shall have to arrange about payments to me from Irina's share, to cover her being here.'

'I shouldn't think that would be difficult, if you really want it.'

'Of course I want it. Wherever anyone's staying, they're always costing something. I don't say anything about Neil's being here –' Phyll flushed brightly and looked at her mother with indignation. 'I say I *don't* say anything about it,' Marcia repeated impatiently, 'but you must remember that I haven't got all that amount of money now. I can't have people using this place as if it were a hotel. But it'll all straighten out, once I *know*. And I shall be very glad if Neil will go back to Moulton and Wingate and find out everything. Do you think he can go today?'

'I wouldn't think today, actually. But if you'll ask him about it this evening, I'm sure he'll go as soon as he can.'

Neil, as usual, telephoned Phyll in the course of the morning. For several days he had been undecided as to what they ought to do about their wedding, but he sometimes found that when he was altogether perplexed, a solution would suddenly come upon him like a ray of sunlight across a stormy landscape. One of these moments of illumination had struck him as he went down to the office that morning; it dispersed all hesitations and doubts; he felt convinced, and so he was able to convince Phyll, that they must get married at the soonest possible date. To wait on the plans of anybody else might mean endless delay and as he and Phyll both wanted the wedding to be dead quiet, no preparations would be necessary, bar the special licence which, as there would be no time to call the banns, must be got, and no doubt could be, without difficulty. Phyll, momentarily taken aback, was then eager in agreement. Neil said they'd be married at Grove End, and by Hilliard Bartram, wouldn't they? He didn't fancy the *ambience* of Carteret Street, and Cousin Louisa would like nothing better than to create a scene of hospitality and joy for a little wedding-party. They did not want to insult the bride's mother by taking the wedding out of her hands; let it be said that she had so much to do in her own affairs, that it was not reasonable to expect her to undertake it. She would, of course, be invited to attend the wedding, but as for depending on her for anything, or altering their plans to fall in with any of hers, it would be ploughing the sand, Neil said, and Phyll agreed entirely. Neil then said he thought he'd spend that night at Grove End, telling Cousin Louisa everything they'd decided, and seeing how the decorators were getting on. While he and Phyll were away – they'd decided on a fortnight at Charmouth – he knew dear old Louisa and Miss Bumpus would work themselves into the ground, getting everything ship-shape. Tense and impatient as he was, he could see no difficulties worth naming; but Phyll came back to the problem of Irina. Neil exclaimed: 'Look here, one thing at a time. It's no good going round and round in circles, or we'll end up exactly where we started. You and I *must* be married, and we *must* move out of Carteret

Street. When all that's done, we'll see what can be thought up for Irina.'

'Could we ask Cousin Louisa to take her?' Neil was momentarily silent. This solution did not appeal to him; first, because he felt it was an imposition on Cousin Louisa; and second, that if Irina were in the same house with them, separated only by lath and plaster, they'd have to – Phyll would want to, and he'd feel they had to – see a great deal of her. The rapture and peace of those early weeks of marriage which he was passionately looking forward to, as a continuation of the honeymoon, would be seriously interfered with. He said: 'I really don't know, darling. After all, there's nothing absolutely frightful about her staying with her mother, even with Mosscrop about the place. He's a swine, but he's not a child-molester. And your mother – of course she'll duck out of anything she can, but she can't duck out of this, she's *got* to provide a home for her own child, and Irina's got the measure of the place pretty well. She's not a kid who wants a lot of society. She's got the playroom and Mrs Mumford will see to her meals.'

'Yes, I know. But if we get married in November and Mummy on January the sixth, that leaves about eight weeks when she's with them by herself –'

'Well, what of it?'

'She'll be very miserable.'

Neil wanted to say, impatiently: 'Selfish little beast!' but he said only: 'I'm sorry, but at the moment I just don't see any help for it. Of course it's tough on her, but we'll be in close touch with her.'

Phyll sighed. 'Yes.'

'So we go right ahead, do we?'

'Yes, I suppose so.' His office was at that moment empty but for himself. He dropped his voice. 'Do you love me?'

'Yes.'

'More than anyone in the world?'

'Yes.' He rang off, and his excellent secretary, who had been waiting on the landing with a file he had asked her to fetch, came in with it.

After her burst of weeping over 'The Three Ravens', Irina, when not actually crying, had relapsed into her pale and silent state. A dread of something, uncertain but frightening, impended over her. She knew that plans must be made for her but that so far nothing had been settled. She sensed a new kind of sternness in Neil's attitude towards her; she did not dare to say to him: 'What's going to happen to me?' She did not ask Phyll, she hardly thought Phyll would know, and, if she did, Irina was afraid to hear the answer.

On the Saturday morning she was particularly unhappy. Saturdays used to be times of delight, looked forward to all the week; now they were blank and dark. The sensation was made worse by the approach of Christmas, which once used to send its fairy light into the last weeks of the winter term. Irina had not been in the study since the news had come. She thought, this morning, that she would just go and sit there, among all her father's things. She crept in at the door. In her father's armchair Ivor Mosscrop was sitting.

He looked up. 'Oh, come in, Irina,' he said. 'Make yourself at home.' She might have said: 'I am at home,' but she remained silent. Ivor meant to be good-natured. He felt he'd got the better of the kid now, and provided she wasn't allowed to make a nuisance of herself as she'd done the other night, he was genuinely willing to be kind to her, within reasonable limits. This was the first time Irina had been alone with him. He was bigger than she had thought, taller, heavier. He smiled, but his face with the large front teeth seemed to her repulsive and frightening. In the chair, on whose arm she used to sit, he sat as solid and immovable as a piece of masonry. She could not think of anything to say. She did not want to say anything. She went silently out of the room again. As she went upstairs, her mother came across the hall and went into the study. She could not hear the words exchanged, only her mother's gay, ringing tones and Ivor Mosscrop's deep ones. Upstairs, she looked about the playroom. For the first time in her life she felt lonely. She began to think about their old house at Grove End, where, to her, her father had been the most important person in it. His presence had filled that house as it had never filled the flat. A longing to see it again rose up in her. She had heard her father say that the people who'd bought it had left it themselves, so perhaps it was empty; even if other people had moved in, she could steal round the garden after dark without anyone's seeing her. The more she dwelt on the idea, the more strongly it took possession of her. It would not be difficult to carry out. She determined that she would make her expedition when she would not be questioned. The journey seemed straightforward: by Underground to Waterloo, and then by one of the frequently running trains to Grove End. She had plenty of money; some she had saved through not wanting to buy anything, and some her father had given her to cover her weekly pocket money for the time he had expected to be away. She began to long, ardently, for the chance to be off.

Ivor Mosscrop was now so much at ease in Carteret Street: having put to Marcia that it would be a useful thing to have old Badger Sneyd's valuation of any things she did not want, and gained her ready agreement, he brought Badger to the flat on Saturday afternoon and, with Marcia at his elbow, showed him where the silver was kept, and the china, and asked him to take a look-round at the furniture as well. Once they'd got his approximate valuations, Marcia would decide what (if anything) she would like to sell. Ivor put Badger in temporary possession and took Marcia off to a football match. She had never experienced this form of hectic amusement before his advent; now she had become enthusiastic for it. Before they went Ivor, with a *sotto voce* curse, pointed out to Badger the objects of which, beside the porcelain shepherdess, the will had deprived them. As his gaze followed Ivor's indications, Badger's face was a study; he said nothing however, but merely chucked his head. Left to himself, he brought out a much-rubbed solid-looking notebook with spirally fastened pages and the stump of a carpenter's flat, indelible pencil, and set about his task. He worked without a pause, passing noiselessly about the rooms, whenever he moved an object, doing so deftly, without the slightest sound. In the pantry he carefully examined the table silver and the china, counting the spoons and forks, noting the assay marks, reckoning up the piles of plates, the cups and saucers, scrutinising the makers' marks on their undersides. Presently he came to the open door of the kitchen where Mrs Mumford was available sometimes at weekends, though naturally she charged a rather higher rate at these times. She was now making preparations for an early tea for herself and Darren, who was sitting writing at a corner of the kitchen table. It was her first sight of Badger, though she had been told of his coming; when she saw him with his ill-shaven neck above the grubby collar of his flannel shirt, his black knitted pullover, his sports jacket too broad for his shoulders, her heart warmed to him. 'Will you come and have your tea, Mr Sneyd?' she called out.

Badger advanced, saying: 'Thank you, I'm sure.'

Darren looked up and slid a small piece of paper under the tea canister. On it he had written: 'The moon was out and they all fell down out of the sky.'

Mrs Mumford said: 'This is my boy.'

'Ah,' said Badger kindly. They sat down at the table. 'Shocking thing that, about your governor,' said Badger, stirring his tea.

Mrs Mumford said with emotion: 'He was a *real* gentleman, not many left like him now.' Darren ate pieces of cake and drank cups of tea, but said nothing. His mother explained: 'He hasn't got much to say in front of strangers.'

Badger said feelingly: 'None the worse for that, and I shouldn't wonder. Sight too much jaw from some of them young ones we got to take now.'

'He writes it down,' Mrs Mumford said with a mixture of bewilderment and pride. Darren shuffled his feet. 'You got another letter for Miss Irina?' she asked. 'Let's put it on her tray so's she won't miss it.' She took the slip of paper and put it under the tumbler on the tray already laid for Irina's supper.

At that moment Irina appeared in the doorway. Mrs Mumford offered tea but Irina shook her head. 'And I won't want any supper put for me. I'm going out this evening.'

'You are, dear?' Mrs Mumford said. 'Somewhere nice you're going?'

'Yes, very, *very*.' As she said this, Irina's eyes lighting on Badger, she recognised him, remembered where she'd seen him before, in the hall with the little china figure. She looked terrified and almost ran out of the room. Badger looked perplexed and sad. 'Ah,' he said, unexpectedly: 'if I'd had kids, I'd "a" tried to keep 'em straight.'

'It's a shame you didn't 'ave 'em,' said Mrs Mumford sympathetically.

9

Sir Geoffrey Galbraith had been asked to give an opinion to a committee sitting at the House of Commons and had stayed afterwards in conversation with a man he'd once known well; they'd been at the Bar together but McGinnis had left off practice and entered the higher ranks of the Civil Service; they hadn't met for years and the *rencontre* had been very interesting and pleasant. He had not known what train he would be able to take, so could not arrange for his car to meet him, but the walk from the station was no hardship. The train was a heavy one: impossible to say whether anyone he knew were on it; there was quite a little crowd getting out on to the dimly-lit platform. He was among the last to come down the flight of concrete stairs to the roadway below, and at the foot of them he was delayed a little further. A boy was singing to a guitar; the notes were plangent, the voice young, hoarse, common, sweet. The guitar case was lying open at the boy's feet with a scattering of coins in it. Sir Geoffrey stopped, felt for some change then dropped in a half-crown, rather more than he had wanted to give, and a great deal more than anyone else had given, but nothing smaller had met his fingers and he did not want to stop by the boy as if he meant to give him something and then pass on.

He got out on to the road leading to the little town. The sky was full of muffled moonlight which revealed more and more of the landscape as the eye grew accustomed to it. The lip of the common, bordering the asphalt pavement, was fringed with tufts of grass; the dew had distilled in them and in the misty moonlight they were loaded with clusters of minute, faintly sparkling drops.

So many excellent friends, but no one there all the time, really to talk to. What used to complete the enjoyment of an interesting or amusing occasion was telling Laura about it, all of it, in detail. She had always wanted to hear every word. The present change was not only one from a supremely contented marriage to loneliness, but in the tenor of life itself. The past had belonged to an era that was freer, calmer, more innocent, in spite of the strain of a career on the Bench, a strain that took its toll, however fitted the temperament was to withstand it: Liverpool Assizes, Cardiff Assizes, it was wonderful how one had got through them; but there had been so much energy, so much mental and bodily strength.

He walked steadily up the road till he came to the place where he must cross. An early nineteenth century pub, The Pheasant, stood squarely at a junction of four roads; these were never empty, but at certain hours, particularly of an evening, the traffic thundered past in a continuous stream; at the cross roads traffic lights had now been installed, but even under this protection the words would sometimes occur to him: 'In the midst of life, we are in death.'

He was standing behind the few foot-passengers who were waiting to cross when he noticed, on the edge of the pavement in front of him, a little girl in a round felt hat looking eagerly across the road, waiting for the lights to change. In another instant he had recognised her. 'Irina!' he said. She turned with a startled look. 'Are you by yourself?'

'Yes.'

'You've come to see your Cousin Louisa?'

'No.' At this moment the lights changed. He took her by the elbow and steered her across. On the opposite pavement, he said: 'What are you doing here, my dear?' She looked up into his face, silently with half-open lips, as if she could not answer. As he was wondering what he ought to do, her replies being so unsatisfactory, his car drew up beside them. Fred, in consultation with Mrs Treadgold, had been to meet the first of the trains the master might have taken, but had drawn a blank. He had now come for the next possibility, and finding, from the empty station-yard, that he'd cut it a bit too fine, was driving slowly back, in case he might find Sir Geoffrey on the road. He jumped out and opened the door, and the master saying to

111

the little girl, 'Come back with me to my house before you do anything else,' they both got in.

Mrs Treadgold was in the hall. He was conscious of a distinct relief at the sight of her. He said: 'You've never seen Phyllida Spedding's little sister. Here she is. Irina, this is my housekeeper, Mrs Treadgold.'

'Has she had her tea?' was Mrs Treadgold's immediate enquiry.

He said quietly: 'If you'll give her something to eat, I'll talk to her presently. We must try to find out what's the matter.'

Irina did not need telling to go with Mrs Treadgold; she followed her into the kitchen without hesitation. The room was warm from the Aga cooker. In the middle of the floor was a large round wooden table and on it, under a crinkled rosy glass shade, an Edwardian lamp adapted for electric light. Beside it were two padded wicker arm-chairs; in one of them a Siamese cat was lying in a sickle shape. Its back legs and tail were laid together, one of its fore-paws thrown across them. Its face with watchful eyes and pointed jaw was like a fox's, brilliant, sly and cruel.

'Oh!' Irina said. 'Is that your cat?'

'Well, no,' said Mrs Treadgold. 'I don't know where he belongs, but he comes in here and we feed him sometimes.' This was not the exact truth; the cat, wherever he might belong, now called in regularly for two meals a day, but she knew she was welcome to have a cat in her kitchen as long as it didn't get under the master's feet. She gave the strange little guest a cup of tea and some home-made bread with butter, showed her the downstairs lavatory, then began to prepare her vegetables at the enamel-topped table in the kitchen window. The cat, she saw, though usually intolerant of human approaches, was lying on the little girl's lap.

Sir Geoffrey meanwhile was in a quandary. If she hadn't come to visit Miss Bassett, had she come to see Neil? But then, why hadn't she said so? Perhaps her sister was at the White House, but the startled face she had turned up to his, the withholding of any expla-nation, the passivity with which she had allowed him to bring her to his house, all discounted such a solution. What he already knew of her domestic situation was displeasing. Ordinarily, he felt, one could

112

rely on Neil and Phyll to take care of the child, but the young pair, rapturously in love and full of cares for their wedding, could not be held entirely responsible for her. He telephoned Miss Bassett, however, and Miss Bumpus answered. Neil was not there, though he had been spending the last few nights in his flat. She thought he might probably be there later. Could she take any message for him? Sir Geoffrey thanked her but said no. After all, the child was safe; it was no use spreading useless alarm. He next rang Carteret Street, with no reply at all. Well: a Saturday evening – that was not surprising. He went to the kitchen where Mrs Treadgold was peeling potatoes and Irina was sprawling in one of the basket chairs, nursing the cat. He said: 'Suppose you come and talk to me, Irina?' and she followed him into the study.

Some colour had come into her cheeks and he did not, now, feel afraid to question her. He said: 'I was surprised to see you there, all by yourself. If you weren't going to see Neil, or your Cousin Louisa, will you tell me what you were doing?'

No longer tense, she looked at him with candid eyes. 'We used to live at The Lodge, which is in Woodside Road,' she said.

'I know you did.' He thought he began to see the explanation.

'And after Daddy – as Daddy – I thought I would like –' She stopped.

'You thought you would like to see your old house again?'

'Just to walk round the garden in the dark, and see the windows.'

'But my dear, the house belongs to somebody else now. It would have been trespassing.'

'But it was our house, we used to live there.' Her intent, luminous gaze was fixed on him. It was clear that she could see no argument beyond that.

'I know, and I see you feel that, in a way, it's still yours; but it isn't, you know. As you want so much to see it again, I expect it can be managed. We will find out who the owners are now, and ask them to let you walk round the garden.' She looked as if this were not what she had wanted to do. He saw he had not carried conviction, and went on, with increased emphasis: 'Irina, there's something I must say to you.' He paused. How, without too much frightening her, to

113

impress on her the seriousness of what he had to say: to conceal from her the image of herself, lying in darkness, half-naked, bleeding, strangled, and yet make her understand its meaning? He said: 'Unfortunately, there are some very wicked people about, nowadays. If they met you by yourself at night, with no one near to help you, they might hurt you very badly, and kill you, perhaps, so that you couldn't tell anybody who they were. I would like you to promise that you won't go anywhere by yourself after dark, if you can possibly help it, certainly not in dark country roads, or any lonely streets in London either. Will you promise that?' She said, at last, with a sigh: 'Yes,' and he believed her. He added gently: 'Your father was my great friend. I'm telling you what he would tell you. Now,' he went on, 'can you tell us when your mother or Phyll will be at home? I should like to let them know that you're here, quite safe.' She said they would both be out till rather late, that was why she'd thought she could – she hung her head. 'Could get there and back before they came in? Well, we must see what we can do.'

He went out to the kitchen, to discuss the situation with Mrs Treadgold. 'I don't like to take her back until we know there's someone there, and that may be so late.'

Mrs Treadgold said in matter-of-fact tones: 'Why not let her stop the night here? Then we can take our time about ringing them. Shan't I make up the bed in the dressing room? She can sleep in her undies, why not? Better than keeping her up till goodness knows when.'

'Well, Mrs Treadgold, it's very kind of you to help out, and I think that *will* be the best way.' They went back to the study. Irina was kneeling on the floor, a large volume of 'The Illustrated London News' for 1880, which she had taken out of one of the lowest bookshelves, propped up on the seat of a chair. Sir Geoffrey told her what they had decided, and she seemed to accept it without question. He said: 'I've told her, Mrs Treadgold, that she mustn't go about by herself after dark and she has promised she won't.'

Mrs Treadgold exclaimed in severe tones: 'She'd never be such a naughty girl, now she's been told not!' It was nearly eight o'clock and she said: 'Shall she sit up to dinner with you, Sir, or have her supper in bed?' Sir Geoffrey had had a tiring day and he felt that interesting, touching, as Irina was, he would prefer the quiet of a solitary dinner to one where he had to make conversation with her. As he hesitated, Mrs Treadgold said: 'I think the sooner she's in bed the better. Will your dinner at quarter to nine suit you, sir?'

'Anytime, anytime at all,' he said thankfully. 'Good night, my dear. I'll let Phyll know as soon as I can where you are. I expect she'll be feeling anxious.' Irina said nothing and walked out after Mrs Treadgold.

At quarter to ten, having finished his dinner and thought matters over carefully, he came to the telephone again. He was not apt to take on unnecessary responsibilities; but what Jasper had told him at their last meeting, and the picture Neil had filled in of a careless, disreputable household, and Irina's own state of repressed misery when he had found her at the crossing, made him feel with uneasy certainty that someone should give her shelter for the time being; and who would do it if he did not? He would hope of course for considerable help from Miss Bassett and ultimately from Neil and Phyll; and he could not undertake such a stint at all without the wholehearted cooperation of Mrs Treadgold, though, as he admitted to himself, cooperation was hardly the word, as almost the whole burden of looking after the child and keeping her company would fall on her, but he was hopeful of her agreement. As she came to take away the dishes, she hardly allowed him time to get the words out of his mouth.

'When she said she'd meant to go to their old house, and walk round the garden in the dark – Woodside Road is so quiet, and with so many trees, it's almost like a wood –' Mrs Treadgold gave one of her characteristic gestures, a movement of the head, which conveyed that no more need be said, things had gone too far already.

'So if you will be so very kind as to undertake to look after her – I am afraid it will almost all fall on you.' Mrs Treadgold declared that it would be no trouble, and gave him the impression that even if it were, that wouldn't matter.

When he telephoned Carteret Street a little later, to his relief Phyll answered. 'I expect you've been wondering where Irina is,' he began.

'I – well, yes, Neil and I have only just got in ourselves; he's gone back to Grove End now. As she wasn't here, I thought Mummy must have taken her somewhere, though she doesn't as a rule.'

'I found her at the crossroads here. She wanted to see your old house again. I thought that didn't seem a very safe plan after dark, so I brought her here. And I've been wondering, my dear, as you've got a lot on your hands at present, and I don't think there'd be room for her with Miss Bassett till the builders are out, how would it be, if she stayed here for a few days? She seems to have settled in already. I think she'd be quite happy with Mrs Treadgold.'

'Oh, I'm *sure* she would. How very, very kind of you!'

'Your mother wouldn't make any objection, I daresay?'

'Oh *no*, she's sure not to. She's very – she can't really think about others things very much, at present.'

'No. Well, let's call that settled. I'll write to your mother, of course. And there's the question of school. I think the journey from here is too far. As there can't be much left of the autumn term, perhaps your mother would agree to her not going back for it?'

'Oh *yes*, I'm sure she would.'

'Then someone ought to let the school know; we can arrange that later. But Irina will want some clothes. If Mrs Treadgold brings her up tomorrow morning, Sunday, about eleven, will someone be there to let her in?'

'Yes, but Irina has her own key, as a matter of fact.'

'Still, I'd like someone to know when she comes and goes.'

'I'll be here, for certain.'

'And will there be some suitcase or bag available?'

'Yes, I'll have one ready.'

'And I hope nobody will be cross with her. I think she's in a very unhappy frame of mind just now.'

'I know she is.' Phyll sounded distressed. 'I haven't been looking after her very well.'

'My dear, I'm sure you've done everything you could. Let somebody else help now. We shall just have to see how we go. But I did tell her very seriously that she mustn't go about by herself after dark.'

'Yes! I never thought of her going off like that. But she does rather get about. She went down to Daddy's club that time.'

'Yes. Well, don't worry any more for the time being. She's quite safe here.' He rang off, thankful that he hadn't been able to speak to the one person to whom he ought to have spoken. Before going to bed, he asked Mrs Treadgold if she would be so kind, tomorrow morning, as to go with Irina to Carteret Street. He said he would tell Fred to drive them there, arriving at eleven; there would be time, on their return, for Fred to drive him over to a lunch engagement with another retired judge and his family who lived some six miles beyond Grove End. Mrs Treadgold said, if there were any doubt about that, they could manage for themselves with the train and taxis. Sir Geoffrey said: 'I should feel more comfortable if Fred were with you.'

Next morning Irina joined him at breakfast. They were both now a little shy. Last night their intercourse had been inspired by a certain dramatic element; now they were into a stretch of commonplace, unrelieved daylight. However, she was obviously pleased to hear of the arrangement to fetch her clothes, since this must mean that she was to stay at The Lawn for a little time, at least. Gradually, her shyness thawed. In between spoonfuls of cereal, she looked round the dining room and her gaze went across the lawn to the screen of trees. 'Is there a pond down there?' she asked.

'Yes, there is.'

'How lovely!'

'Well, yes, but don't go too near the edge of it, will you? You'd find the ground very squashy.' (He hadn't thought of the pond, whose edges shelved to a reach that was deep. What had he done, taking on this child?) His face became not unkind, but stern. 'That's another promise you'll have to make, to keep away from the edge.'

'Yes, I will,' she answered timidly.

To mitigate his severity, he said: 'When my wife and I came to live here first, there was a very wet summer and the water rose all over the garden; we had swans swimming on the lawn.'

She looked rapt. 'Did the water come into the house?'

'No, I'm glad to say it didn't do that.'

'It did once, in Westminster Hall, in the Middle Ages. The

117

Thames came right into the hall, all across it, and people rowed over the floor in boats.'

'I expect your father told you that?'

'Yes, he did.' Her reply was so calm, so natural, he felt relieved and was glad to see her eating scrambled egg with appetite. He telephoned Miss Bassett after breakfast, early, to catch her before she went to church. She was astounded at the tale, and said over and over again, how kind Sir Geoffrey was being. Poor little Phyll, she was sure, did her best, but it could hardly be expected – and it was quite true, it would be difficult to put the child up in The White House while the builders were in – Neil himself was just camping there, till the wedding; but if at any time it seemed too much for Mrs Tread-gold, they would find room *somehow*. He felt it was a minor advantage, at least, to be in touch with another member of Irina's family.

Fred brought the car round at ten and Mrs Treadgold, who was not often seen in a hat, appeared, wearing a rather stately one, of black gros-grain with a large bow athwart the front. Sir Geoffrey thought it became her very well, though of course he did not say so.

'This is a very nice car, isn't it?' Irina said as they drove away.

'Belongs to a very nice gentleman,' said Fred, beneath his breath.

When they had mounted the stairs at Carteret Street, Irina pulled out her key from a little pouch with a press-button on it that she kept in her coat pocket, but before she could put it in the lock, Mrs Treadgold gave the bell a loud decided ring, and instantly Phyll had the door open and Irina was in her arms. 'Irina!' she cried.

At that moment Marcia in a dressing gown appeared at her bedroom door, and Mrs Treadgold advanced. 'Oh yes,' said Marcia, 'come in. You've come to fetch her clothes?' She looked sleepy and bemused. 'It's all right if you want to go and stay with Sir Geoffrey, Irina,' she said, 'but you might have told us you were going.'

Irina said: 'I didn't know I was going. I meant to be back before you were in.'

'Well, never mind now,' Marcia said. 'You'd better go and begin putting your things together.'

Irina went into her bedroom and Phyll asked Mrs Treadgold if she and Fred would like cups of tea? 'No, dear, thank you, we've got to be getting back.' She was beginning to make an enquiry about the wedding preparations, when Marcia's bedroom door opened again and a man, heavily built, good-looking but somewhat frowsy, in crumpled pyjamas, but wearing over them a handsome dressing gown of dark blue piped in red, came out. He saw a man in chauffeur's uniform standing in the hall, his cap lying on the hall table. He sized Fred up immediately as belonging not quite to his own walk of life but nearer to it than he himself was to the Speddings'. If they had met in different circumstances, he would have been hail-fellow well-met with him. As it was, aware of hostile criticism of himself, he found a childish satisfaction in looking down on Fred as someone of inferior status, and walked past him into the bathroom with an almost theatrical toss of the head.

Mrs Treadgold had taken the suitcase Phyll produced and gone with it into Irina's bedroom. The latter had seen Ivor Mosscrop in the hall. She was leaning against the bedpost, her eyes suffused with tears. Her preparations for packing had so far got no further than the laying out on her bed of her sponge-bag and two large volumes – *The Tempest* and *The Sleeping Beauty*, illustrated by Edmund Dulac. Time was pressing. Mrs Treadgold opened the wardrobe and pulled out drawers; as she was packing dresses and coats and nightgowns and underclothes into the case, Irina said: 'That's Daddy's dressing-gown he's got on.'

'More shame to him,' said Mrs Treadgold robustly; 'but never mind; the sooner we're off, the better.'

In the hall, Fred took the suitcase. Mrs Treadgold looked about for Marcia but did not see her. Phyll put her arms round Irina once again. 'How long will you be here?' Irina asked.

'The wedding is tomorrow week. Neil will motor me up to Grove End on Monday morning. We're being married from Cousin Louisa's. I'll tell you all about it in a day or two. Mummy and Ivor won't be coming up for it. They'll stay here till they're married.'

'But *after*?' Irina whispered, clinging to her. 'I don't want to be here with them!'

Phyll looked dismayed. 'We shall have to see, darling,' she said. She did not dare to make a promise even to encourage the hope of one. Neither Marcia nor Ivor showed themselves; Phyll felt that clouds were rising, threateningly, on her radiant horizon.

Fred returned them to The Lawn in excellent time to drive Sir Geoffrey to his lunch engagement. Sir Maurice Meadowes and his wife had a house fronting a pretty village green with a group of chestnut trees at one side, and opposite, a pub, The Three Jolly Bagmen, known locally as The Jollies, where Fred took his lunch on these occasions. He enjoyed the welcome he always received in the bar as a quiet, good sort of chap and one in an interesting position. The Meadowes were also very glad to see Geoffrey Galbraith, as he was to see them; today he was specially glad; he wanted to describe to them the charge he had undertaken. Their own children were married but none of their grandchildren was as yet of Irina's age. Lady Meadowes was much interested and inquired a great deal. It amused her husband to notice how complete a picture she elicited of the whole affair merely by her unstudied questions, inspired by warm personal sympathy. The most skilful cross-examination couldn't have done it better.

During lunch she asked the guest if he'd listened to the radio play the other evening, in which the hero, if so he could be called, was a High Court judge, re-living in agonies of guilty remorse a case in which the prisoner he had sentenced was, morally speaking, much less guilty than the judge himself. Sir Geoffrey had not, and asked if they had? 'For a wonder I did,' Sir Maurice said. 'I usually turn it off if I don't care for it, but I kept this one on – I was curious to see how far the fellow would go before he got to the end.'

'What one would like to know,' said Lady Meadowes gaily, 'is: where *are* these self-condemning judges? *I've* never met any of them.'

Sir Geoffrey laughed. Her husband said with slight impatience: 'We all admit we've made mistakes, but no one capable of that sort of hysterical self-abandonment would ever get through the work.'

Sir Geoffrey said: 'Most ignorant people are very positive; but progressive playwrights dealing with the law are specially so, I think; if they weren't, I daresay it would knock the bottom out of show business.'

Fred returned, as directed, at three o'clock; everyone felt that this was the proper time for the visit to end, and wished that it could have gone on longer. He opened the car door and touched his cap to Sir Maurice who had come out to see the guest off. He had a copy of 'The News of the World' tucked down beside the driver's seat. He had been looking at it in the bar and they had told him to take it if he liked, it had been left behind by a customer, and he was welcome to it.

Sir Geoffrey thought on the drive home how well Fred was looking nowadays: contented, cheerful, bright-eyed. He gave Mrs Treadgold the credit for a good deal of this improvement, but he congratulated himself, too, on a good piece of work.

Irina had been under his roof for less than twenty-four hours but in that time she seemed to have become a settled inmate. The pain of her father's death had re-awakened on her visit to Carteret Street, but it had become somewhat soothed when she returned to The Lawn. She adapted herself instinctively to whatever Mrs Treadgold wanted of her. The latter was preparing for Sir Geoffrey to have his tea at half past four, and Irina, looking for tea things in the china cupboard, saw on an upper shelf a tea-set of white china, thickly sprinkled with violets, the leaves and stems a sombre green, the flower the true, dim purple. She said: 'Oh! couldn't *that* be used?' So when, on Sir Geoffrey's return, Mrs Treadgold went to ask if Irina should have tea with him, or in the kitchen, and he said, rather hesitantly, with him, by all means, she asked at the same time if the violet tea-set might be used? He said yes to that too. It had been a favourite of Laura's, put carefully away since her death. It would have distressed him if any accident had happened to it, but he had not taken any personal pleasure in it; now, when he saw Irina sitting opposite to him with intent downward gaze, her fingers spread in the air over a tea-cup, a plate, he felt a kindling interest in it himself. He said as he took some bread and butter: 'Do you know Gray's "Elegy"?'

'Yes,' she said absently, as she pored over the paintings of leaves and buds and full-blown flowers.

'Do you know the verse about violets that he left out of it?'

She looked up. 'No, I don't.' He repeated:

Here, scattered oft', the earliest of the year,
By hands unseen are showers of violets found;
The red-breast loves to build and warble here,
And little footsteps lightly print the ground.

She listened agog; then she demanded: 'But *why* did he leave it out?'

'Perhaps he thought it wasn't good enough, compared with the rest.'

'But the birds' footprints: why did he leave *them* out?'

'I don't know. Poets have to do what they think best, whatever other people might want them to do.' Irina said nothing. When she was with people she trusted, she did not argue. He was beginning to take conscious pleasure in her society, but he hadn't needed Maurice Meadowes' comments to remind him that he must try to arrange this state of affairs on an official basis. After tea, when Irina was deeply absorbed in the bound volumes of 'The Strand Magazine' which contained the first of Sherlock Holmes' 'adventures', he wrote:- 'Dear Mrs Spedding, This is just to say that I am very glad for Irina to stay here for a short while. My housekeeper Mrs Treadgold will look after her and we will do our best to make her happy. Of course we realise that she is still in a state of shock after this tragic event. I understand that you will be going abroad immediately after your wedding in January. Will you, at your leisure, let me know when you expect to return? So that we can make further arrangements. Meanwhile she is very welcome here. Yours sincerely.'

This letter was opened by Marcia as she breakfasted in bed. Now that Ivor shared her mother's bedroom, Phyll did not carry in the breakfast tray; she laid it overnight in the kitchen, Ivor brought it into the bedroom and plugged in the electric kettle. This morning after he had carried the cups to the bedside, he took the letter from Marcia's hand. Having read it, he laughed and tossed it down on the breakfast tray. 'We can let that ride,' he said, and got into bed beside her.

He was pleased with the position of affairs. Neil Pepperill had moved out and his wedding to Phyll would be in a week's time. Ivor

122

and Marcia had decided that to put off their own wedding till January was an unnecessary delay, so they had arranged to be married before Christmas and depart for a month's honeymoon, though even now they had not decided where to go. He would have liked nothing better than a slap-up hotel in Brighton: every comfort, and not damned cold all the time, as it was in Scotland, for instance; but they both realised it would be wiser to make for some foreign destination from which they couldn't be whistled back immediately. He was already determining that a high-class boarding-school would be the best thing for Irina, (get her out of the light for three-quarters of the year). The fees would be no problem. Since her father had insisted on tying up all that money on her, they could put her into any school that would take her.

10

Marcia felt that she would be glad never to have to see Irina again but for Phyll she had some genuine affection, though not a great deal. She felt obliged to ask, and up to a point, really wanted to know, about the arrangements for the wedding. She made it clear that she and Ivor would not be coming to it, and as Phyll did not want them to, that was got over without difficulty. Marcia said, looking away, 'All this about Daddy has made everything so difficult down there. They're all *his* friends, not mine. Of course, it'll look rather queer, me not being there.'

'It won't matter,' Phyll said. 'We're going to be so very quiet.'

The result of the bride's mother's having opted out of the wedding arrangements was that at Grove End they had become almost a communal undertaking. Neil had wanted to take Phyll away from the church door, but Cousin Louisa had been so disappointed at the idea of not having a small, a *very* small lunch party afterwards, that he and Phyll could only thank her and accept. Miss Bumpus had asked if Irina were to be a bridesmaid? and Neil had almost shuddered as he exclaimed: 'No, no! Nothing of that sort!' He did not intend to have a best man, either. He had several friends, any one of whom he could have approached, but it would have meant getting this chap down to Grove End and altogether making a to-do, such as he was almost neurotically anxious to avoid. Nonetheless, Tom and Nell Mercer had been invited, and Fred had suggested diffidently to them that the loan of some of their greenhouse plants would make Miss Bassett's drawing room look very festive. Somewhat to Cousin Louisa's surprise, he had driven up the day before the wedding with the back of Sir Geoffrey's car carefully loaded with pots of fragile greenery, and in the front a few more pots with substantial dark leaves and rounded, brilliant flowers. Miss Bumpus, who seemed to have been expecting him, was out on the front steps in a moment, and between them they carried the pots into the drawing room, arranging them beneath and around the window.

Fred had had the minutiae of the wedding arrangements explained to him, for practical purposes, and also on the system which makes people tell their family affairs to the bees. Neil was to drive up to Carteret Street betimes on the wedding morning, to fetch Phyll and her luggage. They would come to The White House, where Miss Bumpus insisted they should have a mid-morning lunch. Neil would drive himself, Cousin Louisa and Miss Bumpus to church, the Mercers would bring with them Mrs Treadgold and Irina, then Fred would convey the bride and Sir Geoffrey, who was to give her away. The latter had said to Hilliard Bartram: 'He doesn't need a best man, but somebody must give her away. I didn't see who was to do it if I didn't.'

'I can't see who could be more suitable, however much choice there'd been,' Hilliard said. Although Phyll herself had told him they wanted the wedding to be very quiet, a wish with which he deeply sympathised, even he had heard with some surprise how very quiet it was actually to be. Sir Geoffrey said: 'I think the very sad and distasteful conditions in her home have made them shrink from any sort of publicity, and he had an upbringing with a good deal of nervous distress in it. I think they're finding a refuge in each other.'

'Yes:

124

So silently they one to the other come,
As colours steal into the pear or plum.'

'You know a lot of poetry.'
'I read a lot, once. Some of it's stayed with me.'
The wedding day was calm and clear, ideal, the well-wishers felt, for the long drive to Charmouth. The ceremony was to be at half past eleven, and at quarter to Neil's car drew up on the drive of The White House. Neil was called into Cousin Louisa's dining room, and Phyll went upstairs to what was to be her bedroom, where Miss Bumpus had laid out face towels, and spread a Victorian white cotton and lace runner on the dressing table. Phyll was as anxious as Neil for the wedding to be of the utmost simplicity, but it had never occurred to her not to have wedding-clothes. She put them on now, a silk suit the colour of a tea-rose and a black velvet hat with a large brim. When she came down, everyone in the small gathering was astonished. Her eyes were lowered and she wore a faint smile. Though she was the youngest person present her modest and unselfconscious dignity awed them, and for a moment they were almost afraid to speak to her, but Miss Bumpus then urged a large cup of coffee on her and gave her a chicken sandwich, part of which she ate. Neil, a sandwich in his own hand, could not take his eyes off her, with her head slightly bent, she did not meet his gaze. Nell Mercer, anxious not to delay the party, went out to their own car and in a few moments Tom reappeared at the dining room door and the others felt they should be collecting themselves. On the drive, everyone was there who should have been there except Mrs Treadgold. Sir Geoffrey went back into the house for her. As he came into the hall, he heard sounds of crying in the dining room, loud, childish, uncontrolled weeping. His heart nearly failed him. Was this an outburst of totally unexpected pre-wedding nerves? And what was *he* to do, responsible for getting her to church in twenty minutes' time? As he hesitated, fearfully, he heard Phyll say, between sobs: 'I wanted Daddy to be at my wedding.'
'Of course you did, lovey,' said Mrs Treadgold, 'but Daddy wouldn't like to see you spoiling your face before you get to church.'

Phyll's heaving and sobbing subsided and Mrs Treadgold gently dabbed her eyes, with a clean handkerchief smelling of lavender water. The face was so young, it was not disfigured by a flush over the cheek-bones and eyes under water.

'Well,' he said, coming into the room, 'can you spare Mrs Treadgold, because they're waiting for her?' Mrs Treadgold said courageously, 'Of course she can,' and took herself off.

'Sit down,' he said gently. 'You'll have a lot of standing to do presently.' He pushed one of the leather-seated chairs towards her and she sat. On her lap was a black suede bag with a silver clasp. She saw him look at it admiringly. 'Mummy gave me this as a wedding present,' she said in stifled tones. He was afraid they were returning to dangerous ground. He stood above her, silently exerting all his power, willing her to be calm. By the time Fred appeared in the doorway, looking shy but expectant, her outburst was over and she had no inclination to break down again.

In St James the Less, the wedding party occupied three small front pews while a little crowd of strangers clustered at the back of the church. They had heard there was to be a wedding and had come to look on, but their expectations, they felt, were unfairly disappointed: no flowers, no organ-playing; a dud show altogether. They made audible comments among themselves and stumbled noisily out. Meanwhile Neil was standing with his back to the altar, facing the west door through which his bride was to come; at first the exit of the disgusted strangers blocked the path but in a few seconds they had disappeared and Phyll was coming up the little aisle towards him. Sir Geoffrey had her on his arm, but Neil saw only her. He said afterwards: 'We didn't need anything, except the words and the place.' Until they had to take hands, he stood holding her by the elbow, and Phyll's recollection was: 'It was only half-way through that I remembered who Hilliard was – he seemed to be somebody else.'

Nell Mercer murmured at the close, as the move was being made to the little vestry: 'We had everything laid on that could be laid on, for ours; Hilliard seems rather to approve of bareness – less of an anti-climax if it doesn't last. Still, we've lasted, haven't we?' Tom muttered gruffly: 'That's how they wanted it.' Tom never rose to any occasion in words, but he did in action. She was wearing her ruby brooch.

Sir Geoffrey was sure Miss Bumpus would want to hurry home as she had the buffet lunch on her mind, so he asked Fred to take her at once. Irina, he thought, might as well go at the same time. While the adults were grouped round the table on which Phyll was signing the register, Irina, behind their backs, was standing on a rush-bottomed chair to examine a very small slit-window that contained the church's only piece of original glass, painted in amber and pale crimson, showing a shield with a curious bush behind it. Sir Geoffrey detached her and sent her off. As Miss Bassett came out of the vestry behind the little troop, her large, dim blue eyes had tears in them and he realised for the first time that she must have been a beautiful woman.

The scene in the White House dining room was very joyous. The table was spread with the fine china dishes, so large that they were never, now, in ordinary use. They held two game pies and shoals of canapés in which Sir Geoffrey thought he detected Mrs Treadgold's hand. The snowy wedding cake which had come down from Fortnum's was wreathed with marble-white ribbed shells. When Phyll was called on to cut it she could not make the knife enter. Neil put his hand over hers and the slices fell apart, dark inside, built round with white above a deep strip of honey-coloured almond paste. Cousin Louisa asked Sir Geoffrey to open the champagne, but Tom was doing it already. Guided by Miss Bumpus he had brought the bottles out of the refrigerator. Hilliard arrived on his bicycle just in time to toast the bride and bridegroom, and under the little commotion Sir Geoffrey levered a piece of game pie on to a plate and gave it to him, putting a fork into his hand at the same time. When the company had moved into the drawing room, Neil stood up among the plants in the window, saying he wasn't going to make a speech, only to say that Phyll and he now saw what they'd have missed if they'd gone away straight from the church door. It was such a bisk, if he might use the word, to see people round them, as happy as they could stare, just because he and Phyll were so happy. He'd never be able to thank everybody enough; he'd just tell them that he knew he didn't deserve

127

his enormous luck, but he'd do his utmost, and one other thing, he'd promise them, he wasn't going to drink any more champagne after the glass he'd had already, they needn't worry about the journey! So he'd just say thank you once more to everybody. Phyll, standing by him, said 'Thank you,' blushing and ecstatic. Mrs Treadgold, having been given the time that they wanted to start, now hurried her upstairs to change her clothes. She had asked Miss Bumpus which of them should do this; the latter appreciated the courtesy but said she had enough to do in the dining room. She was as radiant as if the wedding had been her own. When Irina's slice of wedding cake had slipped off its little plate and she had trodden it into the carpet before she realised where it had fallen, Miss Bumpus not only said it didn't matter, she looked as though she were quite glad it had been done. Sir Geoffrey said with compunction: 'Fred ought to have been here when we drank the toast,' and Miss Bumpus said: 'He drank it in the hall, looking through the door.' Sir Geoffrey was shocked. He said: 'I'm sure you've very kindly given him some lunch.' 'He's in the kitchen with it now,' she reassured him.

He went across the hall to the kitchen. Fred was sitting at a scrubbed white table with a little red-checked cloth over part of it, plying a knife and fork at a large section of game pie, a piece of wedding cake on a plate beside him. He got up, but Sir Geoffrey said: 'Don't. I only came to see that you had everything.' Fred half sat down and said: 'This is Mrs Mounser, she comes to help, like.' Sir Geoffrey then noticed that a very thin and small woman, with large, transparent-looking projecting teeth, was sitting at the other end of the table, though she wasn't eating anything. 'How do you do, Mrs Mounser,' he said. 'Aren't you having any lunch?'

Mrs Mounser said: 'I shall have it to take home with me, I'd rather, and Miss Bassett has made me welcome to what's left of the cake for my grandchildren; I've got the three of them with me, while their mum's in hospital.'

'I'm sorry to hear that. Is it your daughter, or your daughter-in-law?'

'It's me daughter, but she's not too bad. Only they'll keep her there another ten days, they reckon.'

'I hope your anxieties will soon be over.' She smiled, then she said: 'Sweet pretty bride she is! Well, she's taken the plunge.' She sighed, as if this were a matter for anxiety rather than congratulation. She herself had found that you never got out of troubles, you only changed one set for another, but Fred said: 'If she's to be all right with anyone, she'll be all right with Mr Neil.' Then he asked: 'What time do you want to be going back, sir?'

'No hurry,' Sir Geoffrey said. 'And you must come out onto the steps to see them off.' He went back to the dining room, where Cousin Louisa, while attending to Hilliard Bartram's wants, was telling him how touching she had found the service. He said nothing, his speaking face told her he agreed with her. Sir Geoffrey said: 'I don't think I was ever more moved by a wedding except my own.'

Tom Mercer had been out on the drive with Neil, examining the wonders and beauties of the Jensen; now he came indoors. The moment had come for the couple's setting off; Phyll came downstairs and the hall was full of people. 'Where is Irina?' cried Nell. Irina was in a corner of the drawing room, looking at a Japanese screen of black satin, embroidered with life-size groups of irises, chrysanthemums and peonies in faint but natural colourings. At Nell's call, she came out. Phyll caught her in her arms: 'We'll be back soon, darling.' The others' kisses and blessings had been given while Sir Geoffrey stood aside. She had cried because she wanted her father at her wedding; he had undertaken the father's part, but he hadn't said anything comforting to her. He was saddened, thinking that though he had acted for the best, she must have thought him stern and cold-hearted. Suddenly he found her arms about his neck and her round, soft, burning cheek pressed against his lean one. 'You've been so -*so*,' she exclaimed. 'I never can thank you enough!'

11

Sir Geoffrey had not seen the couple since their return and when Cousin Louisa asked him to come to lunch and bring Irina, he accepted with pleasure for himself but he suggested he should come without Irina: he would like, he said, to ask Phyll if she had any news of her mother's plans, and he felt it would be more convenient, on this occasion, to leave Irina behind.

He had no fear of leaving her to herself. There was no television downstairs but there was a set in Mrs Treadgold's bed-sitting room which she often invited Irina to view, though Irina seldom accepted the offer unless it were to see some feature of animal life: monkeys chattering and swinging on brilliant creepers, or arctic bears, prowling silently, white in a white mist. He came to the kitchen, to ask that she should have her lunch with Mrs Treadgold, without saying where he was going in case the child should be surprised at not being taken to the White House herself; but Irina was rapt into a world of her own. The cat was rolling on its back, looking sideways out of its slits of brilliant eyes; she had sloughed off one of her slippers, and balancing with her hand on the back of a chair, was stroking its chest with her toes. Two powerful, furred paws clasped her ankle, a purr trilled delicately through the sole of her foot. He smiled without saying anything; he did not want to attract her attention, but before he left the kitchen he stopped to admire the ranks of Christmas cards that had already reached Mrs Treadgold from various quarters of the globe and were now trooping across the mantel-shelf: exotic birds, of green or rose-coloured plumage, carillons of gold and silver bells, wreaths of foreign-looking flowers with gilt messages printed inside them, all more vigorous and colourful than their English counterparts; ranged along the mantelpiece, they shouted a chorus of greeting. Mrs Treadgold smiled happily as he examined them; she looked as contented as if she had been in the middle of her family.

Sir Geoffrey had looked forward with warm interest to seeing Neil and Phyll again. As the latter had kissed him at her wedding, he now kissed her as a matter of course. While she went into the kitchen to do whatever Miss Bumpus would permit, Sir Geoffrey heard from Neil some account of the honeymoon. Much of the time it had been windy and wet and December clouds had often over-hung the shore which the waves pounded and withdrew from as they walked along it. Many young people would have cursed such weather but Neil and Phyll, who had now rejoined them, seemed to have found in the dim air and the pulsating wash of the sea something supremely satisfying. The bright winter sunlight made a sharp contrast to the scene they'd just heard about, sky and sea and shore mingled in sound and wind and twilight. Outside, the garden was spare and neat, the drawing-room window wreathed with pale-yellow winter jasmine, and Sir Geoffrey congratulated Cousin Louisa on the groups of palest green Christmas roses, standing up on the bare, dark beds.

At lunch he said to Phyll: 'Have you any news of your mother's plans?'

Phyll said: 'I've had a postcard – they went to Marbella in the end.'

'And have they said when they're coming back?'

'Mummy said, the middle of January.'

'The place in Carteret Street is shut up, I suppose?'

'Yes, except that Mrs Mumford goes in, once or twice a week.'

'I don't want anyone to feel that there's any hurry about deciding what Irina's to do. I'm happy to have her with me at present, and what's more important, Mrs Treadgold's happy. I couldn't continue this arrangement without her.'

'No, indeed!' said Cousin Louisa.

'As it is, Irina's happy, Mrs Treadgold's happy, the cat's happy and I'm happy. There's no problem at the moment. But I feel that we ought to get down to some idea of the future.'

'Of course we ought,' Neil said. 'What it boils down to is when exactly her mother is coming back, so that she can go home?'

'If you and Phyll and Mr Porteous are satisfied that Mosscrop, however unacceptable, won't do her any harm, then the obvious thing is for her to rejoin her mother. In fact if Mrs Spedding – Mrs

131

Mosscrop, rather, were to demand her return, the law would oblige us to give her up.'

'Yes,' said Neil impatiently. 'But her mother doesn't want her and the kid doesn't want to go.'

'The first consideration is the only valid one. If her mother demands her return, then I'm afraid the child's unwillingness will have to be ignored.' Phyll's face was piteous; her lips trembled and tears began to show themselves on her lower eyelids. Neil was nearly beside himself, at the sight of her grief, and at the threat it posed to their domestic bliss. 'Come off it, darling. We've agreed that no harm will come to her. Of course she'll be unhappy at first. God help us, her father's only just dead, but she'll have school to occupy her, and we would have her with us for some of the weekends.'

'Ethel and I could help with some of that,' said Cousin Louisa. 'Yes, we could,' Miss Bumpus agreed.

'I think,' Sir Geoffrey said, 'the first step must be to establish contact with her mother – your mother, Phyll. We want to hear as soon as she comes home; then we must ask her for a statement as to the date on which she's prepared to have Irina back.' He looked at Phyll compassionately. 'It won't be so bad in the long run. We couldn't expect that your father's death could be got over without a lot of suffering for several people.'

Feeling that some relief was wanted, they began to discuss arrangements for Christmas Day and Boxing Day. Cousin Louisa said to Phyll: 'We still have the Christmas tree ornaments used when I was a child, birds of Paradise with spun glass tails and several coloured glass globes. We don't have a tree but Ethel arranges them about the drawing room and it reminds me so much of how exciting I used to think Christmas was then.' Phyll smiled through tears, and they came to a discussion of dates. Sir Geoffrey said he would like to see everyone at The Lawn for one of the festive meals, but it couldn't be on Boxing Day. He had heard Mrs Treadgold speak, with almost child-like awe, of the star attraction at one of the large stadiums, a skating ballet, *Cinderella on Ice*. Dancing on ice must be a wonderful sight, she had said. He had managed to get, with some difficulty, seats for her and Gertie for the Boxing Day matinée. Mrs Treadgold, hearing of his intention, looked ready to weep. Then she asked if Irina should not go with them? He had said very seriously: 'No, I think you ought to have a day completely free of any responsibility.' For the same reason, he would not arrange for Fred to motor them up. 'He would be on your mind,' he said. 'I would like you to have a day entirely free for enjoyment.' He said he would order a car from Peastone's Garage to take them, and would telephone the box office to find out what time the show ended, so that the driver should know when to collect and bring them back. Mrs Treadgold's dignity and common sense prevented her from marring the occasion by protestations; she sailed out of the room like a galleon with pennants flying. This arrangement therefore made impossible any hospitality at The Lawn on Boxing Day. Cousin Louisa said she knew Ethel would enjoy seeing them all on Christmas Day, and Neil and Phyll asked everyone to tea on Boxing Day afternoon.

12

Mr Porteous had got into touch with Elmfield School, explaining that Irina Spedding would not be coming back for the rest of the term and asking that her place should be kept open for her, to which he received a sympathetic but temporising reply. No response at all had come from Carteret Street as to when Marcia would be able to give her child a home. Sir Geoffrey felt that something might as well be done for Irina's education in the meantime. Hilliard Bartram's talking to him about Lucinda Fairlight made him think that Lucinda might oblige them by giving Irina French lessons. He telephoned a well-known scholastic agency and asked for the going rate and Lucinda agreed to the suggestion, quietly but readily, that she should come to The Lawn three mornings a week. 'One doesn't connect her with the French, somehow,' Hilliard had said, thinking of Lucinda's lank and unmodish appearance, but the first time she had mentioned a French title in talking to him, he had been almost startled by the purity of her accent. He knew several English people who spoke French very well, but Lucinda's was in a different sphere from theirs; to an English ear it had an unattainable perfection.

Lucinda, from her experience of educational publishing, knew several admirable books of French conversation for children, covering journeys by train and motor car, by boat and in the air, shopping for food, for clothes, experiences with doctors and the Post Office. She brought some of these with her and a charming production, *Album Fée*, each of whose pages showed one of two pictures, according to whether you looked at it through a sheet of red gelatine or blue. Irina was interested at once. She was glad to show what she already knew and to learn something fresh. On her next visit Lucinda produced for her the 'Fables' of La Fontaine. So far she had only known the tales of the 'Fox and the Crow' and 'the Grasshopper and the Ant', which thorough-going repetition had made rather flat, and she was delighted by the vivid impression of new ones: of the Heron, 'going on his long feet I don't know where, his long beak helved into a long neck,' and the tart exchanges of the Crayfish and her Daughter: 'What a way you go along! Good God, can't you walk straight?' 'And how do you walk yourself? Am I expected to walk straight, when my family walk crooked?' The pages were full of the significant experiences and sage remarks of lions, bears, cats, rats, rabbits, monkeys, peacocks, wolves, stags, bats, horses, dogs, frogs and owls. Irina was delighted at the prospect of contact with so many creatures. Some, even of the selected fables, were much more difficult to translate than others. Seeing her one evening at the round kitchen table, puzzling over the book, for the vocabulary was not enough to supply her ignorance, Sir Geoffrey had hunted out a French-English pocket-dictionary, rubbed, dog-eared and grey-looking, over half a century old. Irina was very glad to have it, but even when she had discovered the meanings of the separate words she often found she could not fit their sense together into a whole, till Lucinda did it with her at the next visit.

On a morning in Christmas week Sir Geoffrey, coming to breakfast in the dining-room, thought he saw something white under one of the large Chippendale chairs in the hall. He stooped. Under the chair's seat, a large, luxuriously furred white cat was sitting. 'And who asked *you* to come here?' he exclaimed. The cat closed its eyes and turned its head aside in a dismissive gesture. Mrs Treadgold, appearing with the coffee, said apologetically: 'He's been in once or twice. I think he comes to see Miss Irina.' Sir Geoffrey showed that he was a little nettled at this new invasion by the somewhat brusque manner in which he said: 'I should call her Irina, if I were you.' As he took his seat in the dining room, he said: 'We don't want any more of other people's cats in this house, Irina.'

'There aren't any more after this one,' she said, looking up from her boiled egg.

'That's more than you know; but if there are, they must be told to go back to their own homes. This one is Mr and Mrs Mercer's cat. They won't like it if it comes to live here, like that Siamese creature.' Irina sighed; she said nothing. His back was to the window; he thought he detected a fugitive, roseate gleam on polished surfaces in the room; turning round, he saw that the sky was covered with flakes of cloud, a fiery rose colour. Glad of a distraction, he said: 'Oh, look at the sky!' She looked over her left shoulder, then turned again to her plate. She began to say: 'It was like that one morning when we were getting up. Daddy came in, in his dressing-gown and said: come and look out of the passage window. And we went. And he said – he said –' She stopped, looking down in silence, a long silence, then a loud, despairing wail broke from her. He got to his feet in dismay, meaning to fetch Mrs Treadgold but she appeared before he could reach the door. She got Irina out of her chair and disappeared with her into the kitchen, from where Irina's crying could be heard, gradually subsiding. He went on with his breakfast gloomily, telling himself that however well she seemed to be recovering, it was far too soon to expect that she wouldn't still have recurring moments of agony. Presently he moved to the open kitchen door. Irina was lying back in one of the basket chairs. He heard her say passionately in a still thickened, muffled voice: 'I wish *he* had been killed instead of Daddy,' and Mrs Treadgold reply with despairing hopelessness: 'Oh no, *those* aren't the ones that get taken.'

Anxious to do anything he could for Irina's comfort, instead of insisting that the white cat should be summarily turned out, he telephoned Nell Mercer and apologised for its presence. 'I shouldn't like you and Tom to think we had enticed him.'

'Oh no,' said Nell cordially: 'We should be sorry to lose sight of him altogether, but we are very glad he has such a nice place to visit.' She then asked him to come in for a drink before lunch and suggested that he might bring Irina. 'Not that we have anyone nearly young enough for her,' she said regretfully. He said he was sure Irina would like to come very much. Meantime, it turned out that Fred, washing down the car on the drive, knew the cat well.

He told Mrs Treadgold that its name was Caspar. Mrs Treadgold thought that outlandish; she called it White, merely. White had already demonstrated that he had as much right to The Lawn as the Siamese had. The latter had encountered him at the foot of the staircase and, in surprise and indignation, given him a sharp slap in the face. White was not easily roused, but when roused he was formidable. He drew back, then flew at the Siamese and the two rolled on the floor with savage yells, making terrifying lacerations with their powerful hind legs. Mrs Treadgold was aghast; a set-to like this in the hall, and she foresaw the master's ordering both cats out of the house for good. She aimed a kick at the combatants which drove them apart. The Siamese streaked upstairs and found the one spot where the winter sunlight fell on a small area of the landing; here he lay down, curled round, and looked balefully out of half-closed eyes. White walked into the kitchen in a stately manner and sat down in front of the stove.

Sir Geoffrey and Irina came to the Mercers' house at twenty minutes past twelve. The occasion was not a party, only themselves and Colonel Barker. Irina was charmed by the little conservatory, built out over one of the drawing room windows, full of plants and flowers, but her attention was then drawn to Colonel Barker's spaniel, sitting outside on the terrace and gazing longingly into the room. Nell Mercer gave her a tumbler full of tomato juice with ice in it, and handing her a plate, invited her to make a collection from the dishes piled up with interesting little things to eat. Irina was very glad to do this, but presently she sidled up to Colonel Barker and said shyly: 'Your dog seems rather lonely out there. Can I go and talk to him?' He eyed her with dislike and said: 'I'd rather you didn't. It's his business to wait for me. It's what he's there for.' Irina lowered her eyes and walked silently back.

Nell was now saying to Sir Geoffrey: 'I've found a book among the boys' old things upstairs. I don't remember where it came from. I wonder if Irina would like to have it for Christmas?' She went to a side table and came back with *The Arabian Nights*, illustrated by Edmund Dulac.

'My dear Nell!' he exclaimed, 'Irina loves Dulac's illustrations.'

'Perhaps she has this already?'

'Oh *no*,' Irina breathed, almost dumbfounded. 'Oh, I *would* love to have it.'

'But my dear Nell,' said Sir Geoffrey in consternation, 'this is quite valuable now.'

Nell said with radiant kindness: 'She's so welcome to it. No one here wants it.'

'Well, Irina,' he said, 'this is a magnificent Christmas present.'

'Yes, it is,' said Irina under her breath. She sat down on a low chair and became rapt with delight at the picture of the prince riding the magic horse in the sapphire-blue night sky. Nell was meanwhile asking for news of the bridal pair. He said they seemed delightfully happy. Then he asked if she had viewed the television talk on women's being degraded by marriage, which a very emphatic old lady, wrinkled like a walnut, had given the night before.

'I listened to some of it,' Nell said, 'then I turned it off. I get so tired of that sort of thing! We ordinary people know each other's faults, of course. Women say: Really! If that isn't men all over, and men say: Oh! *Women!* but we *don't mind!* We're just frightfully fond of each other's society.'

'Yes. The sexes are very precious to each other.'

'Those women always setting up antagonism between the sexes make one so irritated! Quite apart from husbands, or lovers, ordinary women want a scene with some interest and style, what you get by working with men and being on good terms with them. Imagine an ordinary girl, having to work in an office with nobody but people like that old crab!'

'One would like everybody to have what they want: a society full of antagonism for that old lady, and one of mutual affection for people like you, my dear. And I must say, you seem to have got your choice!' Nell laughed. She refilled his glass and took the decanter over to where Tom and Colonel Barker were discussing brands of cat and dog-food. Sir Geoffrey came in her wake, and Irina, closing the precious book and laying it down, followed him tentatively. Colonel Barker mentioned the brand of tinned dog-food he'd settled on; he always bought it, he said. Irina, primed by eating and drinking and with the delightful idea of having *The Arabian Nights* for her own, was now so stimulated that a phrase gathered from the scattered resources of her French lessons rushed into her head. 'Doesn't your dog get tired of just one kind?' she asked. 'I should think he would get *fatigue de cuisine*.' She crunched a little savoury biscuit and took a gulp of tomato juice. For a moment indignation made Colonel Barker speechless; then he said: 'Any dog of mine who got *fatigue de cuisine* would know what he could do about it.' Irina looked down, abashed. Sir Geoffrey said they must be walking home and in a few minutes they were seen passing the French windows, Irina not venturing to caress the dog, who wagged an eager, entreating tail as they went by.

'How long is Galbraith to be stuck with that child?' Colonel Barker demanded.

Nell said: 'I don't think he feels he's stuck with her. I think he's quite willing to keep her till her mother's affairs are straightened out. After all, she's a dear little thing.'

'She seems to me a thorough little vixen,' said Colonel Barker in feeling tones. 'Not that *I* want to say anything,' he added, turning round to the mantelpiece to pick up his glass.

Sir Geoffrey and Irina walked the short distance beside the thuja hedge, along the pavement which had a thick curb of glistening stone, he, feeling relaxed and comfortable after Tom's excellent sherry, Irina clasping the invaluable book to her chest. Presently she said: 'I don't think Colonel Barker is very nice to his dog.'

138

'There are different ways of being nice to dogs. Colonel Barker's way is not your way, but it's quite a good way.'

She was silent; then she said: 'Are he and his wife going to get divorced?'

For a fraction of a second he stopped dead; then he said: 'My dear! No! Whatever put that into your head?'

'She didn't come with him.'

'She was probably at home, getting his lunch ready.'

'Oh.' With both arms round the book, Irina ran forward and stepped aside, on to the curb. After a few flying paces she jumped off it, then jumped on and ran forward again, jumping down, jumping up, airily as a butterfly.

13

Immediately after breakfast on Christmas morning, Sir Geoffrey's radio filled the drawing room with the exquisite liveliness of Bach's 'Concerto for Four Harpsichords'. Irina already knew that he did not like any interruption when he was listening to music, so she stayed in the kitchen, nursing the Siamese cat and wondering if White would appear. Mrs Treadgold thought he would not and should not. 'He ought to give them some time at home on Christmas Day,' she said.

The Christmas morning service at St James the Less was held at ten-thirty instead of eleven, for the convenience of housewives and their Christmas dinner. In the time she had been under his roof, Sir Geoffrey had not taken Irina to church, though continuing to attend it himself. If she were to stay with him, he wanted to bring up the matter of church-going with her; he meant to consult Neil and Phyll about it. Neil was, at least sporadically, a church-goer, and Phyll would tell him what their father had accustomed them to do, but church on Christmas Day was a mundane as well as a religious observance, that did not need any enquiries. When they came in at the little west door, he began to wonder if it might not have been better to take her to St Michael and All Angels, with its organ, its choir, its colourful decorations and large Christmas attendance; but he would not seriously have considered abandoning Hilliard Bartram's service for another one, and he was feeling heartened by the unusually good congregation and the warm, comforting smell of the large paraffin stoves by which the church was heated, when he noticed Lucinda sitting at a piano that stood aslant from the altar. There was a harmonium in the space under the tower but it needed serious repairs and for several months the services had been conducted without singing. He was charmed, though not surprised, to find how well she played. The congregation sang: 'Good Christian men, rejoice', 'As with gladness men of old', and 'Hark, the herald angels sing', and his voice, melodious and unexpectedly deep, coming from so spare a frame, was a great support to the rest. At the end of the service, Hilliard was surrounded by members of the congregation. Sir Geoffrey did not try to speak to him as he expected to see him at The White House in the course of the afternoon, but he had a word with Lucinda, wishing her a happy Christmas. She smiled but said nothing.

The Christmas lunch at Cousin Louisa's was a scene of enjoyment, reflected in the glitter of the ornaments disposed over the drawing room. Mrs Treadgold had said that she and Fred would have the meal by themselves at The Lawn; after it, she would write her great number of letters, and Fred would make one in a cheerful afternoon in the holly-decorated bar of The Pheasant, among the boys whom he'd known for years, who'd pitied his sufferings with Mavis (while saying *they* wouldn't have stood for it), and now respected his status in a way that soothed him inexpressibly.

In the brightness of Cousin Louisa's table, Sir Geoffrey occasionally directed an anxious glance towards Irina; he was afraid some poignant memory of a family Christmas might occur to her suddenly and bring her down in tears, but her face was placid and bright; when Neil and Phyll had come rushing downstairs, she had hugged them with enthusiasm. Neil was feeling conscience-stricken; he now thought that in his frantic determination to safeguard his domestic joy and peace, he'd not been altogether kind to the kid. He began to pay Irina a good deal of lively attention; without saying anything actually funny, he made her want to laugh; for the first time, she felt that it would be exciting to be grown up. When the Queen's health was to be drunk, Cousin Louisa asked whether Irina should have, perhaps, half a glass of wine? Neil poured her out a full one. Sir Geoffrey recalled having seen her when she was three years old; he was lunching at The Lodge and at the end of the meal she had come in and stood at her father's elbow. It was another occasion on which they were drinking the Queen's health, and Jasper had made her dip her finger in his glass of port and suck it and say: God save the Queen! It was a memory which he must keep to himself for now.

After the Loyal Toast, conversation turned on various drinks. Neil said there was a shot, though he hadn't come across it lately, called Corpse-Reviver. Sir Geoffrey said: 'I think that was what used to be called Wake the Dead, when I was young.'

'What did it taste like?' asked Irina curiously.

'I don't know, I never took it.'

'There's one you'd like better,' Neil told her. 'It's called Glass Slipper. That's a tall, narrow glass called a flute, full of ice-cream with vodka poured over it. You shall have it when you come out with me.'

'I think she'd like it just as much without the vodka,' Sir Geoffrey suggested.

The talk became general and, in Irina's view, less interesting. When Miss Bumpus carried the coffee tray out of the room, she followed her into the kitchen where Mrs Mounser was already making a start on the washing-up. She was free to do this as her daughter was now out of hospital so the grandchildren had gone home. A nice rest, that was; she was ever so fond of them, but they kept you on the go, like nobody's business. Her husband would be out all day, going the round of the pubs, so she preferred to come up to The White House. The large portions of turkey, the mince pies and a scarcely begun bottle of white wine would be welcome, as well as the money for the work, and the Christmas box Miss Bassett came out into the kitchen to give her, with all good wishes and saying she hoped Mrs Mounser would stay and have some hot tea to go home on.

Irina had taken a teacloth and was happily engaged in wiping a pile of dripping plates until Phyll came in to look for her. Hilliard Bartram meanwhile had come up, hoping it was not too early. Several members of his congregation had called on him after the service, to wish him a happy Christmas and drink his cooking sherry. He had had no stomach for anything to eat and would be glad of his tea: he wanted, too, to have a word with Sir Geoffrey if this could be managed. It so happened that they had the drawing room to themselves, and sitting with him in the window, Sir Geoffrey gave him the opening by saying how well Lucinda had played for the Christmas hymns.

'Yes,' said Hilliard, 'yes. I was very grateful to her.'

'And may I ask –' he paused.

'Of course you may. But all I can tell you is: the obstacle she finds in my committed life doesn't seem to get any easier to her; at the same time I am more and more drawn to the idea of living with her as my wife. Once I didn't feel sure that we should be happy – that was when I realised what the stumbling-block would be; now I feel entirely sure that we should be, if only I could persuade her to accept that.'

'And do you make any headway?'

'I sometimes think I do. Our conversations seem to get more and more interesting, though as a rule they're never about anything very much.'

'No. They're interesting because of the people making them.'

'They don't tell me anything new about her, they just give me a clearer view of what I knew before.'

'Which charms you!'

'Yes.' He was silent with a look on his face as if he were re-living some very interesting moments. Then he sighed and said: 'I'll raise the matter of the French lessons. How many more times a week would you like her to come?'

'Every morning, except Sundays, if she could manage it; if not, then as often as she can. What a pity you didn't bring her to tea this afternoon. Miss Bassett would have been so pleased.'

'I didn't suggest it because actually there has been a slight check in our relationship. We were pulled up short by suddenly realising that

142

our life-styles wouldn't be – might not be, compatible. We've always, up till now, met at her house, when I've called on her, but yesterday for the first time I asked her to tea with me. We were sitting very comfortably when two black boys called; they wanted my help in getting up a football club. They didn't stay long but just as we were settling down again, a youth came who'd been to me before. He'd been desperate, he'd said – I believe in something but I don't know what it is. Then he'd said – so harrowing – There's bound to be something outside, bigger than you, isn't there? I think I've just begun to get it across to him. I didn't dare to turn him away. Lucinda got up and said, she'd say goodbye for now. She wasn't angry. I don't even say she was disappointed; but I knew, she'd seen what life with me would be like, this sort of thing would be going on all the time. I've always felt we saw into each other's minds. I knew she was drawing out of it while she could.'

'But perhaps you would adapt –'

'No. My pleasures, my convenience, it would be my duty to adapt. I couldn't adapt the claims of my calling.'

'No; but you haven't given her time to come to a decision. And you haven't even proposed to her! After all, if you were married – you'd still give up as much of your time, but people would realise they must make appointments to see you, not just invade your home without warning.'

'Most of them, but there'd always be a few I couldn't refuse, whenever they came.' Hilliard's voice was so quiet, it was remarkable that in public he was perfectly audible; but his face now looked so worn, Sir Geoffrey was glad to hear the sounds of the early tea approaching. Miss Bumpus, having arranged the tea-table while Cousin Louisa was coming into the room with the others, said to Hilliard:

'Vicar, you're very clever at judging character from handwriting.' Hilliard pulled himself together. 'Not *very* clever, but I can do it up to a point.'

'Well, my niece has become engaged to a young man who seems very nice. I've got a bit of his handwriting here. I *would* like to know how it strikes you.' Hilliard looked a little apprehensive but he put out his hand for the paper. Joy had written to announce the date of the wedding and to ask her aunt specially to come. It was to be at Kidderminster, rather a long way off, but Bernard had gone into the question of trains and worked out a series of connections by which the journey there and back could be accomplished, and had added a few words, saying how much he hoped she'd be with them: Joy had told him Aunt Ethel was one of her favourite relations.

Hilliard sat, looking attentively at the letter, while the others remained in somewhat awed silence and the tea cups tinkled slightly as they went round. He pored over each stroke, occasionally tilting the sheet to right or left. With long pauses between each comment, at last he said: 'The person who wrote this is very trustworthy . . . He may be a little slow off the mark, but I should say he's absolutely reliable . . . he seems to know his own limitations . . . I don't think he goes off on wild-cat schemes, he feels he's got enough to get on with, right in front of him . . . I get the impression, strongly, that once he's developed an affection, he won't be open to new attractions or want new interests . . . I think your niece should be very happy with him.' With a smile, he handed the letter back and then drank his tea thirstily. Miss Bumpus was extremely gratified and passed plates briskly to right and left. Cousin Louisa said: 'Ethel, you shouldn't have made all this hot buttered toast for us, after all your work on the dinner.'

'No,' said Sir Geoffrey, 'but how very nice to have it!'

Irina meantime had slipped out into the hall where her coat was hanging. She came back with a small piece of paper in her hand and stood uncertainly. Neil was saying: 'If you saw something criminal, would you say so?'

'It would depend on how bad it was and where you were. If I saw something really startling, I expect I should say that I couldn't make anything of it, and give it back.'

Sir Geoffrey now said to Irina: 'Is that something you want the Vicar to tell us about?' She went up to Hilliard and put the worn little leaf into his hand. Hilliard's pause was so long that the onlookers became astonished. He scanned the paper with frowning intensity, sometimes turning it upside down, sometimes slanting it. At last he said in bewilderment: 'I never saw anything like this! It's extraordinary!' He looked at her. 'Where did it come from?'

Irina said with great seriousness: 'It's written by somebody who's not quite right in the head.' There was a general burst of laughter, in which after a moment she joined, because everyone else did.

Sir Geoffrey stretched out his hand. 'May I see it?' Hilliard gave him the paper on which was written: 'Them as got money better keep it. We happy on our own.'

Phyll said: 'Was that written by Darren Mumford?'

'Yes, he was always writing little letters for me to get.'

Sir Geoffrey looked severe but non-committal.

Phyll had sorted out some handkerchiefs and a woollen scarf she thought Irina might like to have and now took her upstairs to give them to her. Sir Geoffrey seized the opportunity to say to Hilliard: 'You didn't see any suggestion of violence in the writing?'

'No, none at all; I realise now, it's mentally sub-normal, but nothing dangerous, from what I could see.' This was a relief, as far as it went, but in Sir Geoffrey's view, the presence of a sub-normal boy added one more to the disadvantages of Carteret Street.

When Phyll came downstairs with Irina, whose goods had been put into a little parcel, Sir Geoffrey said they must be getting home. Hilliard Bartram had been obliged to take himself off already and Miss Bumpus was putting Irina into her coat, while Cousin Louisa, who longed to say to the child that she hoped she'd had a happy Christmas, stood there, not daring to utter a word of the kind.

Phyll came up to Sir Geoffrey, full of the gratitude Neil had tried to express. He had hardly seen her since the return from Charmouth. 'So,' he said quizzically, 'the honeymoon was a great success?'

'Oh, it was! It was!' she cried. 'I nearly died of bliss!' He had expected to hear her say she'd been happy but these words both delighted and astounded him. Under his breath, so that Irina shouldn't hear, he said: 'When we were at dinner, I drank to your father in my mind.'

On Boxing Day Mrs Treadgold did not depart with Gertie in the hired car without leaving careful instructions behind her. The master could make his own way to the chaud-froid in the refrigerator and the soup and coffee on the stove, but she left supplementary directions with Irina.

With the silence of the house in her absence and the stillness of the wintry air outside, for the first time in Irina's company a faint apprehension came over him that he might not know what to talk to her about. He would have felt awkward and uneasy if any intimate or emotional topics had come up, but as it turned out she caused him no discomfort of this kind. She seemed to have adopted not only the régime of his household but its social climate, to be altogether undemanding; yet this did not look like apathy; her bright but calm intelligence was alive all the time. Seeing her beginning the meal by cutting an orange in half to eat it with a spoon (as no grape-fruits had been available), he said spontaneously: 'One of my family went out to India as a judge when India was governed by the British, and when he got there, the Rajah who ruled that district sent him a very heavy basket of beautiful oranges; and when Walter picked one of them up, he found there was a slit in the rind; all the inside had been scooped out and the skin packed full of gold coins; and all the oranges in the basket were the same.'

Irina's eyes widened with delight. 'How lovely!' she breathed. She was seeing in her mind's eye the colours of the gold coins stuffed into the red-gold skin. Then she asked: 'So what did he do with them?'

'He thanked the Rajah very much indeed, but said he was sending the oranges back to him.'

'Couldn't he have kept just one?'

He smiled at her. 'No. Judges mustn't take presents from people they may have to try. The Rajah's friends or servants might have come up before him, and if the Rajah had given him money, people would think he'd been bribed to give a favourable verdict.'

'What a pity!' she said; but she said it philosophically. When they had finished, she very carefully and competently stacked the plates and cutlery and the glasses and carried them out to the kitchen. Sir Geoffrey followed her and lit the gas ring under the pan of coffee. 'Oh!' she said, '*I* could have done that!'

146

'Never mind. You shall do it another time.'

As they were to go to tea with Neil and Phyll, he thought they should set out to walk there about four, but during the afternoon Fred came in to ask whether Sir Geoffrey wouldn't like the car to take them to the White House as well as to bring them back? It was getting very cold, he said. The temperature had dropped; the winter moon was showing its hollow-eyed face in unfathomable depths of blue air, throwing faint shadows of hedge and gate which grew stronger as minutes passed. Sir Geoffrey agreed that he would like the car for both journeys, and asked Fred to sit in the kitchen while they were out; Fred said he had already arranged with Mrs Tread-gold that he'd do that. While Sir Geoffrey went round the ground floor, locking the doors, Irina came downstairs wrapped in Phyll's scarf. It was cashmere, of a clear crimson; it made her feel warm as soon as she put it on.

Although the party was upstairs, all the windows in the front of the White House were full of soft light. At the top of the staircase, the new front door had a wreath of holly, loaded with red berries, fastened to the bright knocker. They had barely reached it when it flew open and Phyll burst out on them. The living room was crowded with the few people in it: Cousin Louisa and Miss Bumpus, Tom and Nell Mercer, themselves, the host and hostess. He and Tom sat on either side of the hearth while Neil adjusted the gate-legged table. Tom was saying: 'I hear his car rally days are over.' 'Phyll didn't like the idea of them,' Neil said, 'besides, I don't want to be out all night.' Sir Geoffrey made no comment but he smiled in a somewhat self-satisfied manner. Everyone else strayed about, ending in the kitchen where Phyll was getting tea ready. The kitchen wallpaper was covered in green leaves with a ribbon of bright silver foil winding through them. '*Very* pretty,' Nell said, but added in a low voice to Cousin Louisa: 'A bride's kitchen!' Phyll, flushed, busy but not distracted, piled scones on a dish and gave it to Irina to carry into the living room, telling her to come back for the cake. Neil appeared to take up the tray of china and Phyll made the tea, bringing it in at the end of the procession.

Sir Geoffrey was amused to see the self-possessed, practical manner in which Phyll administered the tea-party, telling Neil what to fetch, what to do, all of which he obeyed devotedly. As for Irina, she was delighted to wander round, a piece of Christmas cake in her hand, looking again at what she'd seen already and noticing what was new. The small bedroom which Phyll had said should be hers when she came to stay was now all ready for a guest, decorated in green and pink, the bed covered with a white counterpane. It was very pretty, but Irina no longer looked forward eagerly to occupying it. She wanted to stay at The Lawn. She had a secret feeling she kept to herself, that safety was only to be found inside that front hedge and gate.

As the conversation went on all round them, Sir Geoffrey and Nell Mercer found a few moments to talk in semi-privacy. Nell was naturally alive to the situation of Hilliard and Lucinda. 'I was talking to her the other day,' she said; 'not a word about Hilliard, of course, but marriage in general had come up. She said she didn't think she could ever do with somebody there *all* the time. She said: Of course one could bolt or commit suicide, but that isn't the object of getting married. I was rather shocked. I said, no, that isn't the object of getting married.'

'All that might clear up, if it came to the point.'

'Yes. And I do feel, though I may be wrong, of course, that what's wanted is for him to show more persistence. I can't tell you how Tom went on and on at *me!*'

'You don't have to tell me! But we can't do his work for him. We must just encourage him when we see the chance. I would feel much more cautious, in the light of what you say, about encouraging *her*. Not that I should ever be called on, but you probably might –'

To his surprise, Nell laughed. 'Perhaps one oughtn't to encourage anybody! We've been reading a feminist book: it made Tom so irritated, I had to take it back to the library!'

'Dear me, that was surely very chauvinistic of him?'

'I didn't mind, as it happened –'

'Or you would have kept it, till you'd finished it!'

'That I would. But it was really too much for both of us.
It said that though men can't take away women's money so easily

148

now, they still steal their emotional energy and psychological resources.'

'And don't men give them anything in return?' he asked, with an air of grave concern.

'No, I believe not,' she answered cheerfully. 'It seems that women are just defrauded all along the line!'

Tom was standing on the hearthrug. 'Does she *know* any women?' he called out, in loud, exasperated tones. Sir Geoffrey said: 'She knows the hard cases. She seems to have done what people used to do in novels about public schools – it was all true, but it wasn't the whole truth. Is that the time? I expect Fred will be here in a moment.'

Fred had had a comfortable tea on his own in the kitchen of The Lawn; he had been wiling away the time with the radio, and as he turned it off to give his attention to a paperback: *Great Stories of Real Life*, he knew that he had heard a sound. His senses were almost as keen as an animal's; slight as the sound had been, he knew he had heard it, on the path coming up beside the lawn. He pulled aside the curtain and looked out, to where he could see the dark bulk of his cottage with one square of window dimly lit. Whoever it was had been able to get down to the cottage without his hearing them, while the radio had been on. He unbolted the back door and came out on to the terrace. There was nothing to see, nothing to hear. He turned the corner of the house; the whole front was bathed by the flood-lighting which he turned on every evening. He would have run down to the cottage but that would have left the house unguarded. He looked about him, making up his mind that if he found everything at the cottage undisturbed, he would say nothing about this; no need to worry anyone for nothing, though he might just mention it, like, to Mrs Treadgold.

He had hardly brought Sir Geoffrey and Irina home and garaged the car, when the hired car drove up with Mrs Treadgold and Gertie. They came into the hall and stood a moment, dazed by the light, and by the weight of their experiences. 'Well, Mrs Treadgold,' said Sir Geoffrey. 'How was it? Did you enjoy it?'

Mrs Treadgold said with a rapt, solemn air: 'It was *wonderfully*

149

beautiful!' Gertie merely moved her head; she couldn't speak.

Sir Geoffrey tried to convince Mrs Treadgold that he and Irina needed nothing for supper but cheese and fruit, but she swept this idea aside. Everything had been left ready in the morning and only needed heating up. She suggested that she should ask Fred to have his supper with her and Gertie, and then he'd see Gertie home afterwards. Fred had now disappeared down the path to his cottage. Irina cried: 'I'll tell him!' and darted out, round the house and down the lawn. Fred heard and saw her and came out. As they returned to the house, he wanted to say: 'Don't you go running about the garden after dark!' but having done her errand, she had bounded ahead of him. Inside the house, everything was warm, happy and secure; but sometime tomorrow, he decided, he *would* mention the footsteps to Mrs Treadgold. Nowadays, you couldn't take no risks.

14

The morning after Boxing Day Fred was due to work in the Mercers' garden; he made his usual early start and was in conversation with Tom Mercer by half past nine. Towards eleven, Mrs Treadgold, looking out of the kitchen window, saw a female figure coming up the path: mature but attractive, solid, pale but healthy-looking, prosperously dressed in a sleek, fawn three-piece with a white silky blouse and an apple-green scarf over her head. She was walking towards the front gate with carefree assurance. Mrs Treadgold went out at once.

'This is Sir Geoffrey Galbraith's house,' she said pleasantly, 'Whom did you want to see?'

'Fred Poulter,' said the apparition. 'He's my husband.'

'Is he, though?' said Mrs Treadgold. 'You've done without him for a good long time, I must say!'

'What business is it of yours?' said Mavis, throwing up her chin.

'None, so long as you don't come here to make trouble.'

Mavis was prepared, would have liked, to make an alliance with some woman on the site who would have understood her position and supported her. Decent women would take the woman's part in any story, no matter for the facts. It was obvious that this one was going to take the man's part. Mavis had met her sort before; they knew which side their bread was buttered. She glanced round at the trim garden and at the back of the house; and realised that this blank scene was a fortress. She lowered her eyelids and said: 'If I come back to my husband, that's my affair.'

'I should think it's his, too. Does he want you to come back?'

Mavis said levelly: 'I want to get into my husband's house, which is my house, but I find it's locked. Have you, or this Sir Geoffrey something, got a key?'

'There is another key, but I can't hand it out till Fred Poulter gives the word.'

Mavis said: 'Do you object to telling me where my husband is?'

'No, not at all. It's his morning for working at Mr Mercer's.'

'Runs two jobs, does he?' Mavis's eyes narrowed in a speculative look. Then she said, 'When'll he be back here?' Mrs Treadgold did not want to answer this, but she saw that continued stalling would be useless; there must be a confrontation, no good putting it off. She said: 'He comes back at his lunch time.'

'Then I'll be back about three o'clock. Please tell him.' She made for the front gate, 'as if the place belonged to her,' Mrs Treadgold thought, indignantly.

Irina was shut up in the drawing room with Lucinda Fairlight. Mrs Treadgold, while working in the kitchen, listened anxiously for Sir Geoffrey's return from a morning walk to the village for one of his routine visits to the chemist. He was in the hall, taking the neatly wrapped white packets out of his overcoat pockets when she appeared before him in unusual agitation and gave him the news. He remained motionless and silent; then he said: 'When you see him, warn him, and tell him we shall do everything to help him.' Half to himself he added: 'I wish I'd urged him more strongly when I advised him to apply for that divorce.'

Fred came back to The Lawn at quarter to one and was setting off down the garden for his cottage when Mrs Treadgold called to him from the back door and said he was wanted. He turned, looking pleased and interested, and came in. She said: 'Your wife's turned up. She's been here while you were out; she wants to join you again; but not to worry, the master's going to see you through.'

He sat for a moment, stunned; then he said: 'But she – she's – where's the other fellow, then?'

'She didn't say about that. She tried to get into the cottage. I caught her coming back.'

'She can't – I won't – It was her, then, that I heard last night.' He told Mrs Treadgold about the stealthy footsteps which the sounds from the radio had partly drowned out.

'Must have been,' she agreed. 'She said to tell you she'd be back at three o'clock.'

Fred's face was discoloured, a clay-like hue. He said hoarsely: 'I won't There's *nothing* I wouldn't do, to stop her, *nothing*!'

His emphasis alarmed Mrs Treadgold. She said sharply: 'Don't talk silly, now. You won't have to do nothing, beyond say you won't have her back.'

'I'll say that, all right.'

'And stick to it.'

He was silent but a mirthless grin, like a rictus, stretched his mouth. She said, 'I'll be taking the lunch in, in a few minutes. Suppose you have a bowl of soup?'

He gave a great indrawn breath and got up shakily. 'I couldn't take it, I'd throw it up.' He walked uncertainly to the door.

As she finished laying the table in the dining room, she heard Sir Geoffrey come out of the study. 'Fred's back, sir,' she said. 'He's taking it very hard.'

'I suppose so. You don't think she'll overbear him and make him agree to take her back?'

'Not without she chloroforms him first.'

'No – well, provided he sticks to that, I don't think there's anything she can do. Of course he must set about divorce proceedings at once.'

'How will he do that, sir?'

'I'll help him. It's not very complicated.' Somewhat reassured, she

152

went back into the kitchen. Sir Geoffrey went into the drawing room, where Irina was collecting exercise books, primers and a copy of 'Paris Soir.' He meant to ask Lucinda Fairlight to stay to lunch, but she had gone.

A little after three, Mavis re-appeared. Fred stood at the door of the cottage, meaning to keep her out, but she pushed past him. The old feeling of helplessness overcame him. She looked round at the shelter of contentment and self-respect he had managed to create: the old easy chair and the small table beside it with the radio on it, the bookcase, empty except for a few paperbacks and Wisden's Cricketers' Almanac, the little hearth where embers glowed all the time and were brought up to a good fire with the coals he was told to take from The Lawn coal-cellar and the wood he picked up on the shore of the mere, the larger table covered with a red serge cloth, the view through the open door of another room divided into two, a small kitchen with a little refrigerator and a smaller one that contained a bath: all this she saw and she despised it, but it would do for a beginning.

Mavis was well-found in clothes and she had a little money by her, but now that she and the dairy-manager had bust up – (he needn't think *he'd* turned *her* out, she wouldn't dream of stopping, not after the way he'd carried on) she was faced with having to find work, and/or living on national assistance, or coming back to be supported by Fred. Her contempt for Fred was unabated and she would not have considered sharing the low class conditions of where he was now, but she'd heard from the gossip of Grove End friends that he was on good terms with a well-to-do employer and could have almost anything he asked for. It was clear, to anyone looking round the place, that he hadn't asked for much, but *she* would know how to put that right. One of the facts of life today was that, good help being so difficult to come by, anyone who made himself thoroughly useful could practically write his own ticket. She wasn't committing herself to the arrangement as a permanency, but it would do for the time being; she really needed it, she was going to have it. After all, in their marriage, Fred had been the lucky one, everybody knew that.

'Well,' she said, 'you never sent to ask after me; but I've come back now.'

'Ask after you! You said you were walking out on me to better yourself –'

'So I was. I needed to do something for myself as you couldn't do nothing for me.'

'Where is he now, then?'

'Where he always was. You don't need to worry about *him*. Him and me understand each other. We agreed to part.'

'Taken up with somebody else, has he?'

Mavis replied haughtily: 'Of course he was free to make other arrangements when he could see I wasn't going to do nothing more for him.'

Fred was silent, then he said with simple finality: 'You don't come back here.'

'I *am* back, aren't I? This is your home and I'm your wife. This is my proper place.'

'No, it isn't, not now. You deserted me and went off to that other chap. That's grounds for divorce. I'd oughter done what the master advised me and got my divorce then. But he'll see me righted now.'

'See you righted! Who's he to interfere, I'd like to know?'

'He's a judge. And he'll interfere because I ask him to. He won't lead me wrong.'

'Oh, he won't, won't he? He can just keep out of this.' Mavis had told herself she wasn't going to argue. She stepped forward into the room and made for the little staircase leading to the one large room above. He stayed like an image, head bent with half-open mouth.

Mavis switched on the light, provided by a single dangling bulb, and looked about her. Pretty poor it all was, but the bed was comfortably made up; she felt the bedclothes, good blankets and eiderdown. (There was room for another bed. They'd have that. It could come up, second hand, from the High Street, tomorrow morning.) On the chest of drawers was a shaving glass, too good for Fred to have bought himself. She judged there must be plenty more, where all that had come from, and that anybody with their head screwed on the right way would be able to work it for all it was worth. She came downstairs and, again ignoring Fred, walked into the kitchen, which seemed quite well-found, then glanced into the bathroom. A come-down from what she'd been used to the last two years, and even from what they'd had in the council house. No water heater? Only those two great kettles on the Calor Gas affairs. Well, it would do as a start. She came back into the living room.

'It isn't much of a place, but I can make it better.'

'It doesn't want making better. I want it as it is.'

She said with an appearance of good humour: 'Go on! You never did know how to make things comfortable. You used to like me to do it for you. There's no reason we shouldn't go back to those days. If *I'm* willing, you'd ought to be.'

'I'm *not* willing. You said you wouldn't stop along of such a *thing* as me. Right: I'm telling you, *don't* stop; get out and stay out. I've got a decent life here, with decent people. I won't have you coming in and making a mucker of it.'

'I shouldn't make a mucker of it, I'd make it a sight better than it is now. I know I did desert you, as they call it, but now I've come back, the desertion's over. I'm back and I'm going to stay back. I'll be sending my luggage here this afternoon. I'll be round tomorrow morning.'

'You don't send no luggage here.'

'I do, Fred, and you'd ought to realise you're lucky.' Her glance went round the room, as if she was already considering alterations to it, then she picked up her bag and walked to the door. As she disappeared, he gave a despairing look about him, like a man taking leave of all he loved.

Within five minutes Mrs Treadgold came to the cottage door. 'Can you take your lunch now,' she asked, 'or is it tea, by this time?' Without laying a finger on him she impelled him towards the house. In the kitchen, Irina was sitting in the window, polishing tea-spoons. At the sight of her, Fred felt obliged to put on a casual air. 'You're busy!' he said. 'She's a good little worker,' said Mrs Treadgold, 'but that'll do for now, lovey. You go and have a nice read, while I give Fred his tea.' Irina left the kitchen with docile indifference.

Fred ate what was put before him and when the tea-pot appeared at his elbow, he drank several cups of hot, strong tea. He did not at first say anything and Mrs Treadgold did not like to ask but after a while he burst out: 'She said she's sending her luggage in. I won't have it. I won't. I'd clear out and leave the whole place to her, rather than that!'

'Leave the place!' exclaimed Mrs Treadgold. 'Whatever do you mean, Fred Poulter?'

'I don't want to. But if she comes there, I'll strangle her. Then I'd have to leave. They'd take me away, then.' He spoke calmly but he was sitting with one powerful hand on each knee. Mrs Treadgold found herself looking at the hands. 'Fred,' she said, feeling as if she were shouting some message of desperate importance to a man who was drifting out of earshot, out of reach: 'Fred! You owe the master a lot?'

'I do, that.'

'And all we're asking you is: don't do nothing till you have his advice. Nothing! Do you get me?'

'Yes.'

'And do you promise?'

'As far as maybe.' The answer was not satisfactory but she saw it was as far as he could go.

She said: 'Don't you go back just yet, you'll only mope. Stop here, in the warm.' Fred raised his head and looking around him, like someone coming-to. 'I'll draw the curtains,' she said. Early as it was, the winter twilight was creeping on, and it's more protection, she thought.

It was almost dark when they heard the throbbing of a car engine and then a heavy tread crunching the gravel. Telling Fred to stop where he was, she hurried out on to the darkening lawn. A stout, rough-looking man was ahead of her, a heavy suitcase in each hand. These he set down outside the cottage door, and turning about, came up the path in a lumbering trot. 'What are you about?' shouted Mrs Treadgold. 'Who told you to put those cases there?'

The man passed her, calling out: 'S'all right, Ma,' and went on up the path.

'All right, indeed!' she cried. 'How dare you?' But the man had reached the front gate and got into a car whose engine had been left running. (Not anyone from Peastone's Garage, by the looks of it.) Mrs Treadgold came in at the back door and went straight to the drawing room. Irina was lying on the hearth, poring over *The Arabian Nights*. Sir Geoffrey, who had been out all the afternoon, was sitting in his armchair, marking items in 'The Radio Times' to which he wanted to listen. At the sight of Mrs Treadgold, pale and anxious-looking, he came out and led the way into the study.

'I don't rightly know how to tell you, sir,' she began.

'Tell me any way you like.'

'That woman has sent her luggage in to Fred's cottage, two suitcases.'

'They'll have to be sent back to her.'

'But it's Fred! I don't want to sound silly –' she stopped.

Sir Geoffrey said with some severity: 'Mrs Treadgold, you know me well enough to know that if you tell me something you think is important, I shall treat it as important. What is it that's troubling you?'

Mrs Treadgold said, somewhat breathlessly: 'He says if she forces her way in, he'll strangle her. And when I saw him sitting there, with his big hands, I believed him. He's never been all that strong in the head, has he, though, for all he's so clever with his hands? And he's in such a state, he might – he might do anything.' After a pause, Sir Geoffrey said: 'We must be careful. I am inclined to think the first thing to do is to get rid of that luggage. Has anyone any idea of where she'd lodging at present?'

'He never said. But what I've thought – it's no good putting it anywhere in Grove End, she'd have it back here inside ten minutes; but if I was to take it – say – to the Waterloo Left Luggage and bring back the tickets for it, that would give him time to turn round. She'd go after it, you may be sure.' After a moment's thought, he said: 'I really think that might be best. Could you – would you be willing, to do that?' She nodded. 'I'd like to, right away.'

'I don't think Fred had better drive you. Just let me make sure that Peastone's has a car available.' He turned to the telephone. 'Shall I say we want it at once?' She nodded again; her usually ready, decisive utterance had failed her. He gave the order, adding one for

157

the return journey. 'This is extremely kind of you,' he said. 'When I see you into the car, I'll ask the driver to carry the cases to the Left Luggage counter. There mayn't be a porter at hand; and we'll get him to bring them up from the cottage.' Mrs Treadgold made one of her movements of the head which conveyed what she could not say. 'And,' he went on, 'don't trouble about the evening meal. We can –' but she said: 'I'd like to tell Fred to bring Gertie up. She wouldn't mind, I know, and it'll be something to take his mind off.'

Sir Geoffrey said: 'Very well. Is he there? If so, I'll have a word with him and tell him about the luggage, and I'll say that when his wife comes tomorrow, I'll see her.' When he spoke to Fred in the kitchen, his manner was so impersonal and severe, Fred might have been standing in the dock, but the sense was encouraging. Fred understood that the baleful luggage was being removed at once and that the moment his wife showed up, he was to let Sir Geoffrey know. 'Don't be drawn into an argument with her yourself.' Fred tried to say, emphatically, that he would not, but his lips only moved soundlessly. 'And now, Mrs Treadgold has suggested that you might ask Gertie to come up and get supper for all of us. If she can, you'll see that she has some herself? Perhaps you'll have it with her?' He felt that for Fred to be given some duties as a member of the household would have a reviving effect on him. Fred responded immediately; he left the house at once and made for Gertie's ground-floor flat, where he found her listening to music-hall favourites on the radio, and working at a tufted rug in a heartening mixture of crimson and blue. She was very glad to come up, and while she put on her big coat and head-scarf Fred went round the two rooms, the bathroom and the kitchen, testing the fastenings of the windows.

On the short walk back to The Lawn he told her what had happened and where Mrs Treadgold had gone off to. Strangely enough, he found it easier to talk about the matter to Gertie than to either the master or Mrs Treadgold. Gertie was always a sympathetic listener, but she was cheerful with it. Tell her anything off-colour, and she was shocked, all right – 'Well, fancy!' she'd say, but she'd leave it at that.

Meanwhile Sir Geoffrey returned to the drawing room where Irina was still prone on the rug. He wondered how much to explain to her

158

of Mrs Treadgold's mission. The whole matter was all too much connected with the painful area of her own experience. He began to say that Mrs Treadgold was going to take some luggage away that Fred didn't want left at the cottage, and that probably Gertie would come up to get their supper for them, but he had already noticed that when she was in company with people she trusted she was quite incurious. She did not ask any questions and he was glad to be spared from giving information at present. Instead he went into the study and telephoned Sir Maurice Meadowes.

'You know my man, Fred,' he said.

'Yes, nice chap.'

Sir Geoffrey then described the situation. 'I never did any divorce work. I know you did.'

'Yes, but a good while ago.'

'You'd be sounder than I am. She's trying to insist on coming back to him. She says if she ends the desertion, he can't divorce her for it.'

'Well, but he can for the adultery, can't he? There was no doubt about that? I suppose no one's going to claim that she lived *quam sororem* with the dairy-manager?'

'No. I thought it sounded straightforward, but I was a little worried about the time that's elapsed without his making any move.'

'Was there any cohabitation during that time?'

'None whatever. He'd never heard of or from her, from the day of her leaving him till she turned up yesterday.'

'Well, of course, one shouldn't speak decisively without having the papers in front of one, but it *sounds* as if he were in the clear. After all, any marriage can be dissolved on the ground of adultery, other things being equal. There's no law, in England, to force the husband or wife to take back an adulterous partner. And it doesn't sound as if he could be said to have condoned it.'

'No. Their separation was absolute from the time she left his house. I don't think he even knew her address, though of course he could have found it.'

'Well, I wish him luck, though I don't think he is likely to need it.' When they had rung off, Sir Maurice said to his wife: 'I used to think – we all did – that Geoffrey was kind, but rather cool. As decent as

159

they come, but a little – unresponsive. But really, what with this child, and his chauffeur's divorce, he seems to have taken the troubles of the world on his shoulders.'

Rosalind Meadowes said: 'I never thought he was unresponsive, exactly; he listens so intently to what you say, he makes you feel you've never been listened to before.'

'Don't *I* listen to you?'

'Yes; but you know all about me, you hardly need telling; his listening, it's like a scientific process, like having a X-ray. I expect on the Bench, with people in front of you that you didn't know, you did just that –'

'We all try to do it there; I've never been as good at it as he was.'

'Of course listening isn't the same as responding; but I think when one knows him really well, as we've got to since Laura died, one can see, gradually, all the human feelings coming out, like stars. At least, I feel *I* can.'

At ten o'clock next morning Irina was shut up in the drawing room with Lucinda Fairlight, repeating and writing down the French word for every object in the room; Mrs Treadgold was keeping the cottage under surveillance from the kitchen window and Fred, looking now more or less in possession of himself, was digging a bed which they meant to plant out. As Mavis bore down on him, he pushed the spade into the cold, stiff earth so that it stood up by itself and said to her: 'Those cases you sent here yesterday afternoon, I told the master I didn't want them here as you wasn't coming back, so Mrs Treadgold took them to Waterloo for me. She put them in the Left Luggage. She's brought back the tickets. You can have 'em to take with you.'

'Waterloo!' Mavis repeated. 'Whatever sort of a carry-on is this?' She was too much astonished even to be angry.

'It's a nice long way off,' Fred said.

'She'd no business to touch my luggage!'

'*You'd* no business to dump your luggage at my house when I'd told you I wouldn't have you back.' Mavis slowly flushed with anger, then paled again.

'Of all the damned cheek!' she ejaculated; her voice was thick. 'You and your Mrs Treadgold, as you call her –'

160

'I calls her that because that's who she is.'

'There's a good deal here that wants straightening out,' Mavis said in menacing tones. '*I'm* not going to be trampled on, I can tell you that! You just let me get to that Mrs Treadgold of yours, and we'll see who's in the rights of it –'

Fred said: 'Get anywhere you like, except in my house; and here's the master, he wants to speak to you.' Sir Geoffrey had appeared on the terrace and was coming towards them.

'Mrs Poulter!' he said courteously. 'I thought we might have a word. Will you come into the house?'

Mavis would have ignored a summons but an invitation was different; besides, she felt inclined to talk to this old man. He was obviously in the know, and it might be more worthwhile talking to him than to Fred; also it would be a chance to give somebody at the top a piece of her mind, and that would be no bad thing, either. She followed him into the house and into the study; he gestured her to a chair and she sat down; he remained standing on the hearth.

'Well, Mrs Poulter,' he said mildly. 'Things seem to have come to an end between you and Fred. He's made up his mind that he doesn't want the marriage to go on.' (*Fred* made up his mind! Her long-standing contempt for her husband made it sound almost unbelievable that *he* should be the one to take decisions.) 'And as you've given him grounds for divorce, I've advised him to apply for one.' He paused and she said indignantly:

'But you're leaving me out of the picture! If I say I don't want a divorce and put an end to the desertion by coming back, why is he to have it all his own way?'

'Well, but, Mrs Poulter, you left him and went to live in adultery with another man. That was putting *yourself* out of the picture!'

'I went off because he couldn't do anything for me. I had a right to. It was *my* life.'

'Yes, but you put a stop to your marriage by leaving him. You haven't now got the right to come back.'

'Why not? If *I* can forget and forgive, surely he can!'

Sir Geoffrey bent a keen, scrutinising look on her. 'Do you mean you had something to forgive, in the way of another woman?'

161

'Oh dear, no,' Mavis said with a sarcastic laugh. 'He wouldn't have had the guts for that!'

'You mean, you found him trying to live with? But I am afraid that doesn't, in itself, add up to grounds for divorce. Adultery does. You gave him ample grounds when you went to live with another man as his mistress.'

The remembrance of all that she'd done for Fred, day in, day out, of how good it had been of her to marry him at all, rose up in Mavis and nearly choked her. 'I'm not going just to be put out of the way with a rubber stamp divorce,' she cried. 'I've heard all about *them*! I'll contest the action!'

'But Mrs Poulter, just suppose for one moment that you did, and that your husband was refused a divorce, what would you be coming back to? Where would you live?'

'Where – why, here, where he is now. That cottage or whatever it is. I can make it a sight more comfortable, and you wouldn't be allowed to ask much more –'

'I'm not asking anything now, Mrs Poulter. Fred is living there rent-free.'

'Well, all the better. It's not worth much anyhow but I could make it –'

'But there's another point. The cottage isn't tied. His living there is quite a separate arrangement from his work for me. I could end that arrangement tomorrow.'

'He'd have to find somewhere else, then.'

'But I don't think he could find accommodation that would suit you both, at a rent he could afford. And his keeping this job with me would depend on his having somewhere to live. If you drive him out of the cottage by trying to make him live in it with you, if he hasn't a house or a job either, are you sure you want to re-start the marriage? He might find the sort of work in the neighbourhood that he had before, but it might end as suddenly as the factory work did. You've had some experience of living with him on Social Security. Do you want to go back to it?'

Mavis looked even more formidable in defeat than she had looked before defeat had overtaken her. As she hesitated for something to

162

say, her face became like a statue's: hard, pallid, thick-featured, immovable. The arguments were on his side, the law was on his side, but he felt it would take all the nervous energy he could summon to get her out of the room. He saw how right he had been to make Fred undertake not to get into argument with her. The contest between her and the dairy manager must, he felt, have been Homeric, outside the range of ordinary mortals. She stood up and said: 'If I do agree to an uncontested divorce, he'll have to pay me maintenance.' He replied: 'You'll have to leave that to the court. Meantime –' he took an envelope from the mantelpiece – 'here are the tickets for your two suitcases in the Left Luggage office at Waterloo. We had them deposited there; it was necessary to get them away from Poulter's cottage and we had no address of yours to send them to.'

'It was that housekeeper of yours had the audacity to take them there. I'll never forget it! And how am I to get them back?'

'Where do you want to bring them back? Are you staying in the neighbourhood?'

'I'm not divorced and I'd ought to be staying in my husband's house.' He waited for an answer to his question. 'If you must know, I'm with friends down the High Street: Bert and Edna Copeland. They're the ironmongers. They've got a flat over the shop and he runs a taxi in his free time. It's not what I'm used to, but it's lucky I've got *some* friends.'

'Then if you bring your luggage back to Grove End Station, you'll be able to tell Mr Copeland what train to meet. I accept the responsibility for having had the cases removed to Waterloo, so if, afterwards, you send me the account for train and taxi fare, I will pay it.' She remained silent. 'Your husband will take steps to present his petition for divorce; all the necessary information will be sent to you, at Mr Copeland's address, unless you inform the court that you've moved somewhere else. You may need a solicitor's advice and help. And one word more, Mrs Poulter. If you harass your husband by any further visits, I shall advise him to appeal to the County Court for an order forbidding you to molest him. If you continued to do it after that, you'd be in contempt of court. That means you'd risk imprisonment.'

163

Mavis drew a long breath and remained silent. Then she said, vindictively: 'So it was you who fixed up this beautiful arrangement, so you could keep me out of my husband's house; you've helped him to bring our marriage to an end, when I wanted to try again. And I suppose you think of yourself as a Do-Gooder.'

He said: 'I don't think we shall get any further by arguing, Mrs Poulter.'

She looked all round the study, at the books, the prints, the case of orders and medals on the wall, and in a massive silver frame, a tinted photograph of a woman in court dress. She said viciously: 'It seems to me there's a lot that's very off-beat going on here. Your precious Mrs Treadgold, for a start, and you – taking all that interest in Fred – that's a right turn-up for the book, isn't it? And that little girl they say you've got here with you, that's another funny thing, I should say!'

He walked to the door and opened it, then walked across the hall to the front door and held that open; she followed him and crossed the threshold without saying anything more. Returning to the study, he thought with some relief that she had not looked as if she were in want of money. There was a sleekness about her; she was angry but self-possessed. The resources of the Welfare State were available while she had no other support and if she wanted work, the Grove End district offered a favourable prospect of women's employment as domestic helpers, shop assistants or factory workers. Mrs Poulter would not be out of paid work if she looked for it, though not, probably, of a kind she would think suitable.

Presently he walked across the garden to where Fred had now dug over the whole bed and was about to put the spade away. 'Well,' he said, 'I impressed on your wife that if she came here again, I should advise you to apply for an order forbidding her to molest you. And if you'll come to the house at eleven tomorrow, I'll put you in the way of making your application for divorce.'

Fred did not even say thank you, he could not get a word out; but Sir Geoffrey noticed the buoyant air with which he carried the spade back to the tool-shed.

*

Mavis's insinuation about the little girl living with him turned Sir Geoffrey's thoughts to Irina and what ought to be done for her, a topic never far from his somewhat anxious mind. He felt that the one thing she ought to have was companions of her own age, the one thing he could not provide. His friends and neighbours were either childless, or their children were grown-up; like the Meadowes' girls, the Mercers' sons. The only young inhabitants of Grove End of whom he knew anything (and that by hearsay) were members of the sub-culture, famous for such acts as raiding the local shops at midnight, or sneaking into the halls of unwary householders and using their telephones to put through calls to their friends long distance. At present the only young person whose society he could call on for her was her own sister, and he now remembered that the cause of her being in his house at all had been her wild-cat scheme of visiting The Lodge garden after dark. She had never spoken of it again, perhaps his very serious warning had put it altogether out of her mind, but he thought it would be a pleasant thing if Phyll would take her there one morning and come back with her to lunch; enjoyable, he hoped, to them, and giving him the chance to put out further enquiries about the state of affairs in Carteret Street. The house agent who had negotiated the sale of The Lodge to the present owners had also acted when Jasper Spedding had sold it. He and Sir Geoffrey were Grove End inhabitants of long standing. When the latter telephoned him Mr Tallant made a cordial reply: the new owners would not take possession till the end of March, and Mrs Pepperill and her little sister were welcome to walk round the garden any time before then. Phyll fell in with the scheme readily and he arranged with Fred to take Irina in the car to The White House, call for Phyll, take them to The Lodge and bring them back to The Lawn in time for lunch.

Fred had now, under Sir Geoffrey's guidance, filed his petition and sent it to the County Court with his marriage certificate, (which, by good luck rather than good management, he'd been able to lay his hands on), and a money order for the fee, which Sir Geoffrey had told him he must produce. As a result he had developed an almost stern confidence; it was now apparent that for all his simplicity and good nature, he was an authoritative, an indispensable member of the household.

When he set them down at the remembered gate, Irina sped on. Phyll was pleased to visit the familiar haunts but only as she would have enjoyed turning over the pages of an old photograph album; her vital interests lay in the present and the future. It was Irina, looking eagerly about, who longed to see the places where she particularly remembered her father. Turning the corner of the house, she ran to where iron supports had held up a row of ivy arches; these concealed a little moss-grown path and she could see her father walking up and down it on summer evenings, smoking his cigar. The steep bank behind the arches, covered with boulders and groups of fern, and in summer the site of wild geranium and wild strawberries, once almost hidden, was now startlingly visible; then she realised that the row of arches had fallen flat on the grass; the iron frames were rusted through, the ivy, limp but still green and glossy, lying in massive wreaths and garlands at their feet. While Irina bent over them, Phyll turned around and looked at the house, at the ground floor windows in the form of a pair of arches with a column between them, the empty rooms behind them giving them a forlorn and gloomy look. It was no wonder, really, that Mummy loathed the place, Phyll thought. Her mind's eye was on her bright kitchen, and on the space of apricot-pink wall in the living room, where she and Neil meant to hang a picture, they hadn't yet decided what it should be. Irina was now hastening back to the façade; above the front door was the landing-window with its frost-flower pattern and borders of deep crimson glass, but this too, glowing in memory, with no light behind it, was colourless and dark. She said yearningly: 'I do wish we could get inside!'

'We can't,' Phyll said, 'and I should think it's a good thing, really. It would all look so different without Daddy's things; you'd much better just think of it as it used to be.'

Irina was silent; then she said: 'Let's just go through the wood.' What she called the wood was a narrow strip of trees and bushes at the edge of the lawn, dividing it from the road. It had always been dark; a secret place. In summer evenings here, just before bed-time;

166

when the sky was liquid gold behind the intricate dark branches, Irina used to think of the stories about witches in Grimm's 'Fairy Tales' and hope they weren't true. She stepped in among the bushes, pressing and swishing through them so far that she was momentarily lost to sight, while Phyll waited at the edge of the lawn. At last she called to Irina to come out, and Irina re-appeared with smudges of black and green grime on her pale face. They made their way down the drive again and, when they reached the car, Fred, who had the door open, touched the peak of his cap as Phyll got in. Irina knew he wouldn't have done that if she'd been by herself.

At The Lawn Mrs Treadgold took possession of her to get her face washed. Sir Geoffrey greeted Phyll with his usual pleasure and had time to ask her if there were any news of her mother's return? Phyll said she'd had another card, announcing this for the end of January and telling her to let Mrs Mumford expect them then. 'What I would like to find out,' he said, 'is Irina's attitude towards Mosscrop. She must resent him, but one wonders if there is a personal antipathy as well?'

'Now I come to think of it, I don't believe I've ever heard her speak about him. I'll ask her when I can.'

'How did you get on, going round The Lodge garden?' 'I think she was disappointed it was so derelict.'

'I'm sorry that she was, but perhaps it's as well. It may help her not to dwell on the past.'

Irina was almost completely silent during lunch. Sir Geoffrey and Phyll talked about Neil's manic enthusiasm for cars and she said how good he'd been to give up car rallies because she thought them dangerous. 'I expect it was rather selfish of me really.' He did not say she was providing Neil with plenty of other amusement but his smile was reassuring. After lunch he ushered them into the drawing room, and when he and Phyll had had their coffee he left them alone in it. As the door closed behind him, Phyll said: 'When Mummy comes home, I expect you ought to go back.'

'When will she?

'She's written to say, at the end of January. That'll be in about a fortnight.'

'But will *he* be there?

'Yes, of course he will. It's dreadfully sad for us, but he's married to her now. We can't alter that. Do you dislike him very much as a person?' After a pause in which she struggled to put her emotions into words, Irina said:

'He took the bear's necklace.'

'What necklace? What do you mean?'

'My necklace of very small pearls that I used to have. I'd put it on the little bear but I'd forgotten. I found it when I was turning out the toy-cupboard. He came into the playroom with Mummy and Mrs Karmiotis that evening. He took it when we weren't looking.'

'Are you absolutely certain?'

'Yes.'

Phyll was appalled. She did not question Irina's clearsightedness or her truth. This revelation tore down the last of the efforts she had been making to think that Ivor Mosscrop's chief drawback was his innate difference from *them*, that in his own way, he was quite a good sort of person. It called up, unanswerably, his taking possession of her father's dressing-gown, her father's bed. She could only keep a horrified silence and thank heaven that she didn't belong to the household any more; then she felt a stab of compunction that she was ready to abandon Irina to it. But Neil had said: 'For God's sake, tell her she *must* give it a trial. We know she won't be happy at first, but we *can't* have her pushed on us altogether. Whoever she stays with, it's *got* to be realised that Carteret Street is her base.' Phyll had agreed, if rather uncertainly. She sighed.

'Do I *have* to go back?'

'I don't know, darling. I think you'll have to, for some of the time.'

'Can't I stay here?'

'It would be rather a business for Sir Geoffrey to have you here for good.'

'I wouldn't be any trouble!'

'No. But you see, if you were here part of the time and with us part of the time, I think you'd have to go to Mummy for part of the time as well. Don't you want to see her at *all*?'

168

'No. Not now, with *him* there.'

Fred had taken lunch in the kitchen so as to be on hand whenever Phyll was ready to leave, and he had already turned the car round on the drive, but while Irina had found the Siamese cat lying on the shelf above the radiator in the hall, and was nursing it, Phyll had the opportunity to repeat to Sir Geoffrey Irina's last saying. As he came back into the house he felt that it highlighted one of the harsh trials with which life visits its victims, which cannot be evaded but must be borne.

At present, it was difficult to see clearly what should be their next step.

Mrs Treadgold, to whom he said something of this, could see no difficulty. She had seen the man Mosscrop and Mrs Spedding, as she then was, when she'd taken Irina to fetch her clothes from Carteret Street. Half past eleven in the morning, and them not properly out of bed! Her solution was: let the child stay here. He appreciated her emotional support but it did not throw much light on their problems.

15

Ivor Mosscrop had found the honeymoon enjoyable. To stay abroad with enough money to do things comfortably was pleasant, and so was the discovery that his influence over Marcia had not waned; on the contrary, it was stronger. Her gaiety in his presence, her anxiety to please him, had disappeared, but they were replaced by a sullen sensuality. She was anxious if he was not there, she demanded that he should take charge of every detail of their affairs; but strangely, seeing that she now had everything that she had so badly wanted, she was drinking a good deal more than she did before. It did not matter. Ivor was not a heavy drinker, he wanted to keep sharp, but he did not mind Marcia's being sometimes in a rather dazed condition; it did not prevent her making a legible signature on a cheque.

He meant now to make a competent use of his good fortune: not to speculate, he hadn't put up with poverty so long to risk throwing money away now he'd got it, but to go into antique dealing seriously – only possible if you had a little capital behind you, but sensibly too, in a practical and cautious manner. Badger had a fund of expertise which they'd never been able to exploit properly for lack of means; now he and Badger would lay their heads together.

When Ivor brought the breakfast tray to their bed a week or so after their homecoming, Marcia, whose mind was clearer in the beginning of the day, remembered how neatly Phyll had always arranged this. On an impulse of friendliness she telephoned Phyll in the course of the morning, by way of announcing their return, and after enquiries about the marriage, about the flat, about Neil, she added a mention of Irina. 'Well, that's it, Mummy,' Phyll said. 'She's very happy at The Lawn but of course Sir Geoffrey wants to know – we all do, when she's to come back to you?' Marcia said: 'Yes, I suppose so, but I must have a little time to decide it. I told you – or if I didn't, I ought to have done, that I'd heard from Elmfield that they couldn't keep her place for her.'

'We hadn't, any of us, heard that.'

'Well, I've had rather a lot on my plate, haven't I? I couldn't keep everybody abreast of everything. So the next item is, we'll have to find a school for her. That'll take some little time. It's no good her coming back here with no school to go to, what on earth would she do with herself? Till that's settled, she's much better off in the country with all of you. Can't you and Neil take it turn and turn about with Sir Geoffrey? After all, he's got that housekeeper and he was always cried up as being such a friend of your father, one would think he'd be glad –'

'Well, he is, he's been wonderfully kind. He's not trying to get rid of her, he just wants to know –'

'All right, but he can't know before I do. As soon as I've arranged anything I'll let him know, but no school would take her in the middle of a term, I'm pretty certain.'

'But Mummy, she'll need some summer clothes; I expect her cotton frocks are done for.'

'Well, you can look through her things, can't you, and get what

170

she needs. All the money for her is in charge of that Porteous person. Can you come up one afternoon? Bring her with you?' Phyll agreed and suggested that they should arrange provisionally for the next Saturday. She then telephoned Sir Geoffrey, who said that Saturday being a half of their precious weekend, wouldn't a weekday be more suitable? That would mean that Neil could not drive them, but Fred would run them up and bring them back. Sir Geoffrey's usual, unvarying kindness made Phyll almost blush as she remembered the slighting, ill-natured way her mother spoke about him. Finally it was arranged with everyone concerned that the girls should go up to Carteret Street the next Tuesday, and when they came back, Neil should join them at The Lawn for dinner.

Now that Marcia had come back, she and Mrs Karmiotis were extremely pleased to see each other, Marcia to talk unrestrainedly about herself and her affairs, Mrs Karmiotis to listen with avid interest. The latter enquired what was to be done about Irina, and agreed vehemently that she ought not to be shipped back to Carteret Street until a school had been found for her; she already knew of Ivor's determination that it should be a boarding school, and undertook to make enquiries and consult entries in a guide to independent schools in the local library. One morning, with Irina in her mind, she told Marcia that one of the bookshops in the Charing Cross Road had a copy of Dulac's *Arabian Nights*, rather expensive, but if Marcia would think it a good thing to get it for her as a *douceur* – A wish to give Irina pleasure was not a strong motive with Marcia, but she saw the force of the suggestion. She offered to write Mrs Karmiotis a cheque, if she would be kind enough to get the book and bring it round, and Mrs Karmiotis said with much good nature that it should be a present from *her*.

Irina was very glad that this visit, which she saw she could not escape, was to be paid with Phyll going with her and Fred to take them and bring them back; connected like this with The Lawn, she felt almost safe. To wander round the deserted garden of The Lodge, peering through its windows into the empty rooms, was something

171

she had longed to do and found comfort in doing; going to Carteret Street was something from which she shrank, and the instant she set foot inside the hall her fear of pain was justified. There was quite a little crowd in the hall, her mother and Mrs Karmiotis and in the kitchen doorway Mrs Mumford and behind her, Darren, ('He'll be over the moon to see you,' Mrs Mumford told Irina) and there was also Ivor. He hadn't meant to be there when they arrived; not that he gave a damn, but there was no point in sticking your neck out. He'd been delayed by the ebullient conversation of Mrs Karmiotis and hadn't got away in time; he found himself in front of Irina, obliged to speak or be conspicuous by not speaking. 'Well,' he said, 'and how's the old merchant?' Irina gazed at him in blank incomprehension. 'Come on,' he said with jovial irritability, 'don't stand mum!' Her mother said, over Phyll's shoulder: 'He's asking you how Sir Geoffrey is.' After a further second's bewilderment Irina said: 'But he isn't a merchant.' Ivor felt that he'd now done all that the social occasion demanded of him, and with a muttered goodbye to the others got himself out of the front door.

As Irina looked round, shrinkingly, she saw overpowering traces of him. A heap of canvas satchels and knapsacks, rubbed and worn, was stacked against the hall table. In the umbrella stand, an extraordinary stick was leaning; its top was a large, grinning, pseudo-oriental head. It was in fact a sword-stick. Badger had come up with it, and Ivor had fancied it. The coat-rack was smothered with his coats, two and three piled on one hook; crushed between a heavy, much worn navy-blue overcoat, in want of brushing, and a bulky windcheater, was a material she thought she recognised; she put out her hand to it; it was her father's Burberry.

Phyll had followed her mother and Mrs Karmiotis into the drawing room, and Mrs Mumford brought in the tea tray. As she went out again, Darren showed himself at the kitchen door. He was a good deal paler than he used to be, hollow-eyed and taller. He was dressed very neatly; his flannel shirt and his blazer were conventional, but his tie was fastened with a brooch that carried a large, four-leaved clover, transparent green enamel over gilt. Surprisingly good of its kind, it had come, without explanation, through one of Gloria's young chaps;

172

presently she had given it to Darren. He was very proud of it and wore it all the time. His mother had said he'd be delighted to see Irina but he merely hovered in the kitchen doorway; not that he would ever have spoken to her of his own accord, but his face used to change at the sight of her in a way that perhaps no one except his mother would have noticed. Now he looked uncertain and upset and she almost wondered if he recognised or remembered her. (He was that pale, nowadays; Mrs Mumford thought she really must take him to the doctor.)

Phyll meanwhile was pouring out tea, since her mother seemed disinclined to do it. Mrs Karmiotis, for the first time she'd known her, thought Phyll decidedly attractive. She had lost that irritating air of remoteness; she was mature and sensible, matronly even, in piquant contrast to her extreme youth. Mrs Karmiotis was having an enjoyable conversation with her, finding out as much as she could about Cousin Louisa and Miss Bumpus, and then about the household at The Lawn. And who kept house for Sir Geoffrey? she wanted to know. Phyll described Mrs Treadgold in glowing terms.

'Oh *really*?' Mrs Karmiotis said with emphasis. 'And what sort of age is she?'

'I don't know exactly, but in the sixties I should think.'

'Oh *really*?' said Mrs Karmiotis again, this time with the volume of an opera-singer's recitative.

'But very well preserved,' said Marcia languidly.

Phyll said in perplexed tones: 'I don't think she *preserves* herself; that's just how she is.'

'Well,' said Mrs Karmiotis, summing up the matter but without committing herself, 'I daresay it's all *selon les règles*. And you say he's very nice?'

'Oh, he *is*,' Phyll exclaimed, 'and he's been so kind to Irina.' This brought Irina into the conversation and Marcia said: 'Irina, Theonoë has found another of Dulac's books for you. Just what you'll like.' She reached out to the sofa table and handed Irina the book.

'But I've got it,' Irina said miserably. Marcia flushed with annoyance. 'You *haven't* got it, Irina,' she said angrily. 'This is one of the ones you haven't got.'

173

'I've got it now,' said Irina doggedly. 'Mrs Mercer gave it to me for Christmas.'

Mrs Karmiotis rose to the situation. 'Oh well,' she said pleasantly, 'then you won't want this one.' Irina hung her head and mumbled something. Phyll put in: 'It was very kind of Mrs Karmiotis to get this one for you. We didn't, any of us, know about the one you'd got already.'

'Yes, it was,' said Irina, shamefaced. She had known this visit would make her very unhappy. As soon as she could she went out of the room and up to the deserted playroom. As she switched on the light, it was revealed in its state of not having been tidied for months. Her paint-box was still on the table with a jar of discoloured water beside it. On the windowsill the bears themselves were sitting with their heads on one side and their forepaws raised in exaggerated gestures. She closed her eyes tightly to prevent the tears from sliding out.

The conversation downstairs languished a little. In Phyll's presence Marcia could not speak altogether as freely to Mrs Karmiotis as she liked to do when they were alone together about various matters, including the iniquitous arrangement in Jasper's will that had left her child's money away from her, and Mrs Karmiotis did not feel able to discuss with complete candour the situation at The Lawn, which she thought sounded interesting and on which she would have liked to know more. So Phyll got up, saying she had better look through Irina's clothes.

She went across to Irina's bedroom and began taking cotton dresses out of drawers and sorting out shoes. She found that the time had come for a good deal of renewal. Besides dresses, there ought to be a new summer coat and though party clothes would hardly be necessary, Irina ought to have one frock that would 'take her anywhere', anywhere that a gingham dress would not take her.

With Phyll out of the room, Marcia realised that Irina was not there either. She supposed the child must have gone up to the playroom and, though she did not want Irina's society for its own sake, she was made slightly uncomfortable at the idea of her withdrawing herself: Marcia felt obscurely that this meant a criticism, a sitting in judgement. Standing in the hall she called out impatiently: 'Irina, why are you staying up there in the cold?' Irina's voice came from above: 'Because I want to.' Marcia went back to the drawing room, muttering: 'She's really too awful!' Mrs Karmiotis felt that, early as it was, a drink would help. She said so and they went into the dining room.

Presently Phyll came back, prepared to tell her mother what Irina needed. Marcia stopped her, putting her hand to her forehead. 'Don't say it all to *me*,' she said wearily. 'Get what you think she ought to have and send the bills to old Porteous. It's nothing to do with me. I've bought every stitch she's had on ever since she was born, but now I'm not thought fit to have control of the money.' Phyll could say nothing to this, except that she'd do her best. At this moment the doorbell rang and Mrs Mumford let in Fred. Phyll rolled up the clothes for further consideration and stowed them in laundry bag that was hanging behind the door. Irina, who had heard the bell, came downstairs at once, carrying her paintbox. Fred, in the hall, took the paintbox from her and the bag from Phyll. Mrs Mumford asked if she should find some carrier bags? 'No need,' said Fred civilly. (Get them both away without hanging about, was his private feeling.) 'Are you ready, Madam?' he asked Phyll.

'Yes, we are,' she said. While she was saying goodbye to Mrs Karmiotis and kissing her mother, Mrs Mumford came up to Irina. She had found the clover-leaf brooch on the dresser by the tea-caddy, just where Darren had been accustomed to leave his letters. She knew what this meant. 'He wants you to have it,' she said in a low voice and put the brooch into Irina's hand. The pin pricked Irina's palm. She stared at Mrs Mumford with hypnotised intensity. Mrs Mumford was satisfied. She went back into the kitchen.

During the drive back, the fear Irina had had of going back to Carteret Street for good was intensified now that she had seen it again, seen Ivor Mosscrop again, a jovial ogre just as she had remembered him, and her mother as hard and impatient as she had always been. The scene of the deserted playroom, so full of memories, made her feel that if she tried to talk she would begin to cry. Phyll,

175

however, did not want to talk; she was thinking about seeing Neil. When the car drew up, she got out, almost stumbling in her eagerness and Neil himself opened the front door to her. Irina got out and went upstairs to put away her coat; Phyll left hers in the hall and went into the drawing room with Neil's arm round her waist. His characteristic look of cutting severity alternating with almost insane glee, gave her a fresh excitement when she saw it after an absence, however short. Sir Geoffrey greeted her with his usual silent delight, and went to draw the curtains, increasing the soft glow inside the room. Neil said: 'This is a perfect house to come to dinner in this time of year, any time, come to that, but spring dinner parties can be absolute hell in some houses: cold, light evenings and because it's spring they give you stewed rhubarb.' Mrs Treadgold now came in to ask if they would like dinner at once? 'Yes, please, we should,' Sir Geoffrey said, adding: 'I don't know what Mrs Treadgold is going to give us, but I feel sure it won't be stewed rhubarb.' Mrs Treadgold said under her breath, like a sort of ritual incantation, 'Baked jam roll,' and went out again. 'Perfect!' Neil exclaimed.

Sir Geoffrey said: 'I daresay Irina will be down in a minute. She'll have dinner with us and when she's gone to bed, you can tell me what you think of the position.' Irina now came in, looking wan and sad. They were summoned to dinner; as she had had nothing to eat at tea-time, her meal put some life into her, though she remained silent. Mrs Treadgold, coming and going, noticed her looks and said as they got up: 'Should you like to go to bed, lovey?' Irina said nothing but started walking towards the stairs. Phyll went after her and said: 'I'll come up before we go, darling.'

Over coffee Neil said: 'The truth is, she ought to go home to her mother and until she's done just that, and given the thing a fair trial, we don't know where we stand.'

Sir Geoffrey turned to Phyll: 'How did you find things this afternoon?'

'Ivor went out almost as soon as we came in.'

'Was he disagreeable?'

'No, not exactly. Of course the way he talks is not what anybody's used to except Mummy. But one thing Mummy did say, and I think she's right, it's no good her going back there till they've found a school for her. I mean, is it?'

'But what about Elmfield?' asked Neil in surprise.

'As they didn't hear, they filled her place.'

'Didn't hear? You mean, you mother just let go the end?'

'I suppose you could call it that.'

'I think Porteous warned her, after the school's letter to him, that that was likely to happen if they didn't hear. Perhaps he – we – ought to have put it to her more strongly.'

'It's no use telling a woman not to be a fool if she is one,' said Neil bitterly.

'Well,' said Sir Geoffrey, 'she and Mosscrop could say I am responsible for the present state of affairs. When Irina came here, I gave an open-ended invitation for her to stay. I didn't think, and Phyll agreed with me, that her mother's household was sufficiently regardful of her. Perhaps, legally speaking, I ought to have put the matter into Miss Bassett's hands, but Mrs Treadgold was here and she stepped in at once, with all the love and care the child needed; and she's more than willing for the arrangement to go on for the time being.'

Neil said: 'I'm simply overwhelmed, and so is Phyll, by your kindness. I know – we both know – that we're in the firing-line, and that if the Carteret Street show collapses, we shall have to cope. But I can't tell you – neither of us can, how much it means to us just now to have our home to ourselves and how enormously grateful we are.'

Sir Geoffrey smiled; then he said: 'Phyll's father was my very dear friend.' He went on: 'Something must be done about Mrs Mosscrop's undertaking to find a suitable school. This is the beginning of the spring term, I think. Let them have as much time as they think they'll need, but aim to have the thing settled by next September.'

Neil groaned. 'She won't do anything without him, and you've never seen him or you wouldn't be able to imagine him cruising round talking to headmistresses.'

'No. Well, perhaps we could all help there. But I suppose it will satisfy everyone if I suggest she should stay here till September?'

'Yes, I should think so, indeed!'

'If I can know that you, and/or Miss Bassett, could step in for a short time if anything here made it desirable, that's all I need for now. I think I must see if Lucinda Fairlight can give us more time for her. Three French lessons a week aren't enough if she's not to have any other schooling.'

'No,' said Neil. 'If Lucinda can give her a thorough grounding in French, that would be an asset for life, and probably teach her more than she'd learn in most schools. After all Victorian girls with governesses –'

'Yes, but education in a Victorian home, a good one, was pretty rigorous. Still, we're only thinking in terms of the next few months.'

Upstairs, Phyll found Irina with her head sunk in the bedclothes. She sat up and locked her arms round Phyll's neck. She was crying.

'Don't, darling!' Phyll implored.

'It was so – so –'

'I know it was, I know. But don't cry, don't!'

'I don't want to go back there.'

'Don't worry about that for now. Sir Geoffrey wants you to stay here for quite a long time yet.' Irina was longing to hear some absolutely firm and final decision. She yearned to be assured that she would never go back, that she should stay here for ever. With unchild-like commonsense she accepted the partial comfort for what it was worth; but what she now wanted was for even Phyll to go away, so that she could cry and cry without being urged to stop. When Phyll left her, she did this for a few minutes, but by the time Mrs Treadgold came up to look in on her she was asleep.

16

Phyll had recently made two visits to Carteret Street, both in the late afternoon and on each of them she had found Marcia slightly bemused, her hair disarranged, her skirt unzipped at the waist; (she had put on some weight). She was obviously drinking, but Phyll, anxious as she was, could think of nothing that could be done. Marcia had never been amenable to advice, and Phyll was the more disturbed because on her second visit she found Mrs Karmiotis there, and the latter had said to her, *sotto voce* outside the drawing room door, 'It won't do for her to get permanently on the bottle.' Mrs Karmiotis was, in Phyll's experience of her, a staunch drinker, and if *she* thought her mother was on the way to drinking too much, that was alarming. From what Mrs Karmiotis told her, she gathered that Ivor Mosscrop's business in antique dealing was growing considerably, that Badger's spy network was frequently reporting fields of action all over the place, which meant that Ivor was often out the whole day, from breakfast time till late in the evening, several times a week. Marcia didn't know what to do with herself. When Ivor was away she would notice, vaguely but uneasily, that the atmosphere of the flat was different from what it had been once; it was untidy. Mrs Mumford kept the place going, but she had lost heart. Darren had been removed to hospital with a tumour on the brain, but she had left it too late; he had died before they could operate. Pale and strange-looking, she went about the work silently, only presenting herself determinedly on Friday mornings to be given her wages. Once there had been a bit of trouble from the money's not being to hand, and as Mr Mosscrop was fortunately at home, she had spoken out and told him that if she wasn't to be paid regular, she wasn't coming no more. Ivor at once recognised the threat to his comfort, gave Mrs Mumford the money himself, out of his wallet, and told her that she would always find what was owing to her under the tea canister on the dresser on Friday mornings. From that time she always had found it.

Marcia herself was contented when Ivor was beside her, but towards evening, if the flat were empty, she felt very lonely and was obliged to have a good many drinks. As a result she had sometimes a strange feeling that somewhere, in one of the rooms, there was someone, she could not remember whom, but some man who had always been kind; but when she trailed, half-drunk, into one room after the other in search of him, there was no one there.

Mrs Karmiotis could, as a rule, see clearly what other people ought to do; what she often couldn't see was how impossibly difficult they would find it. She saw, now, that the solution to Marcia's problem would be for Irina to return to her mother. If Irina could show her some spontaneous affection, behave with natural, childish sympathy, Marcia's response would be – not immediate, perhaps, but certain to be aroused before long. That dangerous loneliness which was leading to her drinking on a rather serious scale would be cured. Irina probably wouldn't want to come back to Carteret Street; from what Mrs Karmiotis could pick up, the child seemed absolutely to have got it made in Sir Geoffrey Galbraith's household, but her unwillingness couldn't be allowed to count. Her mother needed her and her proper place, now, was with her mother. It wouldn't be altogether easy going, Mrs Karmiotis could see that; they might get on each other's nerves to quite an extent, but *anything* would be better than leaving Marcia alone in the flat for so much of her time. A question which had loomed very large before was Irina's schooling. It had been agreed by everybody that she couldn't come back to Carteret Street until another school had been found for her, and so far nobody had done anything about finding one; but the point no sooner occurred to Mrs Karmiotis than she settled it for herself. A daily governess would be the thing; this arrangement would give the child an object, and, incidentally, the education she ought to be getting, with the additional advantage of keeping her in the flat all the time, instead of her being away at some school, five days out of the seven. Once she had come to this decision, Mrs Karmiotis felt that the next step must be to implement it. She did not exactly know the state of the governess market of today; the Victorian era, of ask and have, had of course been superseded long since, but there must be some of them about somewhere, and Irina's trustees could afford the best obtainable. When she had got to this point, Mrs Karmiotis decided that she would approach Sir Geoffrey Galbraith.

Some people might have thought it rather an undertaking to propose to visit him when she was a complete stranger and had not been commissioned by any of Irina's family, but Mrs Karmiotis was courageous and she was attracted to any situation which was arresting and dramatic. Also, what was influencing her was the very usual experience, that when one has heard a name for the first time one is, after that, hearing it frequently, with an accretion of detail. When she first heard Sir Geoffrey mentioned in the Speddings' household, she had taken it for granted that he must be dreary, but since then several references to him in other people's conversation had been building up for her an idea of him which, (though she was quite certain she would never approve of him), made her feel that he was more interesting, more impressive, than she had supposed. With a great deal of confidence in herself, she had none at all in any department of the Establishment. Supported by the comments of writers in the intellectual weeklies, she had had no difficulty in deciding that judges, as a whole, were almost always wrong-headed and often downright incompetent, but nonetheless the picture taking shape in her mind was that their authority and the ceremony and respect with which they were treated made them rather fascinating. She did not expect to see in Sir Geoffrey Galbraith a reminder of Lord Chief Justice Jeffries conducting the Bloody Assize, but she felt an agreeable *frisson*, as if an interview with him might be stimulating. His mental powers and his severe patience were set off by the reputation she was now beginning to hear that he had, of being rather amusing. Her friend Beulah Cotton, several years ago, had appeared before him in a case where the prosecution were set to prove that she had been on intimate terms with the accused. One of his letters to her, unfortunately available, began: 'My own P.P.' The judge, sitting only a little above the court but appearing to address her from a serene height, had said: 'Those are not your initials?' 'No.' 'Then will you tell us what they stand for?'

To avoid further torment, she had said, desperately: 'They stood for Precious Puss.'

'I see,' said counsel, with hideous relish, 'then "My own P.P." meant my own Precious Puss?'

'Yes, but it didn't mean all that much – it was just idiom.'

'You are asking the court to believe that when a gentleman writes to a lady as his Precious Puss –'

'His *own* Precious Puss, Mr Ventress.'

'I am obliged to your Lordship, as his own Precious Puss, that is just idiom?'

It was all over long since, and Mrs Karmiotis, who had keenly enjoyed the tale of her friend's sufferings while it was still new, had almost forgotten it, until it now came back to her that the judge had been Sir Geoffrey Galbraith. She felt that the interview would be interesting, as well as useful in the campaign for getting Irina back to Carteret Street. He was one of her trustees, he was in the solicitor's confidence, he was a friend of both Neil and Phyll and the child at present was living in his house; all in all, the feat couldn't be brought off without his cooperation. Mrs Karmiotis found his address in *Who's Who* and wrote an excellent letter, introducing herself as a friend of the family, anxious about Irina's future, and asking whether they could arrange a meeting? Sir Geoffrey was in fact very willing to do this. He felt it was an advantage to know as many people as possible connected with Irina's mother. He invited Mrs Karmiotis to lunch, very courteously, hoping she would be able to spare the time on a day in the following week; a train was suggested and accepted and Fred was instructed to meet it.

On the day of her arrival, Sir Geoffrey told Irina that she would be having lunch with Mrs Treadgold; Mrs Karmiotis was coming to see them and would talk to Irina afterwards and tell her about her mother. Irina said nothing but she turned a degree paler. Mrs Treadgold received his directions about lunch with an air which was obviously apprehensive.

Mrs Karmiotis arrived in an aura of richness to which the household was quite unaccustomed. Her velvet coat was cut loosely to suit an ample figure, and its lines suggested the robes of some grandee in a Venetian painting of the seventeenth century. Her hat was wreathed with delicate black feathers that trembled as she moved. Her self-confidence and her evident kindness and her voice, hearty and slightly hoarse, made her entry impressive. She was met by Sir Geoffrey with almost ceremonious courtesy. His frame was so spare, and his voice, though deep, so quiet compared with hers, it might at first sight have seemed that he would be overpowered by her; but Mrs Treadgold, asking if the guest would come upstairs, did not think he would be. In the spare bedroom, laying her sumptuous coat on the immaculate counterpane, Mrs Karmiotis took in every detail of Mrs Treadgold's appearance; she admired it and felt an inclination towards friendliness.

'Is the little girl here?' she asked.

'Yes, but the master thought you'd like him and you to have lunch by yourselves and have a talk with her afterwards.'

Mrs Karmiotis thought this an excellent plan and descended the stairs with eagerness. Her stockings were black lace, woven in a pattern of overlapping scales, which gave her legs the look of some giant bird's, as though triangular talons should have protruded from her black slippers. They added to the slightly alarming air she brought into the homely atmosphere of The Lawn. She had determined she must make no adaptations, no concessions. Her usual method was to say, with downright honesty, exactly what she thought, and if this did not convince her opponents, at least it overpowered them with a rain of verbal fireworks. On this occasion she felt particularly keyed up to it.

In the drawing room Sir Geoffrey said modestly that there was a little white wine for lunch; would she like some sherry first? Mrs Karmiotis, who was amused that anyone should think that a little white wine might be all that her head could stand, said she would like some sherry. To her satisfaction she found that it was extremely good. He confirmed that Irina would join her afterwards and meanwhile Mrs Treadgold came to tell them that lunch was ready. An excellent cook herself, Mrs Karmiotis approved of the lamb cutlets and the early peas, and of the apple tart accompanied by cream in a silver-gilt creamer: simple food presented in perfection. The Mouton-Cadet also was well chosen, and she felt comfortable, hospitably treated and ready to explain her mission.

'It's on her mother's account,' she said. 'Of course, there was a good deal of ill-feeling on the child's part; not that Marcia was in any way responsible for the father's death, of course not, but the child connects it with the fact that Marcia had been demanding a divorce.'

'Yes, I'm afraid that's almost inevitable.'

'But it's unfair, as any adult can see. She'll have to be got out of the notion somehow. After all, her mother was within her rights . . .'

'Her rights?' he repeated in surprise.

'I don't mean that he'd committed any matrimonial offence, simply that the thing had broken down; it had meant nothing to her for years.'

'But do you feel that gave her the right to break up his home, so that he couldn't keep his children with him?'

'I daresay she could have gone on with it indefinitely, but then this new attraction came up, and of course that made it hopeless.'

Argument, or in the last resort, abuse, Mrs Karmiotis was ready to withstand, but she was disconcerted by silence; she was altogether unused to it; the people she knew were, as a rule, vociferous, ready to talk their heads off. She had never met anyone who, accustomed to keep silent so as not to interfere with the workings of justice, carried the habit into private life. Finding it increasingly unnerving, she began again: 'Of course, Ivor Mosscrop is a very different type; naturally Jasper's friends resent that . . .'

'But I think we should all have deplored the breaking-up of the marriage, whatever the man had been like.'

'Of course you object to divorce on principle.'

'No. I think unhappy marriages, very unhappy ones, should be put an end to. But one can't help sometimes remembering the protest the Catholic peers made when the Matrimonial Causes Bill was under discussion in 1858. They said increased facilities for divorce would undermine the stability of family relations, on which the well-being of the State is based. Even they could hardly have foreseen what the statistics would be, today.'

'Oh well,' said Mrs Karmiotis hardily, 'one must move with the times. And if you approve of very unhappy marriages being ended . . .'

'I can't agree that the Spedding marriage was so unhappy as to be intolerable.'

'Well, that was not the opinion of the person who had to put up with it.'

'No. Obviously not. However, Jasper is out of it, and Phyll . . .'

'Oh yes, Phyll is taken care of; it's Irina I've come about.'

'We shall all be very glad of any information you can give us. Neil and Phyll, as her sister and brother-in-law, are partly responsible and

184

Miss Bassett is a very kind but distant relation. I am her trustee, but not her guardian. I expect you know I found her alone in Grove End, after dark. I brought her back with me; I could see she wasn't being carefully looked after. Meantime, owing to her mother's not taking up the matter, her place at Elmfield was forfeited. Another school, I think, must be found for her by the autumn . . .'

Mrs Karmiotis said energetically: 'I don't think it's a school that's wanted, it's a competent daily governess.'

'Really? But why . . . ?'

'For her mother's sake, it's essential she should be at home.'

'But her mother's neglect of her, and her refusal to answer letters about the child's future . . .'

'Yes, I daresay. But Marcia has had a very rough passage, you mustn't forget.'

'Has she? She has gained the husband she wanted, her circumstances are comfortable . . .'

Mrs Karmiotis dashed in: 'That's another thing! The will Jasper seems to have made just before he took off – did you know about that?'

'Yes. I advised him to make it.'

'Then *you* advised him to leave the girls' shares tied up like that? Phyll's naturally, but Irina's?'

'Yes.'

Mrs Karmiotis said with an air of displeasure: 'I don't know why you did that.'

Sir Geoffrey laughed outright. 'But Mrs Karmiotis, if *I* knew why I did it, did *you* need to know?'

'Oh well, perhaps not, but it has made things rather awkward for her, just when one hoped everything was going to be all right at last. Ivor naturally expected that they would have the control of the income from Irina's share till she was old enough to have it. An arrangement like that makes them both feel that they haven't been trusted.' After a brief pause, seeing he was not going to reply, she went on: 'The point is, Irina is *needed* at home.'

He gave her a penetrating glance. 'Have you come with a definite decision from her mother, to have her back?'

'No, not yet. I am feeling my way. The fact is Ivor's business keeps him out a good deal at present and Marcia is left alone. She hasn't stood up to it very well and she's got into the way of drinking rather a lot. That sort of thing is apt to grow on people, as I expect you know.' Sir Geoffrey murmured that he did know. 'And one can see that if Irina were at home all the time, it would prevent Marcia's feeling lonely and give her a sort of stable routine, which would be exactly what's wanted.'

He was thoughtful for a moment, then he said: 'One would have first to be assured that Mrs Mosscrop wants the child back, and then that she could take responsible care of her.'

'Yes, I know, but once Marcia has made up her mind to that . . .'

'What grounds have you for thinking she might want, or be persuaded, to want it?'

'As I say, I haven't discussed the matter with her yet . . .'

'And what sort of home life do you think she could provide for the child if Irina did go back to her?'

'Well, I daresay some of it would be rather dot-and-go-one at first. There's been a good deal of disturbance; it'll take some tolerance and unselfishness on Irina's part, but that's an effort it would be good for her to make, better than staying here with spoiling grown-ups, allowed to do whatever she likes . . .'

'Do you feel that she is allowed to do anything she ought not to do?'

'I don't say that, actually.'

He smiled amicably. 'Then I don't see the force of the argument.'

'It's simply that she's needed, genuinely needed, in her mother's household, and one feels that *everyone* ought to be on the side of assuring her that she ought to go back. Of course Jasper queered the pitch originally. When the question of the divorce came up, I told him, myself, it was his duty to let Irina see that *he*, as well as everyone else, wanted her to accept the idea, but he didn't, I'm pretty sure . . .'

'Was it to be expected that he would? He'd had a severe shock, and then he was told, not only that he must accept the position, he must make his child accept it too. Was that reasonable?'

186

Mrs Karmiotis gave a shrug so expressive it was almost theatrical, and repeated: 'As I say, we must move with the times, after all. And as for shock, if he'd been in the least sensitive towards Marcia, he'd have realised long ago how worn-out the marriage was; it *oughtn't* to have come as a shock to him.'

'Well, Mrs Karmiotis, you know your friend, and I knew mine. I don't think we shall gain anything from a post mortem. I think our next step must be to try to get a decision from Mrs Mosscrop, and as you are kindly willing to take up the matter . . .'

'Oh yes. Of course if she says she wants the child at home, that settles the question?'

'Yes. If she makes the demand herself, and if all the parties are agreed that she is in a position to take proper care of her.'

'Well, we shall see.'

'I think that's as far as we can take the matter at present. But you'd like to have a talk with Irina now?' He went to the kitchen door. 'Where is Irina?' he asked.

Mrs Treadgold said with a slightly flurried air: 'She went down to the cottage to take Fred's laundry back.'

'We want her here.' He returned to the drawing room and, finding an ash tray, put it at Mrs Karmiotis' elbow. In a few minutes, Irina appeared; behind her Mrs Treadgold retreated to the kitchen. Her expression was like that of a devoted retainer attending some member of the family at the block. Sir Geoffrey said: 'Mrs Karmiotis wants to talk to you,' and left the room for the study.

Mrs Karmiotis would have kissed her but Irina was standing too far away. The former thought she had grown since their last meeting; she was very pale. 'Won't you sit down?' Mrs Karmiotis said in friendly tones. Irina sat on the edge of a chair, several paces off. 'I've come to give you Mummy's love and to tell you about her.' Irina gazed at her mutely.

'You haven't seen her since you and Phyll came up to Carteret Street that time, have you?'

'No.'

'She wants to see you, very much.'

'What for?'

187

Mrs Karmiotis was not often nonplussed but she was now. Recovering, she said: 'She loves you, Irina. You're her little girl, aren't you? It's natural she wants to see you. Don't you want to see her?'

'No.'

'That's very unkind of you. She's always been kind to you, hasn't she?' Irina said nothing. 'She hasn't been very well lately. If you came back to your home with her, we think she'd get better.'

'Do you?'

'Wouldn't you like to think you could take care of her and make her well? It would be a very grown-up thing to do. Most girls of your age couldn't do it. People wouldn't expect them to. But we think *you* could do it. Wouldn't you like to?'

'No.'

'But what *do* you want to do, then?'

'Stay here.'

'Why are you so anxious to stay here?'

Impressions rose in Irina's mind, disconnectedly: The Lawn, Mrs Treadgold, Fred, the cats, all vaguely commingling in a haze of happiness, with Sir Geoffrey, a momentary vision. She moved uneasily. At last she muttered: 'I don't want to go away.'

'I see they're all very kind to you,' said Mrs Karmiotis encouragingly, 'but however much you enjoy being here, you'll be very selfish if you won't think about anything except where *you* want to be.' Irina sat, looking at the floor. Mrs Karmiotis ventured: 'I suppose you feel that nothing's the same at home now your father isn't there, and we're all very, very sorry for you. But very sad things happen to all of us, and we just have to take them and go on. Well, I won't talk to you any more about it now, I'll leave you to think about it. I hope some ideas will come to you, about how much Mummy wants to have you at home with her, and how much we all want to see you with her.'

Irina thought of the horrible walking-stick with a head like a grinning apple, of all the heavy, untidy coats with her father's Burberry crushed underneath them, of the study, and Ivor Mosscrop sitting in her father's chair.

'So will you think it all over carefully? After all, you could still

188

spend some of your time here, and with Phyll and Neil. We're only asking you to make your home with Mummy as a basis. You will still be able to visit other people. *Will* you think about it?' Irina raised her head, her cheeks flooded with colour. She didn't say: I don't need to think about it. Her meaning was unmistakeable. (Mrs Karmiotis told herself, she'd always said the child had no natural affection. She'd been right.) She made to round off the meeting with general conversation. 'How is Phyll, these days?'

Irina kicked the rung of her chair. 'She's all right.'

'She says you're learning a lot of French.'

'Yes, I am.'

'Were you sorry not to go back to Elmfield?'

'Not specially.'

'Of course when you ran away and came off here, they couldn't keep your place open for you. But when you're at home, I expect you'll have a very nice governess to come every day to give you lessons. You'll enjoy that, I know, because you're a clever girl and like to learn things, don't you?'

'Some things I do.'

She got up. 'Well, Irina, I'm glad to have seen you. I'll give your love to Mummy, shall I, and we'll see what arrangements will be best.'

Irina left the drawing room; seeing her depart, Sir Geoffrey came out and rejoined Mrs Karmiotis, who asked him to order a car for her. He replied that Fred would take her to the station for whatever train she had in mind, but would she not stay for an early cup of tea? Mrs Karmiotis however had decided to go; she had not thought the meeting would be tiring, but she found it had been, unexpectedly so. Fred was in the kitchen awaiting some summons, and Mrs Treadgold came out to go upstairs with her. Mrs Karmiotis, putting on her coat and attending to her face at the glass, said: 'I've been trying to persuade her that she ought to go back to her mother, but I haven't had much success.'

The recollection of the sight she'd had in Carteret Street of Mrs Spedding as she then was, and that fellow, hardly out of bed, was very strong in Mrs Treadgold. 'Does her mother *want* her back all that much?' she demanded bluntly.

Mrs Karmiotis felt sure that Irina would never have been able to present such an impregnable resistance if she hadn't known, consciously or unconsciously, that this household was firmly behind her. It made her feel an irritation towards Mrs Treadgold whom, at first sight, she had been prepared to like. She said in authoritative tones: 'She's *necessary* to her mother; it's that, that's the root of the matter.'

They were coming downstairs, and Sir Geoffrey, waiting in the hall, heard her say impressively: 'You must take the mother's part, or you'll be slighting the importance of women.' He felt that few people could demonstrate the importance of women more effectively than Mrs Treadgold, but he advanced to see Mrs Karmiotis into the car, thanking her warmly for having come; he said that though they could not see their way clearly at present, all the information they could collect on this difficult matter was acceptable. As he shut Mrs Karmiotis into the car and watched it drive away, he realised that he had gained one piece of information, disconcerting but valuable. A shy child of eleven was not a likely person to help a woman who was drinking. Mrs Karmiotis thought the mother's drunkenness was a reason for Irina's returning to her; he was of the opposite opinion.

Mrs Karmiotis, smoking, leaning back comfortably in the railway carriage, was not dissatisfied with her expedition; apart from its success or failure, it had given her a lot to savour keenly, and to relate, vivaciously, at dinner parties.

Sir Geoffrey also was thinking over the visit very carefully. The first thing he felt must be done was to get Neil and Phyll to go to Carteret Street and form a reliable estimate of Marcia's condition. Neil had a long talk with him and arranged, after a telephone call at half past nine to Ivor Mosscrop, whom he fortunately found not yet set out on a proposed rounding-up of the householders of Kings' Lynn, that he and Phyll should call on Saturday afternoon and go into the question.

Ivor Mosscrop was both annoyed and relieved. He had to do some hard thinking. His original idea had been that once they got Irina into some snob boarding-school, her presence in Carteret Street for holidays, shortened as it naturally would be by visits (long visits) to The White House and The Lawn, would be so brief, it would be worth putting up with it for the amount Marcia would be able to claim from the trustees for living expenses. Now he was not so sure. Marcia's condition, which had taken him by surprise, seemed to be getting slightly worse, and if, with the kid in the house, she were to be found more or less permanently sloshed, there would be an amount of interference and trouble, enough to drive a man off his rocker. Better, he now thought, to cut the connection with Irina right away, by saying Marcia had never really recovered from the shock of Jasper's death, and that, coming on her when she was getting towards the change of life, it had made it impossible for her, at present, to take active charge of the kid. When Neil and Phyll arrived in Carteret Street, Ivor opened the door to them, looking serious, and led the way into the dining room, where the remains of an unappetising lunch still stood on the table, among them two pint tumblers lined with brown froth above dark dregs. He said at once, with a plausible air of gravity and concern, that Marcia really wasn't fit to have Irina on her hands; she'd never got over the events of last October; he might have to take her away for a rest and change presently; that, and the fact that while he was at home the business demanded all his energies, made him feel he must act for her, and say that if they and Sir Geoffrey were kind enough to go on with the present arrangement indefinitely, that was far the best thing from Irina's point of view. They were all standing, and now Ivor made a move towards the drawing room.

Marcia was leaning in a corner of the sofa; her face was pale and puffy, her hair unkempt. Her suit was a good one and had not had time to get shabby, but her expensive shoes were creased, dull and down-at-heel.

Phyll went up to her and kissed her. 'How are you, Mummy?' she asked fondly.

Marcia spoke very slowly. 'I'm all right,' she said.

Phyll and Neil sat down.

Ivor said: 'She's usually ready for a little snooze after lunch.'

Neil said bluntly: 'We've come down to talk about Irina.'

191

After a slight pause Marcia said with a struggle: 'What about her?'

Neil gave a smothered exclamation; then he said: 'We want to know if you want her to come back here to you?' Marcia said nothing. 'Well, *do* you?' Neil repeated.

'Who? Me?' said Marcia. She seemed to rouse herself. 'I don't think she'd do any good here. I don't really feel well enough to have people here, and people there, all over the place.'

'Then, Mummy, are you willing for her to stay in Grove End, with Sir Geoffrey part of the time, and us part of the time?'

'I should think so,' Marcia said, in a tone as if wakened from sleep. 'It sounds a very good plan.'

Neil got up. 'You stay with your mother,' he said, 'and Mosscrop and I can have a word meantime.' He walked out of the door and Ivor followed him. In the hall Neil said: 'This is a pretty poor show. How long has she been like it?' Ivor, he noticed, seemed much more responsible and altogether more decent than they had ever seen him: instead of the cheap and flashy clothes he had once worn he was now in solid, commonplace, respectable garments. Now that he had married Marcia, gained possession of the flat and control of the income from her capital, he no longer felt obliged to assert himself. He appeared good-natured and straightforward.

He said: 'It's been coming on since I had to be out so much on the business. I've been working like steam to build it up. It's really taken off, and I felt I couldn't leave it; but I see now, I'll have to take time off for her. A lot of it is driving round to different places and I can take her with me. I think we can check it now; if not, she'd have to be dried out. But of course she's in no state to look after the kid.'

'No. The rest of us will have to sort it out between us. But we want to make sure that if Marcia suddenly comes-to with a click, she won't demand her back.'

'I don't see her doing that.'

'No. But she'd have the legal right to do it. If it *should* happen, could we rely on you to support our decision to take her over?'

'I'll say you could! *I* don't want her here. I'm only too glad . . .'

'Sir Geoffrey doesn't think there need be any legal business about guardianship. It'll just be a family arrangement. But if, as I say, when Marcia's recovered, as one hopes she will, *if* she wants to make any trouble, you'll use your influence?'

'You're dam' right I will.'

'I hear it was Mrs Karmiotis who started this idea . . .'

'Theonoë Karmiotis is a dam' good sort, she's been a very good friend to me, I'd never deny; but sometimes she goes off the rails a bit.'

'Well, she may be of great use in keeping your wife company when you've got to be away. But someone will have to explain to her that the idea of Irina's coming back here is off. That's going to be a bit awkward?'

'She'll take it from me,' said Mosscrop calmly. 'I don't often put my foot down, but when I do, it *is* down, if you get me.'

'Yes. Well, that's about all, I think. Of course my wife will be very anxious and sad till this condition clears up. However, she'll be in touch, and you've got our phone number if there's an emergency.'

Phyll meantime, finding her mother dozing, had made a quick reconnoitre of her bedroom. There were no arrears of soiled linen; Marcia's stacks of clean underclothes were in the drawers. The dressing table was clean and neatly arranged. Obviously Mrs Mumford was still operating. When Neil returned she was sitting on the sofa again, with one of her mother's hands in both of hers. She got up and hung over her, seeming distressed at having to say goodbye. Marcia did not get up; she remained placid and unmoved. Phyll kissed her on the head and said something about seeing her again very soon. In the hall Ivor appeared to her, as he had to Neil, improved to an astonishing degree. His manner was responsible. He reconciled Phyll to leaving her mother in his care. She could never have imagined or foreseen such an alteration.

As they drove away, Neil said: 'If he can cope, that's all right, but we may have to step in.'

Phyll examined an inner pocket in her bag. 'I brought back the latch-key I used to have. I thought I might leave it with them, but perhaps I might as well hang on to it.'

Neil said nothing.

He took Phyll back to The White House, then turned the car about and drove back to The Lawn where Sir Geoffrey was expecting him, to hear the result of their visit. When he had described Marcia's condition there was a long silence. At last Sir Geoffrey said: 'Well, this doesn't really tell us anything we didn't know before. I suggest, and I expect Porteous will agree, that we must now go all-out to find a school that will take her in the autumn. When that's arranged to everybody's satisfaction, we can made tentative plans as to how she spends the holidays.'

'I've been evading that,' Neil said candidly, 'but now I've got to face it. Phyll and I can't go on having our home entirely to ourselves.' He stopped and sighed.

'Phyll agrees with you, I expect?'

Neil burst out: Yes, she did. She was simply the sweetest girl ever known, there'd never been anyone like her for sweetness, there couldn't have been.

Sir Geoffrey smiled; he did not, in his heart, agree that there'd never been another girl as sweet, but he didn't want to argue the point with Neil. He said: 'Then subject to everyone's convenience, I suggest that we should divide the holidays in half. If there's a bit left over, I know Mrs Treadgold will want it.'

'Irina's so different from Phyll,' Neil went on musingly. 'She's like that girl in the Greek tragedy – Electra, was it? – who had it in for her mother because the mother had killed the father in his bath with an axe.' He spoke lightly but Sir Geoffrey was struck with momentary dismay. The characters of Greek tragedy were interesting, no doubt, high-minded even, but not the sort of people you wanted much to do with in private life. He said: 'I think that's putting it rather strongly!' and Neil admitted that he was given to hit-or-miss judgments; but this one stayed in Sir Geoffrey's recollection. When Miss Bassett asked him to lunch so that they could all talk over the plans for Irina (and thank him heartily for his very great kindness) after lunch in the drawing room, surrounded by the blackthorn blossom on the Morris wallpaper, Sir Geoffrey said, up till now he'd had a very easy ride, the child had given no trouble, she'd just been a very well-behaved and interesting little visitor, but if she were to be altogether removed from her mother's care, as a shared responsibility among them, he for one was rather anxious that she should be encouraged to overcome the bitterness against her mother. 'I haven't a word to say for Mrs Mosscrop myself,' he said. 'As Jasper Spedding's friend I could hardly be expected to, but for the child's own sake; and I must own, I don't see at present how it's to be done.'

Cousin Louisa, who at no time could have given an impression of high intelligence, or even, as a rule, of knowing better than other people, now said: 'I don't think we can do anything except treat her with very great kindness – your Mrs Treadgold shows the way. If we all do that, all the time, in the end we may get the splinter of ice out of her heart.' Her dim though still beautiful blue eyes were obviously short-sighted, but they occasionally took on a look as if they could see quite a long distance.

17

The news that Irina would not have to return to Carteret Street but would be taken care of by young Mr and Mrs Pepperill, Miss Bassett and the master, gave deep satisfaction to Mrs Treadgold, which even the prospect of Irina's going away to boarding-school did not much damp; she calculated that most of Irina's holidays would be spent at The Lawn, particularly as she thought it would turn out that young Mrs Neil was expecting. Nothing had been said and she thought it possible that the girl herself might not know it yet, but she had found that something about the look of the nose usually told you. She said nothing, naturally. Time would show.

Mr Porteous collected the prospectuses of four schools, all of which sounded sensible and attractive, and the parties having made a first choice of Beech Hanger, which was smaller than the others, the school was approached and it was learned that Irina would have to sit an entrance examination. This did not much daunt them: her father had been satisfied with her progress at Elmfield, Neil hoped that as a result of Lucinda's care, her French would knock them cold, and

Mrs Treadgold bore witness to her arithmetic; sitting at one side of the kitchen table while Mrs Treadgold did the accounts at the other, Irina, to whom the figures were upside-down, could cast them up correctly and arrive at the answer before Mrs Treadgold could.

Sir Geoffrey and Mr Porteous were asked to arrange for her to take the examination at Beech Hanger. It was suggested that she should arrive in the morning, sit two of the brief papers before lunch and two after; then she could be fetched away after Sir Geoffrey had viewed the premises. Fred drove them over on a fine morning, and then took Sir Geoffrey on to Lewes where he visited the castle and took his lunch, (Fred had been supplied with sandwiches and a thermos of tea by Mrs Treadgold).

Irina sat by the window in a graceful drawing room, at a table with pen and ink and sheets of foolscap, working sums and composing answers to history questions of an elementary nature; after a nice lunch brought to her on a tray by a kind and cheerful lady, she wrote a brief essay in English on 'Books I Enjoy', which in her case included bound volumes of 'The Strand Magazine' and 'The Illustrated London News', and any books illustrated by Edmund Dulac, of which she said: 'I have not got them all now, but I mean to, one day, if I can.' Then she wrote in French a page and a quarter of foolscap on *'Comme je voudrais passer le jour.'* She was able to concentrate the better as the cries and calls of girls playing near the house had been considerately hushed.

Sir Geoffrey arrived at half past three and had a confidential talk with the headmistress, a very tall and very spare lady, plain and elegant, with a charming, silvery voice. Her manner, though simple, gave the idea that she had it in her to be extremely witty, and her somewhat tentative way of speaking did not detract from the impression of an imposing personality.

They liked each other. Sir Geoffrey gave her a resumé of Irina's situation and added that he thought the child very intelligent. She smiled and said: 'That is fortunate. Of course there are people – very successful people – who don't need much intelligence; they have other resources. But we, here, feel we have most to give to children whose minds can be cultivated. We work them up to capacity but we do our very best to make the work enjoyable. If one is not to injure the natural curiosity, the growing-point, enjoying the work is almost as important as doing it – in the end, quite as important. You must have felt that, in your professional education?'

'I did. But talking of enjoyment, do you find that watching television impairs the capacity to concentrate on reading?'

'Not to the degree we have it here. We keep it for weekends unless there's something they specially want to see, then we arrange for that. Is she accustomed to watch a great deal?'

'No. I haven't got it in my part of the house; my housekeeper has a set which she watches sometimes, but unless it's a feature about animals – arctic bears or race-horses, I don't think she's sold on it.'

'That's a good thing, but as the bad cases are so very bad, one feels they are apt to obscure one's view of the ones that aren't so very bad.' Such sense, he thought, combined with so much penetration, gave one confidence.

When Irina had surrendered her last paper, they made a tour of the premises: of form rooms, light and smelling of sun-warmed wood, with a few pieces of beautiful eighteenth century furniture standing in the corners, and bedrooms for two people or three, done up with gaiety and prettiness. Considering the intellectual standard of the headmistress, he found it rather reassuring that in one of them a doll was lying in a cradle beside its small owner's bed.

When the headmistress said goodbye to them in the hall she had not seen Irina's papers, but she said: 'Do you think you will like being here?' Irina said, 'Yes.' The letter which Sir Geoffrey got a week later, offering her a place for the autumn term, added: 'Her French is unusually good for a child who has not lived in France.' This comment was relayed to Lucinda with Sir Geoffrey's congratulations and thanks, and she was asked to stay to lunch after the next French lesson, for he thought it would be a pity to give these up before Irina left for Beech Hanger. He meant the lunch to be a very small celebration. He asked Phyll; Neil he knew would not be available, and since Lucinda would be there, he naturally seized the opportunity to invite Hilliard. He asked the Mercers; Tom was away playing in a golf tournament, but Nell was delighted to come, and had just congratulated Irina warmly on the entrance examination when she saw White standing in the green-painted doorway of the kitchen. 'Dear me, Caspar,' she said, 'how do you do?' Irina said: 'Oh, I *do* wish you could see – when he stands there and the sun is just right, there's a most wonderful emerald green light on his white fur! It's lovely. It makes him look like something out of "Sir Gawain and the Green Knight". Have you got anything painted green in your kitchen?' Nell said: 'I am afraid we haven't. That's something he has to come here for.'

Phyll now arrived, and after she had hugged and kissed Irina, made her way into the kitchen, where Mrs Treadgold was anointing a large pile of fragile profiteroles with darkly shining chocolate. She put the spoon down and kissed Phyll. 'And what's the news with you, lovey?' she asked.

Phyll said: 'I'm going to have a baby.'

'Bless you,' exclaimed Mrs Treadgold. 'Well, I'm not surprised.'

'Aren't you?' said Phyll wonderingly; she had felt that she was imparting a piece of news that must be highly unexpected.

'Why should I be?' Mrs Treadgold enquired, with considerable reason.

Hilliard was of course delighted to hear of Irina's success, which he equated with Lucinda's success, since the French essay was the only question on which the headmistress had particularly commented, but apart from this he did not, for once, contribute much to the pleasurable spirit of the party. He looked worn and paler than usual, and when, after lunch, Nell asked after what she called his 'case load', he told them of an exhausting matter on which Mr Welland had sought his help. Mr Welland, besides having a good deal of parish business on his hands, had always recognised that Hilliard had a degree of intuition beyond his own, and he candidly admitted that this case was beyond him. The youth was not mentally ill, the psychiatrist said, but experiencing difficulty in the development of his personality. He would be found lying on his face, talking to the insects on the floor, and going nearly out of his mind because they didn't answer him. This struck them all with amazement and dismay, except Mrs Treadgold, who, coming in with the coffee, saw the matter in a different light, exclaiming indignantly: 'There didn't ought to *be* insects on the floor!' as she went out again.

Lucinda shrank to hear the story. To give up precious time, precious nervous energy, to people like that, however often she thought of it, (and for anyone on familiar terms with Hilliard Bartram, this had to be very often) filled her with a desperate misery that never grew less. She saw him now, looking at her with a considering, above all with an impersonal, gaze, which was not the way he looked at her as a rule. She knew that he read her mind, that he had always been able to do; well, she read his, if it came to that. Yet in spite of the insurmountable obstacle, the sense of attraction towards him was slowly increasing. The few times that they had talked about religion, religion had not proved, as it might have been expected to do, a stumbling-block. He had said: 'I don't think intellectual difficulties are of the first importance. I could produce several! What one wants is a personal relationship with God: "Draw nigh to God, and He will draw nigh to you".'

'Yes.' She found nothing to deny or even question. She enjoyed conversation with him as she had never enjoyed it with anybody; but she did not think she could bear the certainty of being put aside so often while he poured himself out on people with whom she couldn't sympathise, from either a medical or a Christian standpoint: about whom she could only feel that she didn't want them to be there.

She had to leave The Lawn before the others did; she had a date-line for the text on which she was working.

Hilliard did not stay long after her. Phyll took Irina off to spend the rest of the afternoon at The White House and Fred, who kept an eye on all the comings and goings at The Lawn, asked Mrs Treadgold to find out what time he should call to bring her back. Sir Geoffrey persuaded Nell to stay for a little conversation; before she left, she said: 'One can see they're pining for each other. I wish they'd make haste.'

'They'll take their own time, I suppose.'

A pearl is a temple, built by pain around a grain of sand!

'Oh dear. I daresay that's true of them; I'm glad it wasn't, of Tom and me.'

In her workroom Lucinda sat with the translation in front of her without attending to it. The recent past rose between her and it. In perspective it had a significance she had not noticed when it was actually there. She saw how very near to each other they had come, more than once, and then, she thought, each time I shied away. I have disappointed him so often. I couldn't help it and that made it worse for him. She now began to realise that while her mind had been fixed on the idea of pushing away his wish that she should share his life, his tasks and his wearisome preoccupations, her own feelings for him had been overtaking her, unnoticed like the incoming tide among distant creeks and inlets.

He had got into the habit of calling regularly on a Tuesday evening for a drink and a conversation. She had made a point of being at home and ready to welcome him then. The Tuesday evening after the lunch at Sir Geoffrey's he did not come. She would have thought little of it, but now the memory of his attentive, impersonal gaze made his absence chilling. For the first time in her life she experienced waiting for someone, while every passing five minutes deepened the certainty that he wasn't coming.

She argued that she must ignore these painful feelings. They were, after all, a sign that she was not going to be committed to a life she would find endlessly trying; she would be thoroughly glad, she would feel the benefit of the release, once the natural smart was over. Then she began to think that perhaps she could have borne such a life, for the sake of what it would give, but it was too late now; the memory of his face as he had looked across the lunch table assured her of that. The idea of making any sort of advance to him, and having it evaded, was so painful that anything would be better. When men had been rebuffed beyond a given point they often ceased to want what had been refused. If their reaching this point coincided with a change of your own feelings, that was a calamity so widely known it had its own title: it was called Bad Timing. Hilliard had seen, had decided that there was no future for them together. His face, thin, grey-eyed, intelligent, responsive, had become impassive, impersonal. He had accepted that the sacrifice was too much for her. She wished she could have undertaken it, but all her life she had refused to allow

200

inroads on her leisure, on her self-absorption, and now she had lost the power to make the sacrifice, even if she wanted to. The weakness of her moral nature, which in this direction she had never tried to check, had now caught her out.

The succeeding week was a busy one, and when Tuesday came round again she determined not to wait in the house for someone who wasn't coming. He usually called about half past five; this afternoon she did some late shopping and spent a fair time in the local library. The three books she collected, on top of the purchases, made the basket heavy. She walked slowly along the road, pushed open the gate and came up the path. As she paused, taking the key out of her bag, a man came out of the shelter of the porch and lifted the weighty basket from her arm.

'I thought you were never coming,' Hilliard said.

Inside the house, she said at once: 'I was wrong to be so unsympathetic about the man lying on the floor.'

'Never mind him for now. We've got other things to think about.'

'But have we? I felt you'd decided we'd come to an end?'

'An end? We've hardly reached the beginning. I've not yet asked you to marry me. But will you?'

'If I did, I would try to be more – not to be so very – as I always have been.'

'And I would try not to make your life a burden. Your happiness would be my chief duty, except one. I couldn't put aside that one . . .'

'No. I wouldn't want you to. If we are to get married it must be to the people we really are.'

'It won't be very easy.'

'I've never thought anything was very easy.'

Two days later, as she was leaving The Lawn after Irina's French lesson, Sir Geoffrey came out of the study and said he'd heard some news which gave him the greatest pleasure. Lucinda stopped, holding books and two French newspapers to her chest. She said in a low voice: 'I will try hard to make him happy!'

He said with a sudden, rather mischievous smile: 'Don't try *too* hard!' When he had seen her out, he went to the kitchen. 'You'll be glad to hear they've settled it at last!' he said to Mrs Treadgold. 'One is so glad for them!'

Mrs Treadgold smiled generously. She said: 'That's very nice news!' But as he left the room and she stooped down to open the oven, she said to herself: 'She won't make old bones.'

18

As Irina's future was now settled with regard to the coming September Sir Geoffrey felt this was the time to do some stock-taking on what they were all prepared to undertake for her. Marcia's condition, as described to him by Neil and Phyll, made it plain that she was not in a state to give Irina a home. If she should improve, as he sincerely hoped she might, they could still rely on the massive egotism of Ivor Mosscrop to prevent her from suddenly wrecking their arrangements by demanding her child's return, which, in fact, she had never shown any sign of wanting.

Sir Geoffrey had strongly advised Irina's father to provide for her in case of his death, when neither of them had had the least idea that his death was imminent. He himself was in his late seventies and it was much more pressing than it had appeared to be in her father's case that he should settle, now, what benefits he intended for her. After a great deal of thought he re-drew his will, settling a capital sum on Irina, of which some was to be available for training her in a profession if his death should come about before the end of her schooling; another, large, sum was disposed of in charitable bequests and legacies to his friends, and another between Mrs Treadgold and Fred Poulter, provided they were in his service at the time of his death; as part of Mrs Treadgold's share, he left her the freehold of The Lawn.

The financial aspect of his affairs settled, he had before him the more immediate one of Irina's guardianship, informal though it must be, and somehow divided in case of his death, between Neil and

Phyll and Miss Bassett, though the latter, affectionate and kind, was older than he was.

The position of Neil and Phyll was somewhat perplexing. They were not under a legal responsibility; and no one had sympathised more than he with the idyllic early scene of their marriage, but before he had made up his mind to speak seriously he found he hardly needed to. Naturally Neil was entirely focused on Phyll and on the prospect of the baby. (Neither of them knew whether they wanted a boy or a girl the most; Neil was prepared to discuss, with intense concentration, the future careers of either, but Phyll, left to herself, thought of the child without defining its sex, simply as Baby.) Phyll had always had a family feeling for Irina, but now Neil himself, surprisingly enough, seemed to be taking a more responsible attitude; the idea of the baby and of himself as a father had changed him from an ardent lover into a committed family man, and this consciousness included Irina. He seemed, not older, but more weighty; his face was more fixed in severity, though ready as ever to light up at what struck him as comic or preposterous. In the reach of calm before September he began, feeling he'd been unkind towards Irina, to cultivate her. Sir Geoffrey watched them one afternoon when they had all lunched with Cousin Louisa, sitting in her drawing room window, discussing the field offered to Western engineering by the East, Neil explaining and Irina listening intently, about the basic difference in approach of the two civilisations; of how, not long before, cracks had appeared in the dome of the Taj Mahal, which the Indians had mended by pouring molten silver into them.

'I don't say you couldn't do it like that,' Neil was saying, 'after all, they built the thing themselves in the first place, only their ways are not our ways, so to speak.' Looking at them, Sir Geoffrey noticed acutely what up till then he had merely taken for granted, how attractive Neil was to the opposite sex: something impossible to explain or define, only to be recognised. Neil's humour was endearing, his presence a magnetic attraction; and Irina, though remaining unselfconscious, now behaved differently with him from the way she behaved with anybody else. She was spritely, and instead of being quietly attentive she had a lively movement, a turn of the head like a bird's.

Neil and Phyll, when not lunching at the weekends with Cousin Louisa, now came almost invariably to The Lawn. The following Saturday, after lunch, Phyll went out to the kitchen to have a little talk. Gertie was sitting at the table in the window doing the Master's mending: replacing very small pearl buttons on the front of a shirt, and darning the elbow of a sleeve in a dark blue cardigan. Her thickened and wrinkled fingers were clinically clean and she wore a large brass thimble with 'A present from Worthing' inscribed minutely round the rim. Her colourless face with the sunken cheeks and the protruding chin was so friendly, reassuring and calm, it did Phyll good to look at it. She asked Gertie how she was, and Gertie, re-threading a needle, said, like generations before her, 'I am wonderfully supported'. The kitchen took tea after lunch instead of coffee, and while Mrs Treadgold was preparing the coffee tray, she asked if Phyll would like a cup of tea instead? When Phyll said yes, Fred handed her, with an air of *empressement*, a large cup and saucer with turquoise blue rims and little gilt lines beneath them. He did not like to sit down with her, but went off to collect some garden chairs out of the shed, thinking the master might like to sit on the terrace. This was what Sir Geoffrey and Phyll presently did, while Neil said that he would run Irina into the High Street to get some refills for her paint box at the stationer's. They'd be back in half an hour, he'd said. For the first moment Phyll had looked hurt and disconsolate. What an expressive face she had! Sir Geoffrey thought, settling her into a padded chair with a cushion at her back. She had made no protest, not even a comment; only someone looking at her closely would have seen that her eyes looked on the verge of weeping and her mouth quivered. In a moment, however, she was answering with animation Sir Geoffrey's remarks about bedding-out plants. Presently, because nowadays she was ready to fall asleep at any moment, she had sunk into a doze. 'Bless her!' Mrs Treadgold said beneath her breath as she came to take the coffee tray away. Sir Geoffrey had the newspaper beside him and began to read it thoroughly, as he had not so far had time to do. Something like an hour passed, and then in the warm, still afternoon, with white butterflies hovering over the flower beds, he fell into a gentle sleep himself. He awoke to find Phyll sitting bolt upright, with a face of dismay. All around them in the garden, the light told them that it was now much later. He looked at his watch and saw that it was almost four o'clock. He apologised for having slept, and she said she had been asleep too.

'I thought they would have been back by now,' he said. 'I'll have a look.' He walked through the house into the hall but all was empty. He went back to Phyll who was now on her feet, looking agitated. 'Can something have happened?' she asked. 'The High Street is such a short distance in a car.'

'I don't think so,' he said. 'I expect they'll be back any minute,' but he was thinking of sending Fred out in the car to reconnoitre when Neil's car drove up and he and Irina came through the drawing room onto the terrace. Sir Geoffrey said: 'We were getting quite worried as to what had become of you! You'd said you'd be back in half an hour.'

'I know,' Neil said, 'I ought to have realised how the time was going; but when we'd got the paints, Irina wanted to see that pond on the other side of the common where the arrow-head grows. I'd forgotten exactly where it was and we drove about looking for it. I hope Phyll wasn't upset by our being so late.'

'Well, I think she'll be glad to see you back.'

Mrs Treadgold now appeared, asking if they were to stay for tea? As Neil hesitated, Sir Geoffrey said: 'I think Mrs Neil will probably be glad to get back to her own place.' Neil went out to the terrace, where he could be heard speaking in an exclamatory and apologetic manner, and in a few moments they came out together. Phyll seemed to have been crying a little. As Neil went out to the car, she whispered to Sir Geoffrey in a stifled tone: 'So stupid of me, but it's the first time he's ever – *ever* –' He patted her arm soothingly.

As he and Irina were sitting at their tea, he said: 'It was a pity to upset Phyll by coming back so much later than you said you would.'

'She might have known we'd be all right,' Irina said, helping herself to honey.

'Yes. Only I think she was disappointed that Neil was out for so long. They only have two afternoons in the week with each other.'

'We couldn't help it; we'd lost the way to the pond.'

205

'No, I don't say you could, as it happened; but it would have been better to leave the pond for another afternoon.'

'Neil wanted to see it, too.'

'I know, my dear; but you're getting old enough to know that ladies have sometimes to decide what ought to be done, and then men will fall in with it.'

'Did you ever have to fall in with ladies?' she inquired curiously.

'Sometimes I did. When my wife had said what she felt we ought to do, I used to take her word for it. Another time if you've arranged to be back at a certain time, and then something extra is suggested, it would be better to say: We can't do that now, it might make us late and we told Phyll we'd be back at such and such a time.'

'I see.' He was relieved that she did see, but she had become rather pale. The totally new sensation of being found serious fault with by him, however gently, had given her a painful shock. She said no more, but when tea was finished she went silently away.

He was sorry for the distress which he saw she felt, but he believed it had been an absolute duty to put in this word. The crux of the matter had been, not a selfish lack of consideration for Phyll's lonely afternoon, but that Neil and his little sister-in-law had found each other's company so attractive. No harm had been meant by anyone, but harm sometimes came about without anyone's meaning it, because a dangerous habit had been allowed to grow.

The French Institute was holding a small exhibition of late seventeenth century paintings, of which one of the chief points of interest mentioned in the papers was a portrait of La Fontaine. When it had first been advertised, Lucinda had suggested that Irina might like to see the exhibition, as a background to her reading of the Fables. Irina had said at once that she would like it very much, but as Lucinda's private affairs had occupied her during the last few weeks almost to the exclusion of anything else, she had not made a definite plan for their visit until the exhibition was within a few days of closing. Now it had to be done at once, if at all, and Sir Geoffrey warmly promoted the outing. He felt that the Beech Hanger praise of Irina's French should inspire them all to further efforts.

The visit was most enjoyable; portraits of Louis XIV, of Madame de Montespan and Louise de la Vallière, of Molière and the star attraction, of La Fontaine himself, were eagerly inspected by Irina, who was particularly pleased to find that many figures of the Court had been painted in company with monkeys, lap-dogs and parrots. Everything went as well as possible, Lucinda herself finding that it was soothing and exhilarating to be obliged to concentrate her attention on something apart from her own affairs, until their return to Waterloo. As Irina waited for Lucinda in the booking-hall, she saw a girl whom she was sure she knew: of about her own age but taller, solider, with an expression of repressed discontent and unhappiness. After a moment, Irina realised it was Peggy Cromer. She went rather shyly up to her.

'Hullo,' she said. Peggy Cromer said 'Hullo'. Irina already wished she hadn't made the advance. She managed to say: 'Have you left Elmfield?' Peggy answered with a soundless word and a shrug. She didn't want to speak. The question Irina longed to put was: 'What happened to Turner?' Before she could make the effort, Peggy was rejoined by Mrs Cromer, coming away from the ticket window. Mrs Cromer looked pinched and cross. She paused a second to see if Peggy were wanting to speak to a friend, and finding that she did not, the pair of them disappeared into the thickening crowd of early evening.

When Irina was back at The Lawn she answered mechanically the questions Sir Geoffrey put to her. Yes, she had enjoyed the pictures very much. Yes, the one of La Fontaine was very good, he looked real. Yes, she had had a catalogue but she'd left it in the train. He was disappointed by the tonelessness of her replies. Had he really damaged their relationship? Having put his questions, he asked no further. He was about to pick up the evening paper when she said suddenly: 'There was a girl at Elmfield called Peggy Cromer. We saw her at Waterloo this afternoon.'

He put the paper aside. 'And you talked to her, did you?'

Then she told him the story of the divorce which everybody in the form had known about, and how she'd found Peggy in the cloakroom, crying so dreadfully because it meant they'd have to abandon their trusting dog, Turner.

He said, in a few, heart-felt words, how sad it was. He did not like to speak too freely, for fear of touching the wound of her own experience. To change the subject, he spoke of an idea that had been growing in his mind, strengthened by every sign of her sympathy with animals. He said: 'Do you think that when you're old enough, you might like to be a vet?'

Irina's eyes took on the unseeing look of mental absorption. At last she said: 'I think I would. But is it very difficult?'

'Yes, I think it is, actually. You'd have to pass examinations in chemistry and biology and physics. But you could do all that if you really wanted to do it. And then afterwards I expect you'd need some time on a farm, helping to take care of their animals; and perhaps helping a qualified vet in his practice. Would all that appeal to you?'

'Yes, it would.'

'Well, we can just keep it in our minds, unless something comes along that you'd like better.' He was glad to see that the look of tranquil, bright expectancy which he had grown accustomed to in her face, had come back to it.

Next day he saw her with a stout volume of poetry which he had forgotten the house possessed; it was one of a rather shabby collection, housed in an overflow shelf on the landing. 'What have you got there?' he asked.

'It was something we read at school; I couldn't quite remember it. I wanted to see it again because it is like you.' He saw the poem was 'The Ancient Mariner'.

'Am *I* like the Ancient Mariner?' he asked, somewhat taken aback, (but one must accept, calmly, the verdict of the young). If she heard him she did not attend; she was turning over the pages to the marginal note on part four, about the journeying moon and the stars: 'Everywhere in the blue sky belongs to them . . . and is their own natural home which they enter unannounced, as lords that are certainly expected, and yet there is a silent joy at their arrival.'

'*That's* like you,' she said.